Confessions
of a City Girl

also by Juliette Sobanet

PARIS ROMANCES
Sleeping with Paris
Honeymoon in Paris
Kissed in Paris

PARIS TIME TRAVEL ROMANCES
Midnight Train to Paris
Dancing with Paris
One Night in Paris

MEMOIR
Meet Me in Paris

POETRY
I Loved You in Paris

Confessions
of a City Girl

Around the World Edition

JULIETTE Sobanet

Windswept

Livonia, Michigan

Cover design, interior book design,
and eBook design by Blue Harvest Creative
www.blueharvestcreative.com

Confessions of a City Girl: Around the World Edition
Copyright © 2016 Juliette Sobanet
All rights reserved. Except as permitted under the U.S. Copyright Act of 1976, no part of this publication may be reproduced, distributed, or transmitted in any form or by any means, or stored in a database or retrieval system, without prior written permission of the publisher.

This book is a work of fiction. The characters, incidents, and dialogue are drawn from the author's imagination and are not to be construed as real. Any resemblance to actual events or persons, living or dead, is entirely coincidental.

Published by Windswept
an imprint of BHC Press

Library of Congress Control Number:
2016953384

ISBN-13: 978-1-946006-02-8
ISBN-10: 1-946006-02-5

Visit the author at:
www.juliettesobanet.com &
www.bhcpress.com

Also available in eBook

The Confessions

The First Confession   Los Angeles...11

The Second Confession   San Diego...97

The Third Confession   Washington D.C....165

The Final Confession   Paris...223

*For all of my fabulous girlfriends
Boys may come and go, but we'll always have each other*

Confessions of a City Girl

Los Angeles

Prologue

"Natasha, *darling*," my mother coos softly, her voluptuous pile of platinum blonde curls sprawling over the crisp white hospital pillow.

"Yes, Ava." I take her clammy palm in mine, trying not to notice the silver roots lining her weathered forehead or the way her chest rattles every time she tries to speak.

Even from this sterile Los Angeles hospital room, I can still hear my mother's young, devastatingly glamorous voice belting out tunes in our Hollywood Hills home, see her prancing around in a scarlet negligée, breasts spilling over lace, smudged mascara rolling down rouged cheeks, messy curls tumbling over bare shoulders…and *always* a man waiting in the bedroom.

That ever-present image of the infamous Ava Taylor—who will forever be adored by the film-going masses for her scandalous, dazzling beauty on the silver screen—will haunt my dreams long after we say goodbye.

"The envelope," she whispers, losing strength. "In my purse."

With trembling fingers, I reach for her pink Dior bag, rifle through the make-up, the pill bottles, and finally emerge with a manila envelope.

"Open it," she urges, choking on her words, the glamour being sucked straight out of her with each beep of the machines at her bedside.

I pull a packet of papers from the envelope, combing the first page quickly as I find myself praying she'll hang on just a little longer. For as much pain as this woman has caused me, I'm amazed at how deeply I still love her, at how much I am hanging on to her every word, every breath.

"Downtown DC photography gallery sold to Ava Taylor," I read out loud, instantly recognizing the address as that of a popular gallery I've visited, and adored, many times. "Named *The Natasha Taylor Photography Gallery...*" I trail off, lifting a shocked gaze to my mother. "Ava, what is this?"

"Your photographs, Natasha—it's time for you to release them to the world." The cancer in her lungs has made her voice barely recognizable, but it hasn't stolen that mischievous twinkle in her eyes. "In your very own gallery."

"But you know I take family portraits—wholesome photos of glowing pregnant women and husbands kissing their wives' bellies. Not exactly the kind of photos you'd feature in a prominent DC photography gallery."

The twinkle dissipates as my mother levels a serious gaze at me. "Natasha, *dear*, don't get me started on the misery that is your life." She stops to clear her throat, the way she always does when she's about to judge me. "I simply cannot bear the thought of it—you photographing all of those happy families, shoving it in your face day in and day out that you can't get pregnant with that stuffy professor husband of yours who was *never* suited for you."

"Oh, and you know me so well, do you?" I snap. This isn't the time to let out the years of pent-up anger toward the woman who was supposed to be a mother to me, but after that comment, I can't help myself.

"Better than you might think...and that man—well, he doesn't deserve you, Natasha. He doesn't see the beautiful dancer I once knew." My mother's emerald gaze cuts right through me, and I can't handle it. I never could.

"Well, I'm sorry my life, my choice in a husband, and my body's inability to make a baby have been such a disappointment to you. And we both know that I am not the *only* one to blame for the demise of my dance career."

A maddening grin spreads across her full lips. "Oh, let's not be so dramatic," she taunts. "*I'm* the actress here, after all. Yes, the end of your dance career was...*tragic*...but let's not go there today." With a trembling hand, she points to the cup of water on her bedside tray. I swallow my anger as I press the cup to her mouth. She is only able to take the tiniest of sips—what irony after all those years spent guzzling straight from the bottle.

"Back to the photographs—I'm not referring to your family photography, darling. While beautiful, we both know that *those* aren't the photographs that will draw in the masses and make you a huge success."

Dread coats my stomach as I realize where she is going with this.

"It's time to reveal all of the photographs you've taken *of me* over the years. The good and the bad, my darling. It's time for the public to see the real Ava Taylor. The one only *you* knew."

"But you've seen those photos. They're...they're..." I trail off, a slideshow of images flashing through my mind.

Ava in the glamorous emerald evening gown she wore to the Oscars, sobbing and slumped on the kitchen floor, a cigarette pressed between her lips, a bottle of whiskey in hand; Ava lounging naked on the back deck, legs spread for the world to see, downing a martini; Ava in a jealous rage, hurling a black vase at one of her lovers.

Ever since I was a little girl, I've been photographing every disastrous, glitzy, humiliating moment of growing up with my troubled Hollywood mother. It was my way of dealing with her, with my lack of a childhood—documenting the mess instead of partaking in it.

"They're raw," she says, interrupting my stream of memories. "They're me. And I'm not giving you this gallery unless you agree to feature them in your opening exhibit."

I sigh, exhausted by her, by years of her unreasonable demands. "You've got to be kidding me."

"The stipulations are all there in my will. The date for the exhibit has already been set. Six weeks from today."

"Six weeks? But you know I'm in the middle of my third round of IVF, and I have shoots scheduled every single weekend for months...shoots that I can't cancel or we'll lose the house in Georgetown. I don't have the time or the energy to put this together right now. And besides, you *don't* want me to release those photographs to the public."

She snatches the papers from my hands and gives me a slight scratch with her long red nails in the process. "Do you hear yourself? Don't you see the train wreck that has become your life?" Her voice wavers, swallowed up by her raspy lungs. "It's too late for me, darling...my train has already wrecked and burned. But it's not too late for you." She sucks in a loud, wheezing breath before continuing on her final diatribe.

"I know I wasn't always there for you, not in the way you needed me, but just this once, let me try. I'm giving you a chance to change your life, make your career dreams come true. Screw IVF, screw that dreadfully boring husband of yours, and screw that godforsaken house that you've never been able to afford. This obsession you have with creating a *normal* family...it's time to let it go, Natasha." She coughs deeply, her sick, withering body shuddering underneath the sheets.

"You came from *my* womb, and you will forever be unique because of that. Normal just isn't in our genes, darling." A nauseating shade of gray spreads down her face as she shakes the papers at me. "*This* is your story, Natasha. And it's time for you to tell it."

I take the papers from my mother, nodding numbly, realizing that even on her deathbed, even as she is giving me the first true gift she has ever given me, she has still found a way to make this all about her.

But then another thought—one that I do not want to give any credit to—pops into my mind. I wonder if somewhere, deep down, she does have a maternal instinct, after all.

Ava glances around the bleak white hospital room, down at the tubes in her arms, and finally to the machines at her bedside, and there it is. That impenetrable sadness, spilling down her porcelain skin. I am so used to seeing this look of desperation in her eyes—the look she has only ever shown to me—and yet every time, it pains me. Rips my heart to shreds.

I both hate her and love her immensely.

But above all, I cannot bear to see her suffer a moment longer.

"Promise me, Natasha. Promise me you'll do it," she begs softly.

Her outburst has taken every last ounce of energy she had left. Tears cloud her beautiful green eyes, and I know I must give her what she wants.

I squeeze her hands in mine and lean over to kiss her forehead. "I promise, Mom. I promise."

Her breathing slows, and just when I think she's leaving me forever, a whisper escapes her lips. "It's *Ava*, darling," she corrects. "You know the 'M' word makes me feel old."

With a dramatic bat of her eyelashes and one sharp inhale, *those* are my mother's last words.

One

Six weeks later

Flashes of Ava Taylor in all her disastrous glory span the dimly lit walls of the gallery as I pace its sleek hardwood floors, feeling as though my heart may burst if I have to look into her intoxicating emerald gaze one more time.

She's everywhere. The broken mess of my mother, documented from my very own lens, on display for the world to see.

Catching my reflection in the shiny glass of one of her portraits, my gaze wanders down my petite frame, over my strapless violet dress and tall black pumps, and once again I am reminded of how I didn't inherit *any* of Ava's voluptuous curves. My long, golden brown hair and bright blue eyes don't bear a resemblance to my famous mother either. In fact, nothing about my appearance does, *except* for that gleaming Hollywood smile we share. I'll have to turn it on tonight, I tell myself, if only to sell this gallery.

Just as I am checking my phone for the millionth time that hour for word from my husband, a familiar voice echoes through the space.

"Natasha Taylor, when was the last time that snow-white skin of yours saw the sun? It's August in DC and you're still as pale as a ghost."

Swiveling away from a photograph of my mother sporting a cherry-red bikini and heart-shaped sunglasses, passed out drunk on a raft in our Hollywood pool, I turn to find my sweet-yet-blunt best friend Liz Valentine, smiling her cheeky grin. Liz is practically the only friend I have left who isn't pregnant or popping out babies like she's a human PEZ dispenser, which—after my three-year infertility adventure—means she can insult my pale skin all she wants.

Plus, she's right. Ever since Ava's funeral, I've been so busy preparing for my first real exhibit—an obscenely edgy departure from my usual brand of heartwarming family portraits—that I haven't seen the sun in weeks.

I reach for Liz, wrapping my arms around her tiny shoulders like I'm hanging onto a life raft. "Thank you for being here," I say. "Seriously, Liz, thank you."

And although Liz isn't one for public displays of affection, she squeezes me back. She knows there's a lot riding on tonight.

When I finally give her room to breathe, she casts a quick glance around the chic DC gallery, her curious eyes combing the life-sized portraits of my mother, and finally hovering over the sinful selection of twenty-something male servers dressed in slick black tuxes, trays of champagne and hors d'oeuvres in hand.

"Damn…not bad," she murmurs under her breath.

Liz's insane work hours at the State Department have put a major damper on her sex life—meaning that she has none. She won't admit—even to me—how long it's actually been, but by the way she is salivating over these boys, I suspect it has been a *long* time.

"Still in heat?" I ask my friend, noticing how pretty she looks in her tight black cocktail dress, batting those long lashes that could melt a man from miles away.

Liz nods, her lips parted as she flashes a grin at one of the cutest ones—a tall, preppy stud who couldn't be older than twenty-two.

"You have no idea," she whispers.

"Well, you can have your way with lover boy over there as soon as the exhibit is over. But not a moment sooner," I order.

"Oh, please," Liz says, finally peeling her gaze from his boyish blue eyes. "Why would I break my no-sex streak now, Natasha? I mean, this whole living to work thing is just *too* much fun."

Liz's dry sense of humor gets a brief laugh out of me until I spot Sienna—the gallery director and PR angel who has managed to give my first exhibit more press than I ever could've hoped for—pacing toward us in her tall gray heels. Her sixteen-week baby bump looks impossibly chic in the slim blue dress she's wearing, and as she chews on the end of her chunky black glasses, I find myself wishing I didn't know she was pregnant. Wishing I could go to an island where no one ever got pregnant so I wouldn't feel so empty, especially on the most important night of my career.

Sienna grips my arm. "Only five minutes until go time. I think everything is ready."

"Thank you so much, Sienna. Really, you've been—"

"Where's your husband?" she cuts in, scanning the gallery for signs of Ethan. "Didn't you want him to be here with you before we open the exhibit?"

My heart constricts inside my chest, but I smile all the same. "Oh, he'll be here any minute. He had to go to New York this weekend, but his train should've arrived back in DC by now."

"Are you kidding me?" Liz places a hand on her hip, anger flashing through her pretty hazel eyes. "This is the biggest night of your career, Natasha. He should've been home this weekend, helping you prepare for the exhibit, or at the very least offering moral support. What's he doing in New York anyway?"

I sigh, exhausted from all the years of making excuses for why Ethan isn't going to show up to yet another important event in my life, or for why he consistently acts as if his career endeavors in the worlds of academia and publishing take precedence over mine. No matter the fact that my family photography business has kept us afloat ever since Georgetown's Political Science Department turned him down for tenure and he was bumped to his current position—a meagerly paid adjunct professor who spends more time with his head in a book than seeking out tangible opportunities that could help dig us out of debt and save our beautiful house in Georgetown, which we are on the verge of losing.

"Ethan connected with an editorial assistant at Random House recently and scheduled a dinner with her to pitch a book idea he's been working on," I say.

What I haven't yet found the courage to tell my best friend is that three weeks ago, after our most recent failed IVF attempt, Ethan decided to "take a break" and promptly packed his trusty rolling suitcase and rolled it right out the front door of that charming brick home of ours.

He said he was staying *alone* in a hotel in DC, but I'm not naïve—I've smelled the perfume on his shirt after all those late nights at the library; I've heard him whispering into the phone in his study after he thinks I'd fallen asleep.

But last night, it was *me* he called in the middle of the night, drunken and sorry. He told me he missed me, that he made a mistake walking out on me, and that he wanted to make an effort to put the pieces back together. Maybe even try once more for a baby.

And despite the downward spiral of our marriage, of our love, I am still clinging to the ten years of history we've shared, to the good times we once had, to the way he *used to* love me, look at me, adore me. And most of all, I cannot force myself to let go of the idea of having a baby with him, of starting our own little family together.

I've been ignoring his indiscretions, hoping that somehow, we can salvage what used to be and create something new, something that will save us from total and utter marital failure.

So, I asked him to start by showing up tonight.

There's still time, I think as I check my phone once more. But Liz's impatient voice drowns out my hope.

"A dinner with an editorial *assistant*? Couldn't he have scheduled it another weekend?" she hisses. "I mean, your mother just passed away last month, for God's sake, and you're revealing your disaster of a childhood in a public photography exhibit. If Reluctant Hubs doesn't show, I'll personally kill him for you, Natasha."

Sienna lifts a brow in my direction, and I give her another reassuring smile, even though I feel anything but reassured by my husband's inability to answer his phone or show up on time after the desperate promises he made to me the night before.

"No one will be killing anyone tonight," I say. "He'll be here, Liz. It was his first real opening with a big publishing house, so he felt he had to take this opportunity."

"But this is *your* first real exhibit, and it's a game changer, Natasha. I mean, look at these photos you've taken of Ava…they're magnificent." Her gaze rests on a photograph at the back of the gallery, where my mother is standing on the ledge of a New York City balcony, laughing manically at the full moon overhead, one high-heeled foot dangling carelessly in the air. I was sixteen when I took that photo, and like so many other moments in my life with Ava, I remember thinking that *this* could be the moment it all comes crashing down.

Liz's voice breaks into my memories. "*Disturbing*…but magnificent," she finishes. "And Reluctant Hubs needs to be here. No excuses this time."

"*He'll be here*. And please, Liz, call him Ethan tonight. He really doesn't appreciate the Reluctant Hubs reference."

Ethan earned the endearing nickname *Reluctant Hubs* within the first year of our foray into the world of infertility. Things only worsened after two subsequent years of administering hormone shots and showing up—albeit reluctantly—for scheduled sex. By the time he decided to take a break from our marriage, he'd become about as excited to climb into bed with me as he would be about a lifelong prison sentence.

And, if I'm being honest, he isn't the *only* reluctant one in this pair.

But sex just for the fun of it—does such a thing even exist?

As Sienna bustles off through the gallery, a smack of nerves hits me, making me forget all about the lack of pleasurable sex in my life.

This is it. And Ethan really isn't here. I check my phone once more to see if he's responded to my barrage of texts and calls, but there's nothing.

Liz's hand lands on my shoulder. "Forget about him. I didn't mean to get you riled up. Tonight is a big night, and *you* are the star, Natasha. You've really captured your mother… in a way I've never quite seen before. And I know everyone else who sets foot in this gallery tonight will feel the same."

A shaky smile graces my lips as I glance around the chic space and down at my watch. "Let's hope so. I need to sell every last one of these photographs *and* this gallery if Ethan and I want any chance at trying one last time for a baby and saving our house…or the marriage, for that matter."

Liz shakes her head, crossing her arms over her chest. "Such a shame you have to sell the one thing your mother left to you. Right after your first major exhibit here, no less. This could make your career, Natasha. Are you absolutely sure there isn't another way?"

I shake my head, not wanting to think about the second mortgage we had to take out on the house or the piles of debt Ethan and I have accumulated after years of fertility treatments, acupuncture sessions, rage-inducing hormones, and *three* failed IVF attempts. I don't want to think about the devastating ways infertility has chipped away at our happiness, at our marriage, and most of all, at my soul.

I resent the stacks of baby shower invites sitting on my kitchen table, the ever-constant reminder that so many of my closest friends have gotten knocked up it seems simply by *looking* at their husbands.

Even more so, I hate myself for not being able to be happy for them.

"Natasha, are you in there?" Liz prods, snapping me back to the present.

I avoid her truth-seeking gaze. The look that says: *Why are you still trying? What's the point?* I don't want to face that question, so instead, I tell her, "No, there's no other way. The gallery has to sell. The photographs have to go. And it's all riding on tonight."

"No pressure, though. Jeez." Liz sighs as a waiter clad in his sleek black tuxedo approaches us with a tray of champagne.

"Ladies?" he offers with a provocative brow raise. He's young, naïve, and flirty; he has no clue how much of my life is riding on the successful execution of this event. "A glass of bubbly before the crowds descend upon your photographic masterpieces?"

Liz plucks up two glasses and thrusts one in my direction. "Drink it," she orders. "I promise I won't tell Reluctant Hubs."

Eyeing the champagne swirling in the glass, I catch a whiff of its fruity scent and realize I've never craved a sip of alcohol so badly in my life.

"*Natasha.*" Liz squeezes my arm. "Unless you're so pale because you're actually pregnant this time and you've been sick all week, I demand that you drink this glass of champagne. You need something to take the edge off and bring a little color to those gorgeous cheekbones of yours. You don't want to look like a fucking Eskimo while you're showing off your dazzling collection."

"God, it's been so long," I admit, totally unfazed by Liz's frequent use of profanity or by the fact that she just called me an Eskimo.

The cute waiter boy nods. "C'mon, Mrs. Taylor. Live a little." He gestures at the half-naked photograph of my mother dangling overhead. "Sure looks like your mom did."

I raise a suggestive brow back at this slick young stud who thinks a glass of champagne will cure all of my problems. As if.

But still….*what the hell.*

My fingers wrap around the stem of the glass before I can stop them, and within seconds, the fizzy alcohol is pouring down my throat, soothing my frazzled nerves, bringing a jolt of life back to this shell-shocked, tired, thirty-two-going-on-fifty-year-old body of mine.

I finish the glass, set it back on his tray and wink at him. "Keep 'em coming tonight."

"Yes, ma'am." He leans a little closer to me, the scent of his cologne making me remember a distant time when sex *was* fun.

Before I can delve too far into that thought, he whispers, "For what it's worth, Mrs. Taylor, you're a fucking gorgeous Eskimo…the hottest one I've ever laid eyes on. You'll knock 'em dead tonight."

And with that, our sexy twenty-something champagne boy is off, my cheeks are burning, and Liz is staring at me with her mouth agape. "You know, I never could wrap my mind around the fact that you were Ava Taylor's daughter, because you're just so normal. So grounded. So buttoned-up. But tonight, my friend…" Liz pauses, nodding in approval at the short hem of my dress, then down at the three-inch heels on my feet. "I think you *do* have a little bit of your mother's scandalous Hollywood glam in you after all."

I turn to face the double glass doors, where a line of chicly dressed strangers are waiting to storm the gallery, to see the never-before released photo collection of America's favorite actress…gone bad.

"Let's hope so," I say. "For tonight anyway, I'm going to need it."

Just as Sienna is about to open the front doors, my phone buzzes in my hand.

A surge of hope courses through me as a text from Ethan pops up on the screen.

> *Having drinks with two senior editors, but will try to take a late train to DC to catch the end of the opening. So sorry. I'm sure it will be a hit, Nat. Have fun. xx*

I *hate* when he calls me *Nat*.

I fight the tears gathering at the corners of my eyes, shoving them deep into the compartment where all of the other unshed tears have gone over the years. Then I turn my phone off, hand it to Liz, and nod toward the door.

"Let's do this."

Two

Hours of schmoozing later, I stand alone in the back of the gallery, gazing up at the only photograph of my mother that hasn't yet sold.

A dim spotlight illuminates her tragic gaze, the tears dripping from her thick black lashes wrapping me up in their comfort, their familiarity.

Despite myself, I miss her...I even miss those tears.

I take one last glance toward the front of the gallery to see if Ethan has arrived at the last minute like he said he would, but with only a sprinkling of my friends and a few die-hard Ava fans still mingling and drinking champagne, I know he isn't coming.

Ava's final rampage echoes loudly in my head, magnified by the three glasses of champagne I downed earlier.

This obsession you have with creating a normal family, it's time to let it go, Natasha. You came from my womb, and you will forever be unique because of that.

Normal just isn't in our genes, darling.

"Well, my so-called *normal* husband couldn't even be bothered to show," I whisper. "But at least we sold all of your photographs." I look straight into her glassy eyes. "Are you happy now, Ava?"

"Not *all* of them have sold." A deep voice echoes through my ears, startling me to the point where I actually jump.

Embarrassed, I flip around to find a dark-haired stranger invading my space. His disarming grin sets me on edge immediately.

"Excuse me?" I say, crossing my arms over my chest—a reflex I have with men like him.

He takes a step closer to me, his slate-blue eyes and crisp gray suit commanding attention.

"This photograph," he says, not breaking my gaze. "The one you were talking to. If I'm not mistaken, it hasn't sold yet…and neither has the gallery."

I arch a brow at him, inhaling the alluring scent of his cologne…and immediately regretting it.

"You're an interested party, I take it?" I place one hand on my hip, hoping against all hope that this dashing mystery man who has shown up at the end of the night will be the one to make an offer.

He tilts his head to the side, his sultry gaze combing down my neck, rolling over my minimal cleavage, and lingering on my hips. He finally finds his way back up to my mouth, but by that point, the strapless violet dress I'm wearing feels irrelevant. I may as well be naked.

He flashes me a cunning grin. "You could say that."

Before I can get myself together to respond and mentally put my dress back on, he extends a hand. "Nicholas Reyes. Photographer turned investor."

Just as I slide my hand into his, that name, *Nicholas Reyes*, sends a jolt of recognition through my dazed, slightly drunken mind. I take a bold step closer to examine the way the spotlight shines down over the hint of stubble on his cheeks, running along his defined cheekbones all the way up to a small scar over his left eye.

"Natash—" I begin to introduce myself, but he cuts me off.

"Natasha Taylor. How could I ever forget those stunning blue eyes?" He's still holding onto my hand, his warmth radiating shock waves through my chilled, tired body.

A white-hot flush spreads across my chest as a memory of him—*and* his photos—soars through my brain. I want to back away immediately, but my tall black pumps will not budge.

"You photographed my mother for the cover of *Rolling Stone* ten years ago. How could I ever forget those photos?" I say, not hiding the sarcasm that drips from my tongue.

I was twenty-two at the time, a college senior, visiting our Hollywood home for the holidays. In an alcohol-and-drug-induced tantrum, my mother insisted that I drive her to the *Rolling Stone* cover shoot. Nicholas sauntered in late, the magazine's star photographer who clearly had free rein over the women he photographed. I remember the ease with which he handled Ava's drama, using his slick professional charm to maneuver her mostly naked body into all sorts of scandalous poses, which would later be splashed all over every newsstand in America and devoured by the public.

The *only* man I knew who hadn't been interested in the infamous cover photo of Ava wrapping one arm around her voluptuous, bare breasts was Ethan Roberts, the man who would become my husband only six months later.

Of course prior to the *Rolling Stone* spread, Ava had certainly done her fair share of racy—and in my opinion, *tacky*—photographs. But there was something so sensual about the way Nicholas photographed her...something so intimate and revealing, that I felt naked just watching him work.

As I stand before him now, with only a few inches and two clasped hands between us, I remember that feeling well...and I also remember hating him for it.

"It was quite a shoot," he admits. "And your mother was quite a woman. But it's clear that no one truly knew what lied behind the Hollywood façade... no one, except for you, Natasha." His voice is intense and sultry as he says my name, and I realize that I haven't heard my own husband say my name that way in years...maybe not ever.

Even though the voice in my head is telling me to pull away, take a step back, and focus on *selling the gallery*, I stand there, mesmerized by the heated look he is giving me, by the memory of the day I first laid eyes on him.

"Can I ask what you're doing in family photography when you have this kind of talent?" Nicholas' hand finally slides from mine as he gestures around the gallery.

The heat swimming through my core quickly sparks to anger. "My career choices are none of your business, Mr. Reyes. Just because you photographed my mother naked ten years ago doesn't mean you know anything about *me*."

He raises a brow, clearly aroused by the challenge. "What I know about you, Natasha Taylor...or rather what I *see*, is that you survived an incredibly tumultuous childhood with Hollywood's favorite sweetheart, a closet drug and sex addict, who wasn't much of a mother at all. But despite it all, you've grown into a talented, successful, *gorgeous* woman, and you take some of the most raw, stunning photographs I've ever seen."

Of all the praise I've received throughout tonight's exhibit, Nicholas' bold words are the ones that cut straight to my heart. While I am standing before him, trying to form a coherent response, his gaze shoots down to my left hand.

"Why isn't your husband here tonight?" he asks.

"How did you—"

He nods to the nearest photograph of Ava. "I couldn't help but overhear you when I walked in."

I bite the inside of my cheek, willing the knot forming in my throat to go away, willing myself to stay strong, to make just one more excuse for why my own husband has not shown up for me on such an important night.

But I can't. I just cannot do it.

Swiveling away from Nicholas, I focus on Ava's tears instead of the ones that are threatening to pour down my face.

"My life, my *marriage*, is none of your business, Mr. Reyes."

"Excuse me for pointing out the obvious, Ms. Taylor—"

"*Mrs.* Taylor," I snap, flipping back around.

He ignores my correction, moving right along. "But when you grow up with a mother like Ava Taylor, then showcase your lives in an exhibit like this, your life becomes *everyone's* business."

"Is this your way of making an offer on the gallery?" I cut in. "If so, you sure have a fucked-up way of going about it."

"Am I wrong?" he taunts.

Rage courses through my veins, and I have the sudden urge to shove Nicholas Reyes straight into the portrait of Ava at his back.

"For your information, I never wanted to show these photos to another living soul. But Ava wanted to make one final splash, one last statement to the world...it was her dying wish."

"And of all the photos that have been taken of her over the years—including my own—she chose *yours*." Nicholas steps closer, his broad chest cornering me, blocking the rest of the gallery from sight. "For that, your mother was a genius."

Emotions twist around in my gut like a tornado, and suddenly I feel tears stinging my eyelids. I blink them away, pushing past Nicholas. I'm not sure where I'm going, but all I know is that I cannot allow him to strip another layer from the crumbling wall I have built around myself. Not tonight.

"Natasha," he calls after me. "I'd like to make an offer."

My heels stop dead in their tracks, even though my heart is telling me to run—not walk— as fast as I can from this man.

He paces up behind me, rests a strong hand on my arm. I turn slowly, forcing myself to look him in the eye.

"I'll buy the final photograph *and* the gallery...on one condition," he says.

"And that would be?"

"I'd like you to meet me in LA next weekend to do a photo shoot for a contemporary dance company I recently invested in. Your photographs of the dancers will be featured in a gallery I'm opening in downtown LA next month. This should be right up your alley, considering your days as a dancer."

"How did you know I used to dance?"

The light catches the hint of gray in his blue eyes as he shoots me a smoldering grin. "I'm an investor; I did my research."

I think back to his illustrious career at *Rolling Stone* and realize that shortly after my mother's issue was released, Nicholas Reyes the photographer dropped off the map. "I'm curious, Mr. Reyes. Why would a photographer at the height of his career, photographing movie stars and rock legends for *Rolling Stone*, stop all of that momentum to become an investor?"

Nicholas' smile fades, and for the first time I notice a sadness permeating through his edgy exterior.

But he still doesn't miss a beat. "Sometimes it's better to stop while you're ahead and find other, more lucrative ways to follow your passions. The photography world was too limiting for me in some respects; I wanted to be involved in all of the arts—so now I invest in them. Galleries, dance companies, theaters, music."

"That's all fine and good, but I don't understand why you need me to fly all the way out to LA to do these photographs. With your contacts, I'm sure you know dozens of other more qualified photographers."

"I want you to capture the dancers the way you've captured your mother. Raw, honest, alive. After what I've seen tonight, Ms. Taylor, I won't be happy with anyone else. Which leads me to the next stipulation in my offer."

"With men like you, there's always more, isn't there?"

Nicholas responds by slipping a hand around my waist and lowering his lips to my ear. "When you come to LA next weekend, you'll have your own room in my suite at the W Hotel, and I'm taking you out for a night on the town. Seems like you could stand to blow off some steam, no?"

His breath on my skin makes my cheeks blaze with heat, but I don't move away from his embrace. "Mr. Reyes," I whisper, tipping my chin up to meet his. "Are you forgetting that I'm a married woman?"

He shoots a quick glance around the gallery. "This husband of yours who didn't show. Should we consult him first?"

"You don't even know him."

"I know that it's a crime he wasn't here for you tonight. And I know that you need to sell this gallery, and I'm your only bidder."

I can almost feel the steam billowing between us as Nicholas hovers over me, waiting for my response.

"Just one night?" I say, not believing the words as they trickle from my mouth.

He nods. "Only one night, Natasha. And like I said, you'll have your own room...*if* you want it."

He pulls me in tighter, brushing his lips over my cheek. The feel of his mouth on my skin is a dangerous enticement, a perfectly timed tease, one which makes me remember that whole sex-just-for-the-fun-of-it thing that has been missing from my life for *so* long.

He runs his lips along my cheekbone up to my ear, before whispering, "Do we have a deal?"

I feel myself falling, my entire body yielding to the heat of him, to the pure, unadulterated freedom I feel for this brief second in his arms. And in a moment of complete irrationality, a moment where I don't even recognize the woman saying the word, I hear it pass through my lips.

"*Yes*."

Three

I bustle out of LAX, squinting beneath the blinding California sun as it beats down on the sleek black town car awaiting my arrival.

A driver with long, thick dreads and a trendy black vest greets me with a polite nod. "Mrs. Taylor, welcome back to Los Angeles. Let me take those for you." He relieves me of the heavy camera equipment I have strung over my shoulders and opens the door for me.

Before I climb in, I breathe in the fresh, seventy-five degree air that flitters past, and realize I have left more than just the suffocating DC humidity behind. Stacks of baby shower invites, my withering marriage with Ethan, the perfect little families I photograph every weekend—there are no traces of *that* life here, in sunny Los Angeles.

There are memories, though, of a childhood gone terribly wrong, but as I settle my gaze on a tall palm tree swaying in the breeze, I realize this will be the first time I've seen this city through my own eyes, without Ava's shadow looming over me.

"Mr. Reyes is waiting for you at the theater," the driver says, snapping me from my thoughts. "In the meantime, please make yourself comfortable. You'll find champagne, compliments of Mr. Reyes, to accompany you for the ride."

Suddenly the details of what I have agreed to *do* on this quick trip to LA smack me over the head.

Champagne? A driver?

Mr. Reyes…waiting for me?

My chest tightens as I nod, silently, and climb into the backseat of the fancy car.

What have I gotten myself into?

Plucking the champagne flute from the console, I let the bubbles fizz down my throat and remind myself for the millionth time that day of all of the concrete, valid reasons I said yes to Nicholas' offer. I need to sell the gallery to save the house, to pay down our mountains of debt, and, if we can figure out a way to salvage the marriage—if we even *want* to salvage it—the money could help us try one last time for a baby.

But for the first time in years, the thought of having a child with my husband sends a wave of nausea straight through my core.

Or am I nauseous over the fact that I've agreed to spend the evening with a man I barely know, a man who makes my entire body flush with heat…and over the fact that I have lied to my husband about the real reason I'm here?

Head in my hands, I push a heavy breath through my lungs while I replay the conversation I had with Ethan the day after the gallery opening—when he finally decided to saunter home after his three-week departure, only mildly apologetic for missing my big night. Instead he glossed over the "break" and went on and on about his amazing New York trip, and the editors who cannot wait to read the book he has yet to begin writing.

Then, in his nonchalant, your-career-never-matters-as-much-as-mine tone, he offhandedly asked how the gallery opening went.

I told him that it was a massive success, and that I had to fly to LA to meet with a potential investor and shoot a troupe of dancers to seal the deal.

And then, surprising even myself, I told him that as far as I was concerned, the "break" was still on, and we could reevaluate once I returned from LA.

He nodded, poured himself a glass of sherry and headed upstairs for a nap, as if this were all totally normal.

Despite the blast of hot air wafting in through our dining room window that day, I remember standing there, shivering, wondering where the man I'd fallen in love with ten years ago had gone.

I did this, I'd told myself. I sucked the love from this marriage with my demands to have a baby…to create a child who I believed would bring the love, the joy, the happiness back to our empty, cold home.

But that afternoon, after Ethan settled in for one of his usual three-hour naps, above all, I was irate that he'd deserted me on the night I needed him most.

And I didn't feel the least bit guilty that I'd lied.

It is only as I sit in the back of this town car, drinking champagne, that the guilt over lying to my husband is hitting me; the reality of what I am about to do cannot be ignored.

As the town car slows to a stop amid the usual gridlock on the 110, I lift my eyes to find a silver envelope lying next to the champagne bottle, *Natasha* scrawled in jet black ink across the front.

I slide a shaky finger underneath the flap and remove a small card.

> *Natasha,*
> *Raoul will escort you to the shoot, which begins at four p.m. In the meantime, please enjoy a glass (or two) of champagne…and relax. We're going to have an incredible night, I promise you. I'll be waiting…eagerly…at the theater, to see those magnificent blue eyes of yours once more.*
> *—Nicholas*

My core shakes with what could only be called desire…but I haven't felt anything even remotely close to this in so long that I'm honestly not sure what to call it. I tuck the card back into the envelope, in total and complete disbelief that a man as sexy and alluring as Nicholas Reyes is waiting for *me*.

Surely he can have any woman he wants.

And I imagine that he does.

So why would he insist on spending one night with *me*?

Confessions of a City Girl

I ponder this mystery for our entire traffic-filled journey through Los Angeles, but as the town car winds its way downtown, I realize that I am only trying to avoid the real question at hand:

How could I have agreed to do something so bold, so out of character, and so utterly *Ava* as to accept his invitation?

By the time we reach the theater, I am a bundle of nerves. Despite the glass of champagne I've downed, the inside of my mouth has turned desert dry, my hands are shaking, and as I reach for the door handle, I realize I can barely feel the breath passing through my lips.

It is not only the fact that I am about to do one of the most important shoots of my career that has me all tied up in knots. It's the fact that in a few seconds, I'm going to see Nicholas again.

With each blink, I recall flashes of him from the night of the gallery opening. That defined jaw line, the small scar over his left eye, and his mysterious slate-blue gaze piercing straight into mine as he first approached me, as the scent of him overtook me, moments before I agreed to this...*affair*.

That forbidden word twists through my head, drilling holes in my perfectly constructed world.

Of course Nicholas promised I could have my own room in his penthouse suite, but who are we kidding? I don't have time to question my decision for another second, though, because Raoul is already opening the car door for me.

And suddenly, *there he is*.

Tall, rugged, and as devastatingly handsome as ever, Nicholas extends a hand while a suggestive grin slides across his lips. He is dressed impeccably in a black suit jacket, dark jeans, and a crisp white collared shirt that is open just enough to give me a glimpse of his broad chest that lies beneath.

I slide my hand into his, noticing how natural it feels there. As I stand to greet him, I immediately regret not having that second glass of champagne. I'm an absolute nervous wreck.

"Natasha," he says, sliding his arm around my waist and kissing me softly on the cheek. "Happy to see you made it."

"Did you think I wouldn't come?" I tease, wondering if he can sense my heart pounding underneath this façade of composure.

As Raoul carries my photography equipment into the theater, Nicholas' piercing gaze runs the length of my body…down, down, down, until once again, I feel completely naked standing before him.

"I knew you'd be here," he says with an air of confidence that gets right under my skin.

"Aren't we cocky?" I say with a lift of my brow.

He shrugs as we head toward the theater. "Not cocky, just certain."

"I'm sure you don't get turned down often."

He laughs, the smile lighting up his eyes. "I can only imagine what you must think of me…but you of all people should know that appearances are not all that they seem."

Before I can dig any deeper into the mystery of Nicholas Reyes, he opens the theater door and ushers me through. "After you, Ms. Taylor."

Surprising myself, I stop and place a firm hand on his chest. "It's *Mrs.* Taylor. No matter what happens this weekend, it's still *Mrs.*"

He nods, a knowing smirk passing over his impossibly smooth features. "That feistiness in your eyes—you got that from Ava."

As I slip past him into the darkened theater, I can almost hear my mother laughing.

And I wonder, will I ever escape her?

Four

An impressive troupe of contemporary dancers are stretching and laughing onstage as Nicholas leads me down the central aisle of the theater.

A man dressed in a tight black T-shirt with a pencil behind his ear and a pad of paper in hand flicks his gaze up to us. "Ahh, this must be the star photographer I've been hearing so much about." His smile immediately eases the tension balled up in my stomach.

I have to stop myself from turning around to see who this star photographer is. But when he says my name, it's clear that he is, in fact, referring to *me*.

Nicholas places a hand on my back as he introduces us. "Yes, Drew, this is her—*the* Natasha Taylor. You're in good hands today, my man. And Natasha, this is Drew Hanover, the artistic director and founder of the company."

Drew shakes my hand before giving Nicholas a nod of approval. "Not only talented, but gorgeous. I would expect nothing less from you, Nick." Drew pauses to scan my body—*not* in the sensual way that Nicholas has a habit of doing, but in the way that all dance instructors do. "And clearly a beautiful dancer body. Why did you ever stop, love?"

The truth about why my dance career ended so abruptly at the age of eighteen is too painful to relive at the moment, nor is it appropriate to tell in a professional setting, so instead, I keep it simple.

"Oh, you know, the life of a dancer just wasn't for me in the end." But as I glimpse a striking couple rehearsing onstage, their bodies intertwining and spinning and flowing freely to the passionate lyrics of Jessie Ware, I know that I'm lying.

Taking photographs was my coping mechanism, a skill I developed to deal with Ava, which rolled into a career that I do genuinely enjoy.

But *dance*—that was my dream.

I swallow up the memories, the regrets, and nod at Drew. "Shall we get started?"

I ask Drew to leave the music on as I photograph his dancers. The endless flow of notes keeps them in their element—more graceful, less posed—and me too. I glide around the stage with my camera, snapping away until I lose track of time, until I forget that Nicholas is somewhere in the theater watching my every move, until I forget that I ever stopped dancing.

With each shot of the dancers' elegant extensions, their edgy poses, their muscular, slim bodies that twist and bend and stretch in ways I only wish I could still do, I feel myself remembering a time when the stage, the movement, the music would sweep me away from my life with Ava, would take me to another world…a peaceful abyss I could only ever access through the freedom of dance.

The hours pass by in a haze of beauty until I have captured every dancer in the most raw, honest light I can manage behind the limited view of my lens. After the shoot, many of the dancers come up to thank me, not one of them mentioning my connection to Ava Taylor. It is a breath of fresh air, and a first for me—even the rich Georgetown mothers I photograph always find a way to weave her name into the conversation somehow, never able to separate me from the legend of my famous mother.

I do have her Hollywood smile, after all.

But here in this theater, I feel a shift taking place. I am not *only* the daughter of Ava Taylor today—I am my own woman.

Confessions of a City Girl

And while I cannot grasp what exactly that means for me, or for the life I've built back in DC with Ethan, I can only recognize the way it feels in this moment. Like a curtain has been lifted, the blinders gone.

I am blinking, struggling to see through all this light.

But there it is anyway…the light that feels like *me*.

After all of the dancers have left, I am packing up my equipment when I notice that Nicholas has disappeared. Probably off taking an important call…or perhaps talking to one of his many female admirers, I imagine.

As I kneel down to zip up my camera bag, "Wildest Moments"—that same heartbreaking Jessie Ware song from earlier—filters through the theater once again. Drew crosses the stage and hands me a pair of ballet slippers.

"You were a ballet dancer, right, love?" he says with a knowing grin.

I hesitate before taking the shoes. "How'd you know?"

"Those legs, that graceful posture, those long locks. It was obvious the minute I laid eyes on you." He nods to the slippers. "I know you're itching to have this stage to yourself. I could see it the whole time you were up here photographing. I'll be back in an hour to close up…until then, it's all yours, love."

Drew doesn't wait for me to respond, but instead dims the lights and slips silently from the theater, leaving me alone in its vast beauty, an empty vessel waiting for one last dance to fill it up.

Before I can look at my watch or be practical or think about all the reasons why it would be silly to slip on this pair of ballet shoes after all these years, I have kicked off my boots, peeled off my top and stripped down to my black leggings and a white tank.

The ballet shoes are just my size, and the simple act of putting them on my feet makes me smile bigger than I have in years.

I push my equipment into the wings and take the stage, letting the poignant lyrics flow freely through these tired limbs of mine until I feel them waking up, coming alive.

And before I know it...*I am dancing again.*

The développés, piqué turns, pirouettes, and jetés flood right back to me—rusty though I am after years away from the dance floor, but it doesn't matter. The arches of my feet and my port de bras haven't lost their grace or their spark...but most of all, it is that resilient, passionate spirit within me—the one I thought had died long ago—that is rising to the surface again. Clamoring to be heard.

As the dance takes over my body, my soul, my spirit, I notice that the crushing pain over not being able to conceive is leaking out of me—*slowly*—but leaving me nonetheless. I don't want it anymore, I realize. And for the first time since this harrowing journey began three years ago, I wonder what I have been trying for.

I don't question that I've genuinely wanted my own child...that is a desire so deep, I couldn't fabricate it if I tried.

But I do wonder if I've ever actually wanted to have that child *with* Ethan.

The song comes to a close, flowing into the next, and the next, until I have danced for so long that I have lost my breath, and blisters are forming on my feet. It is in this exhausted, vulnerable state that my mother's final words on Ethan flood my head.

He doesn't deserve you, Natasha. He doesn't see the beautiful dancer I once knew.

Ava was right. Ethan doesn't see the true me—he never has.

But have I ever really given him the chance to?

Just then the music stops, and when I lift my teary face out into the darkened theater, I find Nicholas holding a camera in his hands, his eyes locked on me...mesmerized, burning.

The pounding of my heart is the only sound that travels between us as he holds my gaze in a way that makes it impossible for me to move, to breathe, to think.

All I know in this moment is that Nicholas *sees* me.

Five

An hour and a half later, I am feeling more vibrant, alive, and excited about life than I have felt in years. I've showered alone in Nicholas' stylish penthouse suite at the W Hotel, put on a splash of make-up—okay, perhaps more than a splash—and slipped on a slinky black cocktail dress and tall pink stilettos.

As I ride the chic elevator down to the lobby where I'm meeting Nicholas before our night out on the town, I steal a quick glance in the mirror, not recognizing the woman staring back at me.

She certainly doesn't look like a woman who has just lived through her third failed IVF attempt, a woman who has spent hours crying alone on the bathroom floor over the loss of a child who has yet to exist, or a woman whose husband hasn't taken her out on a real date in over two years.

No, *this* woman looks confident, strong, sexy…happy even.

Like a woman who knows what she wants.

I bottle up the confidence I haven't felt in so long and carry it with me as I strut through the glitzy lobby, past a crew of photographers and wannabe stars, and down a set of red velvet stairs. Nicholas is standing beneath a dazzling crystal chandelier, tilting his head to the side and shooting me a bold, deadly grin—the kind of grin that makes a woman want to do things she's never done before."

He slides a hand around my waist, and I know the minute he's touched me that the damaged, lost soul who lives underneath this dolled-up exterior is a long way away. Perhaps just for tonight, I won't even acknowledge her existence.

Nicholas leans into my ear, whispering, "I'm going to have to keep you close tonight; otherwise, you'll be stolen away from me in seconds. You look ravishing, Natasha." Then he steps back to take me in once more, shaking his head. "*My God.*"

Nicholas has surely been out with women who are younger, more glamorous, and hotter than me. Women who are much more comfortable in their skin than I am. But I stop myself from saying as much, because what he has just said to me—no matter how overtly bold it may have been—is the nicest thing a man has said to me in years.

And by the way he cannot take his eyes off me, I can tell that he actually means it. None of the budding actresses with legs for miles and four-inch heels strutting past are even getting a sideways glance from this man.

A girl could get used to this.

I suppress the nervous giggle that wants to escape and instead place a smooth hand on his arm. "Where are you taking me tonight, Casanova?"

"Dinner first, then cocktails, dancing, and a little burlesque. Sound good?"

I can hardly contain my excitement at the thought of a real night out on the town—or over the fact that Nicholas has planned all of this in advance just for *me*. I'm tempted to pinch myself to see if I'm dreaming, but instead I smile and say, "Perfect."

With a hand on my back, he escorts me out of the hotel, into the warm Los Angeles evening. Two stretch limos line the driveway of the W while a group of twenty-something blondes in absurdly tight dresses smoke cigarettes and let out obnoxious high-pitched laughs. The typical Hollywood vibe of trashy meets money hasn't changed since I was a young girl, following my own celebrity mother around town. But I am unfazed by it all tonight, simply happy to be with Nicholas, no matter where we are.

Raoul is waiting for us with the black town car, and just as I am about to slip into the backseat with Nicholas, the lamplight above catches on my wedding ring. The diamond which has been a permanent fixture on my left ring finger for the past ten years glints and sparkles, making me remember Ethan and the days when we were so in love.

It feels so far away, a distant memory that has been covered up by years of heartbreak.

Nicolas slides up behind me, placing a soft hand on my shoulder. "Everything okay?"

I glance back, finding a genuine look of concern in those gorgeous eyes of his.

This would be the moment to call it off. To tell him I can't take the night any further. That I'm still technically married, and while I'm almost positive my husband has been seeking pleasure elsewhere, that doesn't mean *I* should spend the night with another man...even if it means losing the sale of the gallery, and the financial relief that this could provide.

But with the heat of Nicholas' chest pressing into my back, the warmth of his breath on my skin...I realize that while I know logically how *wrong* this is, something about tonight—something about *him*—feels so right. More right than anything in my life has felt in a long, long time.

I smile boldly at Nicholas. "Yes, everything's fine."

I slide into the car, knowing that I am taking a step in a dangerous direction.

But I also know that I won't turn back now; I want to go wherever Nicholas is taking me.

One glass of champagne and a quick car ride later, we arrive at the Sunset Marquis Restaurant in West Hollywood. The maître d', a dapper older gentleman with a head of salt-and-pepper hair, grins as he welcomes us into the charming dining room.

"Mr. Reyes, wonderful to have you back. And this is Mrs. Taylor, I presume?"

"Please, it's Natasha," I say, not accustomed to all of this pomp and circumstance. I extend my hand for a polite shake, but instead the maître d' kisses the back of my hand.

"Lovely to meet you, Natasha," he says as he retrieves two menus and leads us over to a cozy corner booth. A sheer, tan curtain wraps around our seats, and a flashy chandelier ball hangs overhead, giving us our own private little slice of romance. Outside, the twinkling lights weaving up vine-covered pillars only add to the intimate atmosphere on this beautiful summer night.

After the maître d' delivers a fancy bottle of Sauvignon Blanc to our table and takes our orders, Nicholas shoots me that killer grin and lifts his glass in a toast.

"To new adventures," he says.

You are the biggest adventure of my life, I think as I smile back at him.

"To new adventures," I echo.

I can hardly concentrate on the exquisite taste of the wine as it rolls down my throat because Nicholas is already sliding closer to me in the booth, his legs finding mine underneath the table.

He takes a long sip of his wine before locking his intense gaze on me once again.

"So, what is the *real* reason you stopped dancing, Natasha?"

I shift uncomfortably in my seat; I really don't want to start off the first romantic dinner I've had in years with the tragic story of how my dance career ended.

"Like I told Drew, I decided that I didn't want the life of a dancer in the end—it just wasn't for me."

Nicholas shakes his head, clearly not buying my cop-out response. "When I saw you dancing up there today, you looked..." He trails off, combing my face as if he's searching for the perfect words. "*In love*," he finishes.

The truth pulls at my heart. He's right: dance was—and perhaps still *is*—my one true love. One that I've never shared with Ethan, the man who should know me better than anyone on this earth.

I wonder then, how it would come to pass that in only a few hours with Nicholas, he would recognize and bring to light this deep truth within me. A truth I've been ignoring for so many years.

"How long were you watching me dance?" I ask him.

"Long enough to see how absolutely stunning you are. Not that I didn't already know that, of course," he says, brushing his hand over my arm. "But when you moved up on that stage, you really came alive, Natasha. You were a completely different person from the one I saw in the gallery last week...You were *free*."

It is staggering, the way he sees right to the heart of the matter, to the heart of *me*, already, on this first and only night we will ever spend together.

Once again, I feel naked and vulnerable in his presence, but in a different way from before. In a way that actually feels comfortable...*right*.

"So tell me, what's the real reason that you would stop doing something you love so deeply, something you are clearly meant to be doing?" he presses.

"No one knows the truth," I tell him, wondering how I have managed to keep such a massive secret for so long. "Not even my husband."

He squeezes my arm, the surprising depth in his eyes telling me it's okay to go on. And despite the fact that I barely know him, I realize that for the first time ever, I actually *want* to tell this story.

"I trained at a studio in LA for fifteen years—from the time I was three until I turned eighteen. It was one of the *only* things my mother did right when I was a child—letting me have something that was mine, something that had nothing to do with her fame."

Another sip of wine calms my nerves only slightly as I continue. "The studio was owned by this French couple, Jacques and Delphine Tourneau. They were very prominent in the LA dance community back then, and they were the only ones who knew the truth about my mom. For many years, they were like my second family...or really, my *only* family.

"In the weeks leading up to my eighteenth birthday, I'd been training exclusively with Jacques to prepare for a big audition with a Paris-based dance company that Jacques used to dance for. He'd invited them to the studio specifically to meet me, and it was the career opportunity of a lifetime.

If I was accepted, I would move to Paris and live out my dream of being a professional dancer…"

"Nowhere near your mother," Nicholas finishes for me.

I nod. "Exactly."

"So what happened?"

"The night before my audition, my mother overdosed on a mixture of narcotics and whiskey. I rode in the ambulance with her, watched her get her stomach pumped…you know, all of those heartwarming memories that go with having a responsible mother like Ava Taylor," I say dryly. "I missed my last rehearsal with Jacques, but that night, once my mom was stabilized, I left the hospital and showed up at his house, a total mess. He took me in, gave me a drink to calm me down, told me that he would push the audition back a day so I could have some time to recover. He really listened that night, really understood what I was going through. Delphine was off traveling, and he told me they'd been fighting a lot lately…that he wasn't sure if they were going to make it." I close my eyes, a flash of hands, lips, clothes flying invading my mind. "One minute we were just talking, the next I was in his arms."

Even as an adult, I can still see that lost eighteen-year-old girl, remember how safe she felt wrapped up in Jacques' embrace.

I take another drink before peering up at Nicholas, finding only concern in his eyes where I expected to see disdain.

"He was my first," I continue. "I knew it was wrong, but he was the only man who had ever been there for me, who had ever understood the hell I was living through. And I loved him for that. Two days later, I auditioned and soon after, learned that I was accepted into the company. Jacques and I continued seeing each other in secret, and while my mother normally couldn't have cared less what I was doing, she noticed that I wasn't as attentive or as tolerant to her antics as I normally was. Unbeknownst to me, she'd been snooping through my room, and she found two things that to this day, I wish I had destroyed: my journal and a positive pregnancy test."

Nicholas doesn't flinch, but nods instead, urging me to go on, to finish my story.

"I found out about the baby the week before I was supposed to leave for Paris. When my mom discovered the test, she went ballistic, stormed the studio and told Delphine everything. Delphine divorced Jacques, slandered my name in the dance community, and Jacques' reputation was ruined as well. It's hard to earn a living teaching young girls how to do ballet when all of the mothers in town learn you've gotten one of them pregnant. The studio closed down shortly after, I missed my flight to Paris, and I never danced again...until today."

"And the baby?" Nicholas asks softly.

"I carried the baby for six months. I had only just learned it was a girl when I found out her heart had stopped beating..." My hand instinctively goes to my stomach, tears pooling at the corners of my eyes. "I named her Clara."

Reaching up to wipe my eyes, I find that Nicholas' hand is already there, drying my tears.

"Clara is a beautiful name," he says. "I'm sorry you lost her."

I take a deep breath, trying to compose myself, trying not to remember that traumatizing night I spent alone in the hospital, giving birth to a tiny baby who would never take her first breath. "So your husband doesn't know that this happened to you?" he asks.

An all-too-familiar veil of shame forces my gaze down to the table, but Nicholas' hand on mine gives me the courage to keep going.

"When I met Ethan, I'd done everything possible to erase that part of my past. I'd given up dance, separated from my mother by moving across the country to DC, gone to college, and poured myself into my photography. There were no traces of that young, damaged dancer left when he met me. And I didn't want to bring her back. I didn't want to relive it. Plus, even if I had tried to explain what had happened, he would never have understood. He wouldn't have believed that his *Nat* could have been involved in such a scandalous scenario."

Considering the candor with which Nicholas has analyzed my life in the short time I've known him, I am fully expecting judgment or advice, or at least a disapproving nod from his side of the table.

But instead, he only squeezes my hand and says, "I understand why you didn't tell him then."

"Thank you," I say softly. "Thanks for listening. It feels good to say it out loud, to acknowledge that it happened. That she existed."

He nods, a knowing look passing over those mysterious eyes of his, making me wonder why it seems that he understands me on a deeper level than I can comprehend.

Our food arrives just when I am feeling shaky from having shown so much of myself to Nicholas.

A comfortable silence settles over the table as I take a bite of my beautifully prepared lemon and thyme chicken dish, but after a few moments I notice that Nicholas still hasn't touched his food. Instead, he is studying me intensely.

Placing my fork down on my plate, I dab at the corners of my mouth with my napkin and wonder if I've revealed too much. I still don't know anything about Nicholas or his past, or even what he is doing here, with me.

But instead of asking him all of that, my hand instinctively slides over his. "What is it?" I ask.

He runs his thumb along his jawline, letting out a long sigh. "Last week, when I saw you standing there alone in the gallery, I had this feeling that we had more in common than our connection with your mother." He shakes his head, as if in disbelief. "And now I know that we do."

"What do you mean?"

"I know what it's like," he says. "To lose an unborn child."

This is the absolute last thing I expect to come from Nicholas—the smooth-talking playboy—but then I remember that pained expression that crossed his face back in the gallery, when I'd asked why he would abandon such a successful photography career. "I'm so sorry," I say. "Does this have something to do with why you stopped photographing all those years ago?"

"It does…I'm just not sure this is where we wanted our romantic dinner conversation to go. Maybe better told another time."

"Will there be another time?" The words shoot from my mouth before I can stop them.

"I hope so." There isn't an ounce of hesitation in Nicholas' voice, or in those alluring eyes of his as he says this.

A tense moment passes between us as I think about what it would be like to see Nicholas again...and what that would mean for my future with Ethan...if there even will be a future with Ethan.

Dismissing those dangerous thoughts as quickly as they stormed in, I turn back to the subject at hand. "I just told you the most devastating, private story of my life," I remind him. "And I barely know you...but maybe that's why. Maybe there's comfort in revealing something intimate about yourself to someone you hardly know. Less risk that way perhaps?"

After another drink of his wine, he finally looks me square in the eye.

"You can tell me, Nicholas. Whatever it is, you can tell me."

He shrugs, sighing. "I'm surprised you didn't read about it in the news—or the tabloids—all those years ago."

"Having Ava as a mother, I made a firm commitment to avoid both the news *and* the tabloids from the time I was a teenager. It was too damaging."

"Ahh, makes sense," he says. "I would've avoided them too. They weren't always too kind to her."

I shake my head. "No...no, they weren't."

"Well, right around the time I photographed your mother for *Rolling Stone*, I was seeing a young actress...a young, *married* actress."

Lifting a brow, I smile at him. "This is nothing new for you then, I see."

A low laugh lightens up his serious expression. "I know you probably won't believe me, but I honestly don't make a habit of seducing married women. Rebecca was in a bad marriage—her husband was abusive. She was going to leave him for me, but..." He trails off, seemingly lost in a wistful memory.

The name Rebecca suddenly makes me recall a story I did get wind of all those years ago via Ava—my Hollywood gossip queen mother. It was a story about a plane crash involving a young actress and a photographer; the photographer survived....but the actress did not.

"Rebecca Stone," I say quietly. "She was killed in a plane crash...but you..." I pause, taking in the scar above his left eye. "You survived."

Nicholas looks up, surprised. "I thought you didn't read the news."

"Ava told me." I can still see her sitting in the kitchen, smoking a joint, half naked as usual, the newspaper splashed over her bare legs. "She was about to read a review of her latest film when she spotted the story on the front page. She focused on Rebecca, though, and only briefly mentioned a photographer being involved in the crash, but I don't remember her mentioning your name."

What I don't tell Nicholas is that upon learning of Rebecca Stone's untimely death, my mother let out a loud, evil cackle before launching into a diatribe about how all of these young, no-talent actresses had been swooping in, stealing her roles, and how Hollywood, and perhaps the entire universe, would be better off without one more Rebecca Stone.

"Your mother was so out of it the day of our shoot, I doubt she even recognized my name when she read it," Nicholas says.

"It's more than likely that she didn't," I admit.

"It never should have happened," he says quietly. "Rebecca flew out from New York for a *Rolling Stone* cover shoot. That night, after I photographed her, she confessed that she wanted to leave her husband for me, but she was terrified of what he would do when she told him. I convinced her to stay an extra night so we could figure it all out, make a plan. Since she missed her flight, I arranged a private flight for the two of us from LA to New York, so that I could be there with her when she told him...make sure nothing happened to her." Nicholas goes quiet, his eyes darkening with the memory. "But in the end, it was all for nothing."

A startling realization takes hold as I think back to how this conversation began.

"She was pregnant?" I ask.

He nods, his gaze deadpanning into mine. "I didn't find out until the autopsy report came in after the crash. I'd been seeing her for almost a year at that point, and she hadn't been intimate with her husband in months."

"So the baby was yours."

His silence is my answer.

As I glance down at the fancy meal on my plate, I remember what Nicholas said to me outside the theater earlier today—that appearances aren't all that they seem. Maybe he isn't the playboy I've assumed he is. Gazing around the swanky hotel restaurant, I wonder if this elaborate lifestyle he leads is just a distraction, a façade he has built to cover up what's really going on underneath—much like my family photography business...and for that matter, my marriage with Ethan.

"You never photographed again, after you lost her," I say, putting all of the pieces together.

He shakes his head. "No...not until today."

A flash of Nicholas standing in the theater, camera in hand, gazing at me like he'd seen a ghost, runs through my mind. "You photographed me dancing?"

His strong hand finds my leg underneath the table. "It was impossible not to. You were an angel up there, Natasha."

We finish our dinner in silence after that, both of us having revealed more than we surely ever planned to on what was supposed to be a simple arrangement—one night out on the town, no strings attached.

But as Nicholas's burning gaze tears straight through all of my carefully placed layers of protection, there is no question that this *arrangement* has jumped to a whole new level—one I'm not sure either of us is ready for.

Six

After a quick drive down Santa Monica Boulevard, we arrive at La Descarga, which, according to Nicholas, is a trendy, Havana-style cocktail bar. From the entrance, though, it looks more like a dirty, ghetto warehouse. I shoot my sexy date a questioning glance as he leads me up a dingy flight of stairs, but he only grins in response.

A dark room at the top of the staircase reveals a beautiful blonde woman perching over a desk.

"Have you been here before?" she asks, sizing us both up.

Nicholas responds for the two of us. "I have, but the lady has not."

"Are you on the list?" she quips.

Nicholas tells her his name, and after she has checked the guest list, she gives him a knowing nod before leading us into the next room.

I am just about to ask Nicholas where in the hell he has taken us when our blonde receptionist opens the doors to a tall armoire, pushes aside a stack of clothing, and gestures to a hidden door at the back of the closet. Nicholas takes my hand, leading us through the door and onto a high, narrow balcony which overlooks a smoking-hot club. Below us, live music is booming, men are smoking cigars, and scantily dressed burlesque dancers are spicing up the already smoldering atmosphere.

"Wow, what a dramatic entrance," I say to him, fully impressed.

He laughs. "I knew you would like it."

This is a far cry from the stuffy professor gatherings Ethan used to take me to…back when we still socialized together. And although I should feel totally out of my element, the way Nicholas confidently takes my hand and leads me downstairs to the bar—as if for tonight, I am his, and he is mine—makes me feel like there is nowhere in the world I'd rather be.

Nicholas hands me the cocktail menu, which I study meticulously.

Soon, his unabashed laughter interrupts my decision-making process.

"What?"

"You haven't done this in a while, have you?" He lifts a curious brow, that deep voice of his making my insides quiver.

"What are you talking about?"

"You know, having fun? Drinking a cocktail. Going out just to have a good time."

Damn, I really thought I had him fooled.

I had myself fooled, anyway.

"Oh, God. Is it that obvious?" The nervous laughter I'd been bottling up spills over now.

He leans against the bar, impossibly sexy in his crisp white shirt and dark jeans. "Don't worry, I won't tell anyone." He plucks the menu from my hands and scans it quickly. "How about a mojito?"

"Mmm, those used to be my favorite. How'd you know?"

"Minty, fresh, and sweet. Definitely your kind of cocktail." He leans over the bar, orders our drinks, and then turns to me, the smile on his face all smug and sly.

"You still think you have me all figured out, don't you?" I say, placing a hand on my hip. "Besides our extremely revealing dinner confessions, shall I remind you that before today, we've only met twice, *briefly*."

He wipes the smile from his face, inching closer to me, his legs brushing against mine underneath the bar. And there is that intense look again—the same one that stopped me in my tracks back in the theater as he'd watched me dance.

Finally, he speaks. "It feels like longer, though, doesn't it?"

Once again the allure of those gray-blue eyes of his has me enthralled, hanging on his every word. I swallow hard, unable to tear my gaze from his.

"Yes, I know what you mean." And strangely enough, I *do*. I know exactly what he means. The energy between us, the chemistry that flows effortlessly every time he's near, is palpable, undeniable.

When I think back to the day we first met ten years ago at my mother's *Rolling Stone* shoot, I realize I'd felt this inexplicable connection the moment I laid eyes on him. Within minutes of entering the room, Nicholas left Ava's side to come over and introduce himself—something most men would *never* do. I remember how that disarming smile of his left me stumbling over my words like an idiot, but he didn't seem to notice. And when he shook my hand, we lingered there, the physical connection so immediately strong and electrifying, I wasn't sure what to do with it.

Looking back, I know that I was simply too young and too humiliated by my mother to acknowledge the way he made me feel.

But the events of today—the photo shoot, my dance, our revealing conversation over dinner, and now this night out on the town together—have left me more awakened, more alive than I have felt in years. And in this new, heightened state of mind, it is impossible to ignore the fact that I haven't *ever* felt this excited, enraptured, or comfortable in another man's presence...not even in the early days with Ethan.

Our drinks arrive, and I take mine with haste, sucking down the minty fresh alcohol, hoping it will soothe the butterflies that are suddenly wreaking havoc in my stomach, making me feel all light-headed and dizzy—a thirty-two-year-old teenager in heat.

After Nicholas slides his empty glass down the bar, he takes my hand and nods toward the dance floor where couples are draped all over each other, laughing and grooving underneath the dim lights in this steamy club.

"Dance with me, Natasha." The intensity in his voice means there is only one answer to that question.

I let Nicholas guide me out to the center of the floor, vaguely recalling all of the tiring arguments I've had with Ethan in recent years, begging him to put off his work for just one night so we could do something *fun*. All the times I suggested that we take a weekend off from our insanely busy lives, from infertility, from writing and researching and photo shoots, to go somewhere exciting together. To remember who we were as a couple, why we'd fallen for each other all those years ago.

But the nights out, the weekends away—they never did happen. Ethan just wouldn't carve out the time, make the commitment. It was never important enough to him. Everything else came first.

And now, here I am in the middle of a booming Los Angeles dance floor, finding the excitement and romance I've been craving for so long with a man I've only met a handful of times, a man who cannot keep his eyes or his hands off me.

And I must admit—it feels *incredible*.

So incredible, in fact, that any hints of guilt I may have been harboring over my decision to say yes to Nicholas' proposal have been abandoned at the door of this club.

A sultry piano and sax tune moves over the dance floor, prompting Nicholas to wrap his arms around my waist and pull me snugly into his chest. Our hips find each other instantly, a perfect fit as they sway in time to the music, grinding together in urgent, passionate waves. He presses his cheek to mine, the heat of his breath running down my neck and over my breasts, making my core throb with desire.

Song after song, we dance like this—our bodies intertwined, not able to get enough. And with each new song, I feel myself unraveling even further in his arms, marveling at the way his body moves so naturally with mine, at how comfortable I feel letting loose in front of him.

As the beat slows down, Nicholas threads his fingers through my long hair and dips me back, running his hungry lips down my neck. When we resurface, I am flushed, hot, and ready.

His mouth finds my ear. "I want nothing more than to ravage you right now."

I don't wait for him to say more. Instead, the inner seductress I didn't know I had gives him a suggestive grin, takes his hand, and leads him out of the club.

Raoul cannot whisk us back to the W fast enough. For the entire drive, I am writhing with heat, dying for Nicholas to kiss me. And while his hands certainly are not showing any restraint—wrapping around my waist, running over my knees and so high up my thighs I can hardly breathe—he has yet to go in for the first kiss.

The dreamy, feminine side of me can't help but think that maybe Nicholas wants our first kiss to be special, and not just some animalistic urge in the backseat of a car.

But my practical side doesn't waste a moment to chime in and remind me that despite the depth of Nicholas' confession over dinner, I am most definitely one of *many* women he has fondled in this backseat, with Raoul at the wheel.

I tell myself that it doesn't matter if I mean nothing to Nicholas, in the end. I am still married, after all. I'm doing this to sell the gallery, to save our house, to try to make it work with Ethan…and perhaps try once more for a baby.

But as the car slides up to the entrance of the W, I am at once painfully aware of how ludicrous it is that I would agree to an affair in order to try to have a baby with my husband.

Have I lost my mind?

One look at Nicholas' outstretched hand, the desire in his eyes, and I realize that maybe none of this was for the money, the house, or the nonexistent baby with my absent husband.

Maybe, in the end, I did this for me.

Seven

Inside the expansive suite, I gravitate to the floor-to-ceiling windows and gaze down at the city lights, at all of the Hollywood glitz and glam whizzing around below, thinking about how odd it is that I am back where it all began. In this sinful city, about to commit a forbidden act in a penthouse suite, with a man I will most likely never see again.

Nicholas walks up behind me and slips a glass of white wine into my hands as he kisses my neck.

After all the years of trying so hard to be nothing like my mother, I know now that it was all in vain.

She was right.

Normal just isn't in our genes.

Why has it taken me so long to realize this?

The wine slides down my throat easily, coating my stomach in heat before I set the glass down on the window ledge.

I am not the woman I always thought I wanted to be. I am not the wholesome, fertile, faithful professor's wife.

And I will never be her.

It's time to let it all go.

Turning to face Nicholas, I wrap my hands around his neck, run my fingers through his thick, dark hair and look deeply into that hooded gaze.

We speak without words, first his breath rising, then a whimper from my lips as he presses me back against the window. He covers me with his tall, broad body, a blanket of steamy lust that pulses up against my breasts and hips, making me ache in places I didn't even know existed.

He lifts a hand to my neck, runs his fingers up over my cheek, and finally, the man who has invaded my dreams all week relieves me with his sweet, hot kiss.

Our lips lock together forcefully at first, years of pent-up desire pouring out of me at the feel of his mouth on mine, at the aggressive way he is holding me, pressing into me. I cannot get enough of him. My hands roam his neck, his broad shoulders, and finally find their way to the buttons on his shirt. I work my way down, ripping at them as he continues kissing me, passionately, deeply, his fingers running through my hair, before rolling down my back and lower still until he reaches the hem of my dress.

He slips one hand underneath, sliding all the way up in between my legs, his fingers finding the wetness that is there only for him, that has been there since he walked into my gallery opening the week before.

His fingers lace underneath my thong, twisting it around as I wrap one leg around his waist and move my lips down his neck, an invitation for him to come closer, go deeper.

He takes my enticement without hesitation, wrapping my other leg around his waist and hoisting me up so that I am straddling him. His lips find mine once more, and this time his kiss is sweeter, softer, more intimate than the first.

He carries me into the bedroom, lays me down on the bed, and climbs on top of me, continuing this intense kiss. He cups my chin in his hands, then runs his fingers softly down my neck before slipping the straps of my tiny black dress over my shoulders.

"Natasha," he breathes into my ear before pulling back to look at me underneath the dim bedroom light. "You are the most beautiful woman I've ever known."

The glow of the moon through the window illuminates the sincerity in his eyes, making me smile bigger than I have in years. I grab his face and kiss him madly, deeply, uncontrollably.

We roll around on the sheets until we have removed every last bit of clothing. Until he has my body naked, pulsing, waiting for him. He is stronger than I realized, the muscles wrapping around his biceps, shoulders, and back a magnificent picture of strength. I run my hands down his chest, finding a larger scar that runs along his left side, spanning almost the entire length of his torso. I take all of him in—the muscles, the scars, the desire and lust that is flooding his eyes as he lays his bare skin on top of mine, as our hips find each other once more, as I wrap my legs around him and invite him in.

He kisses me first, slow and sensual before finally completing this intense connection by thrusting inside me. He fills me up so fully, so deeply that I am momentarily stunned, out of breath, silent. I grip his shoulders, look into his eyes, and feel a scalding heat emanating from him as he moves over me, slow and smooth.

Our bodies roll and flow together in a beautiful rhythm like nothing I have ever experienced. I didn't know such perfection was possible, but with each kiss, each touch of his strong hands on my breasts and thighs, each rock of our hips, I am reminded that it is indeed possible, and against all odds, it is happening to me.

It is really happening.

Nicholas rolls me on top of him, wrapping those heavenly hands tightly around my hips as he watches me move, drinking me in like he could do this all night.

I certainly could.

I let his hands roam wherever they want to go as I keep dancing over him, climbing higher and higher until I feel the climax coming, a ringing of bells in my ears as I burst and collapse over him, moaning in his ear, intense pleasure rolling off my skin.

He holds me close, continues thrusting beneath me as I catch my breath and recover from the most intense orgasm I can ever remember experiencing. I kiss him everywhere: on his cheeks, lips, chest, neck. He tastes salty and sweet all at the same time, the most fulfilling treat of my life.

Soon I feel him expanding and pulsing even harder, his thrusts coming deeper than before. His jaw tenses, his hands pulling my hips down hard and fast until he pulls me in close, tight, holding me sweetly against his chest as he releases.

I close my eyes, reveling in the blissful feel of him throbbing inside me, the fulfillment of our bodies finding ultimate pleasure together, in this hotel far away, where the real world cannot touch this perfect moment we have shared.

Nicholas stays inside me as he brushes his lips over mine. Then he smiles, devious and satisfied.

I kiss him back, pressing my hips down for one last burst of pleasure before rolling to the side and letting him wrap me up in his arms.

Nicholas fits behind me, his knees pressed into mine, our hips happy to stay melded.

He runs his smoldering lips up my neck, wrapping one hand around my breasts, the other pulling my hips in closer, making me forget all about the other life I have, the one that doesn't include him.

"I've never met anyone like you, Natasha," he whispers in my ear. "You're not like all the rest. You're talented, smart, gorgeous...but it's more than that." He props himself up and gazes down into my eyes as he brushes his hand over my cheek. "It's the way I feel when I'm with you. I felt it the first time I laid eyes on you ten years ago. Then when I heard about the gallery opening, I knew I had to see you again. And today, when you danced... you took me to another world, Natasha. Somewhere I never thought I could go...How do you do that?" He shakes his head, blinking down at me with a level of emotion that I didn't expect him to exhibit during our steamy one-night adventure.

I don't know what to say—I am flattered and touched beyond measure. Surprised by his sweet words, by his need to stop in the heat of the moment and tell me this...and stunned at how happy I feel knowing he sees me as different from all of the other women who must flow in and out of his life.

And I realize that ever since he propositioned me last week at the gallery, I've been secretly hoping there would be more to this than just one meaningless night of illicit sex.

Because I feel it too.

"You take me to another world too," I tell him. "And I felt it, all those years ago. I was just too young to understand it."

I reach up, caressing his cheek until I find that small scar over his left eye. Pulling him toward me, I kiss him there, and then again on his forehead, over his eyelids, and finally, I work my way back to his moist, soft lips. After our tender kiss, Nicholas wraps me up in his arms once more, fitting me perfectly into the curves of his strong body. "I could lay here like this with you all night," he says.

I smile, tipping my chin back to meet his. "Me too, Nick. Me too."

He shakes his head, laughing and nuzzling his face into my neck, the way lovers do after they've bared it all. "I did not see you coming, beautiful. You have rocked my world."

And as we roll around under the sheets, kissing, holding each other, and pleasuring each other so many more times I lose count, I realize that the minute Nicholas walked into my gallery opening last week, my world, too, was forever changed.

Eight

I awake in the middle of the night and roll over, instinctively reaching for Nicholas to wrap my arms around his chest, lay my head on his shoulder.

But the other side of the bed is empty, the sheets ruffled and cold.

Was it all a dream? Was *he* a dream?

I sit up, waiting for my eyes to adjust to the darkness.

Soon the outline of Nicholas' muscular, barely clothed body comes into focus. He is standing at the floor-to-ceiling window, wearing only his black boxer briefs and gazing down at the lights below.

Naked, I climb out of bed and slide up beside him. Without saying a word, he wraps his arms around me, pulling me close. His skin is so warm and smooth that I have no desire to climb back into bed without him.

"I couldn't sleep," he says.

"Thinking too much?" I ask, tipping my chin up.

He nods, kissing me softly on the forehead. "Something like that."

"Why don't we take a walk, get some fresh air?" Strolling around Hollywood in the middle of the night wouldn't normally be my cup of tea, but I can hear the restlessness in Nicholas' voice, and he isn't going to fall back asleep anytime soon.

Plus, I could use a dose of reality, a smack of nighttime air to make me remember that there is a world outside this steamy hotel room, a world I will have to re-enter tomorrow when I fly back to DC.

Nicholas runs his hand down the small of my back as he brushes his lips over my bare shoulder. "Good idea, beautiful."

We dress in silence, but my mind is anything but silent. I'm wondering what Nicholas was thinking about alone at the window, how long he has been awake…and if he ever fell asleep at all.

But most of all I'm wondering how will I ever go back to my life with Ethan and move on as if this incredible night, as if *Nicholas*, never happened.

Outside, the streets of Hollywood are still alive at two in the morning. A group of short-skirted girls and hipster boys sporting skinny jeans stumble past the Pantages Theatre across the street, whooping and hollering after what must have been a wild night out at the clubs.

Nicholas takes my hand as we set off down the Walk of Fame on Hollywood Boulevard, our feet skimming over stars' names before we leave all the late-night riffraff behind and round the corner onto Vine Street. We walk a few blocks in silence, take another left, and wind through the side streets of the town I grew up in. I know this neighborhood well, but with the full moon dipping low in the night sky, casting a warm yellow glow over the thick darkness around us, everything about my hometown feels different tonight.

Or maybe it's just that *I* feel different.

How could I not after what I've just done?

I am lost in thought, and not quite sure how long we've walked when Nicholas stops and nods to our right. A neon sign that reads "Psychic" burns in the window of a small, broken-down storefront.

"Have you ever been to one?" he asks.

I shake my head, about to tell him that I've never been, but that Ava used to go regularly. I stop myself, though, when I recognize my instinct to answer for *her* instead of myself.

"No. Have you?" I say finally.

"No, but I've always been curious." A sly grin slides over his lips. It's the first time he's smiled since we set off on our walk. "What do you say? Should we see if she's open?"

An uneasy feeling settles in the pit of my stomach, but I push it aside and tell myself to live a little. I've made it this far, haven't I? Besides, it's doubtful she's open at this late hour.

"Why not?" I say with a shrug.

We walk up the rickety stairs to the front door, and Nicholas wraps loudly.

A few long moments pass, and I am gazing up at that full moon the whole time, wondering how exactly I got here, at a psychic's doorstep in the middle of the night in Hollywood with a man who is not my husband...but who feels so strangely right.

The door snaps open suddenly, startling me. I tear my gaze from the moon to find a pair of piercing silvery eyes and a head of blazing red hair. The older woman who stands in the doorway shoots us a knowing smile before gesturing for us to follow her.

Her low, raspy voice breaks the silence. "Come in."

The smells of incense and cigarette smoke assault me the minute we walk through the door, and the only light in this dim, dank space comes from the flickering of a few white candles in the far corner.

She gestures for us to sit in a pair of red armchairs as she tosses her violet scarf over her shoulder and gingerly takes a seat across from us.

She folds her hands in her lap, sizing us up with an inquisitive glare.

"I was expecting you," she says finally.

A cold chill slithers up my spine as I dodge her gaze and glance over at Nicholas. *What have we gotten ourselves into?*

He smiles back at me in reassurance before addressing the woman. "We were just taking a late-night stroll when we saw your light on. Neither of us has seen a psychic before, and we're just...curious."

Her gaze darts back and forth between the two of us as her long gold earrings jingle in the silence. "*Indeed* you are...Well, let's get started then, shall we? Tell me your names, please."

"Nicholas."

"Natasha."

"Nicholas and Natasha," she says slowly, pronouncing each syllable as if it's the first time she's ever heard these names.

Before I know what she's going to do next, she scoots closer to me and takes my hand. Her skin is hot and leathery, her perfume pungent. She closes her eyes, breathing softly for a few moments before she speaks.

"Natasha, my dear child, I feel an intense sadness coming from you. Oh my. It runs deep into the womb...you're having issues with pregnancy, no?" She opens her eyes briefly for confirmation, and I nod, stunned that she has picked up on this so quickly.

Closing her eyes again, she continues. "You need to let this go as it serves you no more than the relationship you're currently in. You have outgrown both the man and the ideas you once had for a future and a family with him."

Those flashing silver eyes pop open again. "But of course you already know this in your heart, don't you?"

When I don't respond, she squeezes my hand and closes her eyes once more.

"This isn't to say that there will never be a baby, though. It just has to be with the right person. You must listen to what your body is telling you, dear one. Listen to those primal instincts you have. You've been ignoring them for years now, but I can feel a shift happening in you. You're ready to listen now. You're ready for a change...a big one."

My stomach is tied in knots, my voice caught in my throat. This woman is good...*too* good. I'm afraid of what she may say next, especially in front of Nicholas. But there's no stopping her now—she's in the zone.

"I'm getting something else from you...something a little more *exciting*, shall we say? It's a deep desire to live, to move, grow, and dance. To truly let go and experience your passions, your sexual fantasies, your dreams and desires at a whole new level. A level you've never allowed yourself to go to before. I get the feeling that you've been holding back for quite some time now, possibly because of the husband...but mostly because of someone else..."

She pauses, and in this heavy silence, I feel a shift in the air.

"I'm seeing a woman, a glamorous blonde woman. She passed over recently. She's here now…and she has your lips, your smile. Your mother, perhaps?"

A flash of chilled air sweeps in through the open window, blowing out all of the candles except one. I shift uncomfortably in my seat, wishing we could leave. This is ridiculous. She must've recognized me as Ava Taylor's daughter. There's no possible—

"Yes, I'm getting a message from her, actually." The psychic's intense voice cuts through my doubts. Then the woman opens her eyes, and for a moment, they appear as green as emeralds, just like my mother's.

"She wants you to know that she's sorry for what she said to you at the end, for her last words."

Ava's raspy voice dances through my head, taunting my sense of rationality, of what's real and what's not.

It's Ava, darling…You know the 'M' word makes me feel old.

The last candle flickers wildly in the darkness as the woman continues. "She's saying a girl's name…Claire? No, no, not Claire. *Clara.* She's with her, she says. She wants you to know that Clara is okay, that this was how it was all supposed to turn out. You weren't ready to have this child, and she wasn't ready to arrive yet. There is nothing more you could've done. And Clara, she sends you great love."

Tears stream down my cheeks now. I am unable to stop them. The breeze wafting in through the window picks up, swirling the curtains around and blowing out the final candle. Nicholas' hand rests on my shoulder, but I barely feel it. Instead, I feel my mother's presence more strongly than I have ever felt it, as crazy as I know it is.

"She has to go now, your mother, but she has one last message for you, Natasha…'*Keep this one,*' she says."

Blinking through the tears, I ask, "What does she mean?"

The clairvoyant woman smiles, squeezing my hand. "Why, you know, dear. And if you don't tonight, then you'll surely figure it out *quite* soon. Now, onto your handsome boyfriend here."

She switches over to Nicholas abruptly, and I catch a serious flash of hesitation in his eyes. He obviously thought this would be something fun to do with the time before I leave, *not* a channel to connect with dead relatives or unborn children, which has now induced a late-night cry session on my part.

But the redhead is already holding onto his hands, eyes closed, reading him. "Interesting..." she says slowly.

"You know, I'm not sure this is such a good idea," he cuts in, ready to bolt.

But she ignores him. "I see that just like Natasha, you have experienced deep sadness in your life. You lost someone dear to you...actually there were two: a woman and a child. A little girl, I'm seeing a little girl."

Goose bumps run up my arms. *It was a girl.* Surely Nicholas didn't know that yet if Rebecca was so early on in her pregnancy when she was killed.

"They are smiling, happy now, and they each send you warmth and love," she continues. "You *must* forgive yourself before you can truly move forward. What happened was not your fault, dear one. What you must understand is that when it's a person's time to go, nothing can stop the universe from taking them home. You have no control over that, Nicholas."

I am expecting to see tears or sadness pass over his handsome features, but instead, he lets out a relieved breath. Like this is something he has needed to hear for a long time.

"I do see a recent shift in your life, though," she continues. "Something you used to love to do...paint, draw...no, I see photographs. You were a photographer?" She looks up for confirmation, and he nods.

"You let this go for a long time; in the sadness, you couldn't create anymore. But something, or *someone* has brought the spark back to your life. Oh, yes, her aura is *all* over you. You must pay attention to this, see where it leads you. Now is not the time to hold back in your career or in your personal life. Do you understand?" She opens one eye, peeking up at him with a lifted brow.

He clears his throat, giving her a serious nod.

Next she takes my hand, holding tightly onto both of us.

"There is a deep connection here, between the two of you. It is a connection at the level of soul, a connection which transcends the so-called rules which we have created to govern relationships. That is to say, even though you think by all normal standards that what you are doing together is wrong, you know in your hearts that it feels quite the opposite. You may not be ready to admit the truth about what you've found here, with each other, but life doesn't always wait for you to get your act together, dear ones. If you're stuck, the universe will give you opportunities—sometimes masked as great hardships or challenges—to move past whatever is stopping you, but you must *take* these opportunities and breathe life into them. Otherwise, they will pass you by like a storm in the night."

The wind that was sweeping through the room has calmed by the time she is finished, but my head is now spinning enough to create a small tornado in its place.

We stand in the darkness, and Nicholas slips a wad of cash into the woman's hands. The glow of the full moon outside streams in through the window, revealing a gleam in her silver eyes. I can see that she is happy with the work she has done here…but as for me, I'm not sure what to make of these insights, or revelations…or whatever they are.

She ushers us toward the door, but just as I am about to step outside, back into the real world, she takes my hand and pulls me close.

"There is one last thing, Natasha," she whispers in my ear. "You must take good care of your health over these next few weeks and months. This is of utmost importance, as you don't have *only* yourself to think about."

With her final cryptic words twisting through my brain, I follow Nicholas out onto the Hollywood streets, noticing how much higher the moon has climbed in the sky since we first entered the psychic's lair.

Sunrise will hit Los Angeles soon, but now, more than ever, I am not ready. I am not ready to face the day.

Nine

Morning arrives with no warning—a bright blast of sunlight through the wispy white drapes in Nicholas' penthouse suite.

Squinting, I push myself up in bed and immediately recall the unexpected, strangely enlightening encounter with our redheaded Hollywood psychic, her words flooding back to me in waves.

A barefooted Nicholas is seated next to me, his dark jeans, gray T-shirt, wet hair, and tired eyes proof that he probably never fell back asleep last night. He pushes a large tray of breakfast my way.

"I thought you might be hungry," he says with a smile.

I take a long sip of orange juice as I attempt to gather my thoughts, but it's no use. I'm a mess.

"You know, it's so like Ava to come back from the dead and tell me *now* that she's sorry," I say. "I'm not surprised at all."

We both break into laughter—the only thing you can do after such an intense experience with someone who, for all intents and purposes, you don't know very well.

But as our laughter dies down and Nicholas' sweet smile lights up the room more than the Los Angeles sun could ever do, I realize I can't keep using that excuse—the one about not knowing him very well. In one night, we have confessed our darkest moments, our most intimate secrets; he has made love to me endlessly and so, *so* perfectly; and a psychic has told us that our souls are connected.

I can barely wrap my head around it all.

At a loss for words, I reach for a piece of buttery toast. But Nicholas' hand finds mine first.

"Natasha, I want to see you again."

His words hang in the air between us as my gaze catches my sparkling diamond ring once again.

The reality of what I have done washes over me like a shot of ice water to the face.

"I'll see you at the gallery opening here in LA next month," I say all nonchalant, knowing this is *not* what he means.

"Natasha, I want to *see* you again."

"I have to go home," I say numbly. "My life is back in DC. You know that."

"I know, but you can't deny the connection we have. And I'm not saying this just because of what that woman told us last night. I already knew…already felt it. And I know you do too."

"I do, but…"

"But what?"

"But I'm still technically in my marriage! This was just supposed to be a night, Nick. *One night.* For the sale of the gallery."

"I still plan to buy the gallery from you. But that's not what I'm concerned with. I'm concerned with *you*. What if this could be more? More than just one mind-blowing night?"

Before I can answer him, my phone buzzes on the nightstand. I glance over to find Ethan's name flashing on the screen. A wave of nausea rolls through my stomach as tears fill my eyes.

"I have to go, Nick," I say, pushing the sheets off me and reaching for my phone. "My plane leaves in a few hours. I have to leave."

He rushes around the bed, stops me before I can dash into the bathroom and hide from his truth-seeking glare.

His hands find the sides of my face, cradling it gently. "I know you have to leave today. I know you have to go home and face your life there. All I'm asking is that you think about what happened here last night, think about what you really want with your life, and what could be with us."

I shake my head, wishing I could stop the tear that is making its way down my cheek, gliding onto Nicholas' hand. "This is crazy," I whisper.

He smiles. "Maybe, but I've never felt more right about anything in my life. Promise me you'll think about it, Natasha." His lips brush over mine, sending a jolt of desire…and confusion through my weary body. "Promise me."

I nod, swallowing back the rest of my tears. "Okay, I promise."

Nicholas kisses me once more, wrapping his strong arms around my waist, holding me so tightly, so securely that I never want to leave his embrace.

It is in this moment, knowing that in a matter of hours I will be without him, without his touch, his kiss, his voice in my ear, that I am certain I've never felt more right about anything in my life either.

But the truth remains. I have to go home, face Ethan, deal with our own personal financial crisis…and figure out what in the hell the psychic meant when she told me I don't *only* have myself to think about anymore.

Ten

"Natasha Taylor?" A familiar voice calls out to me in LAX, just after I've passed through security.

I turn to find my most scandalous friend from college. "Violet Bell, what are you doing in LA?"

Her silky dark hair swishes over her shoulders as she runs up and wraps her arms around me. "What are *you* doing in LA? God, I haven't talked to you in ages!"

"I know. Jeez, it's been years, hasn't it?"

"When is your flight? Do you have time for a coffee?" She is talking so quickly I can barely keep up. It's the New York in her.

I glance down at my watch, wanting to tell her that my flight leaves in five minutes so I can dodge this talk. It's not that I don't want to catch up with Violet; it's that she always has a way of seeing through my bullshit...which is probably why we lost touch. She never bought into my whole "I want to have a baby so badly with Ethan that I'm willing to go thousands of dollars into debt while pumping my body full of rage-inducing hormones" situation.

"I have some time," I say, trying not to show my hesitation. But I can see right away in her smoky eyes that she caught it.

"Perfect. Me too." She leads the way, not giving me a chance to back out.

After ordering coffees at Starbucks, we settle into a corner table.

"So, I heard about the gallery opening in DC," she launches in. "Liz told me it was a smashing success. I'm so sorry I wasn't there."

I wave my hand. "Oh, that's okay."

"She also told me that Ethan didn't show."

That's my old friend, Violet. Getting right to the point.

"No...no, he didn't."

Violet shakes her head, shooting me a curious glance. "Hmm...if things aren't great with the marriage, then why are you glowing right now?"

"What?" I say, feeling my cheeks blaze with heat. Surely I'm not *glowing*.

"I know that glow," she says, leaning back in her chair with an air of confidence that only a girl as beautiful as Violet can pull off. "I know it well... from personal experience. Come on, Natasha. What's his name?"

"Honestly, Vi, what are you talking about?" I'm beginning to think Violet is psychic too.

"Don't even say his name is Ethan. That man hasn't made you happy in years. What are you doing out in LA—you used to hate making trips out here. Or should I say *who* are you doing?"

Violet stares me down from across the table. I reach for my coffee, but notice that my hands are shaking.

"Oh, fuck it," I concede.

"Now we're talking," Violet says, smirking in her triumph. "What's his name?"

"Nick," I say. "Nicholas Reyes."

Thirty minutes later, I have spilled all of the juicy details, and Violet is staring back at me, mouth agape.

"Natasha, girlfriend, I always knew you had it in you! You couldn't have grown up with that outrageous Hollywood mother of yours and not taken *any* of her with you. It took long enough though, didn't it? So you're going to go home and finally leave Ethan and run away with this amazing man, right?"

I suck down the last few sips of my coffee before letting out a long sigh. "It's not that simple, Vi. We've been married for ten years. You don't just walk away from that after a one-night stand."

"Um, a psychic who called up your dead mother said that the two of you have a soul connection...not to mention the fact that this man gave you your first orgasm in years. What further proof do you need that this is the path you should be on?"

"Just because he gave me an orgasm—okay, so many orgasms I can't even count, and the best of my life—doesn't mean I should end my marriage and run away with the man. I need to at least try to see if things can be repaired with Ethan."

Violet's eyes flash with impatience. "I'm sorry to be so blunt, but let's not pretend that Ethan hasn't been running around on you for years."

A long silence follows, until Violet reaches across the table and takes my hand. "Listen, I have to go catch my flight, but before I do, I have one question for you."

"Yes?"

"Are you happy with Ethan? Truly happy? Can you envision yourself with him, the way it is now, for the rest of your life?"

"That's three questions," I say.

"*Natasha.*"

I answer with a long sigh and a shake of my head. "No, I'm not happy. I haven't been happy...not for a very long time."

"Then whose life are you living, Natasha?"

There it is: the mirror of truth, in a friend I haven't even seen in years.

"You know, for all her faults, your mother gave you a gift when she left you that gallery," Violet says. "Now don't waste it." Violet throws her black Coach bag over her shoulder and stands from the table. "I know all about divorce, honey. It's not pretty—in fact it's downright hell—but you'll survive."

It's only then that I notice Violet isn't wearing her wedding band. "You and Josh?"

She shrugs like it's no big deal, but I can see the pain flashing in her eyes.

"Violet, I had no idea. I'm so sorry."

"It happens. And really, it's just the beginning of a new life. You can't be so afraid. Can it be any worse than what you've lived through the past few years?"

I stand and wrap my arms around her. "Thanks for getting to the bottom of things, as you always do. Let's catch up soon. I want to hear how *you're* doing."

"Oh, I have *loads* of gossip for you. If you ever want to feel better about your life, all you need to do is call me." She pulls away, then reaches back for my hand, squeezing it tightly. "It's time to live your life, girlfriend. The one you were always meant to live."

And with that, my dear New York friend is off in a flash, and I am left alone in the airport, wishing I could wave a magic wand to get that perfect life so easily, without hurting anyone.

I know all too well, though, that it's too late for that.

Eleven

The cab drops me in front of our perfect little Georgetown town house late that night. I grip the handle of my suitcase, gazing at the purple and white hydrangeas I planted last week by the front steps, and then up at the pale blue shutters which line the window of the bedroom that would've belonged to our baby.

Inside the dark foyer, I call out for Ethan, but am only met with the ticking of the clock over the doorway. I wonder if he'll come home tonight and face me in person, or if he's already run back to the hotel.

Dropping my bags on the floor, I climb the stairs in a numb haze, then pad down the hallway to that bedroom, the one I've been saving for a little one.

A little one who never came.

I've kept the door closed since our last IVF attempt failed a few weeks back, and while I know that opening it up again is only going to tear this deep wound inside me to shreds, I cannot stop myself.

Inside, sadness and rage pour through me as I take in my white Pottery Barn desk, which is covered with stacks of fertility books, detailed IVF instructions, and temperature charts. The drawers are filled with thermometers, untaken pregnancy tests, and the pink and blue rattles I bought back in the very beginning, on the day Ethan agreed to try for a baby.

Before I have time to think about what I am doing, my hands are grasping for the charts, ripping them to shreds. Piles of torn papers litter the floor around me as I take each fertility book, one by one, and hurl them against the wall. Slumping to the floor, I grab at the books, tear out the pages, screaming into the darkness.

I snap each pregnancy test in half, and then smash the rattles against the desk, watching as little pieces of pink and blue plastic tumble at my feet.

It doesn't take long to destroy years of work, of research, of hope.

When I am finished dismantling a life that never came to be, I collapse against the wall, sliding down to the floor, out of breath, heaving for air.

"Natasha?"

I lift my tear-stained face to the doorway, where Ethan stands, a confused professor, at a loss for what to do with his crazy wife.

"It's over," I say, my hands in my hair, my head spinning from years of ravaging hormones, late-night arguments, and an unimaginable amount of debt…but mostly from this loveless marriage.

"It's all over," I whisper.

He nods, gazing down at me in disapproval, the way he might look at a student who didn't turn in her term paper on time.

"*Nat.*"

"*No!*" I yell. "Don't call me Nat. You know I hate when you call me that. I've always hated it."

By the grave look in his dark eyes, it's clear that he knows it's not only my quest to have a baby with him that is over tonight.

He knows that it is *us*, this marriage, this relationship, that has failed miserably, that has nowhere else to go but into the trash with all of the hopes and dreams I once had.

Those hopes and dreams for a normal family were all mine, after all. They were never really his. Ethan could have been content living his days in a library—reading, writing, and researching. He never shared my deep desire for creating a family, for the joys that could come with giving a child a loving home—the home I never had. Those were *my* wishes, and I pushed them onto him.

Just as I think Ethan is going to turn around and leave me alone in this wreckage, he walks over, slumps down beside me, and cries.

I haven't seen my husband cry since his father died six years ago. After every failed IVF attempt, when I would break down night after night, he never let a single tear fall.

It was maddening the way he showed no emotion; his robotic state was almost more heartbreaking to me than the loss of each possible pregnancy because it showed me that I was alone on this journey. I had the husband, but it didn't matter—I was completely alone.

Tonight, though, he has finally snapped; he is broken…perhaps even more than I am.

We hold each other there, in the rubble of our marriage, knowing that we have to let each other go. We have to let it all go.

"I'm so sorry. I'm so sorry." He repeats these words over and over as sobs rake through him. "I did love you. I really did. I just didn't want what you wanted, Natasha."

I lay my head on his shoulder, for once knowing exactly how he feels. "I know you didn't. I'm so sorry I pushed it on you."

And while it breaks me to see him this way, I am relieved to see that he is not made of stone, after all.

.

Twelve

Four weeks later

My best friend Liz is waiting on my front steps when I arrive back from a quick trip to the drugstore. She surprises me by throwing her tiny arms around my shoulders and squeezing me tight.

A chilly fall wind blasts past us, swirling orange and yellow leaves over the redbrick sidewalks at our feet, but Liz doesn't let go.

"I feel awful that I wasn't here," she says. Liz has been in Afghanistan for the past month doing God knows what for her work at the State Department, so she wasn't here for the intense week of divorce talks that ensued after the night I returned from LA.

She wasn't here for that very next morning when I confessed my Los Angeles affair to Ethan, and he in turn confessed an affair he's been carrying on for the past year with a twenty-six-year-old graduate student named Gabrielle, with whom he is madly in love.

She missed the day Ethan moved out of our Georgetown home and into Gabrielle's apartment, only five blocks away.

I've been keeping Liz up to date on everything over email—well, on the divorce front anyway. She has no clue why I've just made an urgent trip to the drugstore, or that I cannot stop thinking about the one magical night I spent with Nicholas Reyes—the man who she only believes I know because he bought my photography gallery.

We walk into my half-empty home, and as Liz jets straight to the kitchen and reaches for a bottle of red wine on the counter, I place a hand on her arm.

"That will have to wait."

"Natasha, honestly. You really should be drinking wine daily at this point," Liz scolds. "You're getting a divorce, and your husband just moved in with some hussy down the street! Do you really want to deal with all of this sober?"

Liz never fails to make me laugh, even when my life is in a complete and utter upheaval. I smile at my friend, so grateful that she's home, and that she could be here for me today. I need her now more than ever.

Just as Liz is reaching for two wine glasses—clearly ignoring my protest—I place my drugstore bag on the counter and pull out the pregnancy test, flashing it in front of her face.

"Holy shit," she says, her eyes widening. "You can't be serious."

"I missed my period."

"By how long?"

"I'm two weeks late."

"Well, that's not entirely abnormal. I mean, you're in the beginning stages of a divorce—your body is probably just rebelling against all this change. Plus your last round of IVF wasn't that many months ago. Your system is probably still getting back to normal."

I shake my head at her. "It's different this time, Liz."

The pity I've seen in her eyes countless times in the past few years returns in full force.

"Natasha, I'm sorry, but how? How is it different?"

"If I *am* pregnant, the baby isn't Ethan's."

The wine glass slips from her hand and tumbles onto the counter. "What are you talking about?"

"Ethan and I hadn't had sex in months before our split. He'd been having it elsewhere, remember?"

She cocks her head to the side, looking at me like she's seen a ghost. "And you have, too—been having it *elsewhere*, I'm gathering?"

I bite my bottom lip, feeling a flush of guilt creep over my cheeks. "Well, it was only one night…but yes."

"Natasha Taylor. You slut. I want *all* the dirty details."

Liz has downed over half the bottle of red wine by the time I finish telling her about Nicholas' proposition in the gallery, my first time on the stage in more than fourteen years, my scandalous Hollywood night in Nicholas' penthouse suite, our wild psychic experience, and finally, his final request—that we continue seeing each other.

"I'm speechless," she says after I've stopped talking. "How could I have missed all of this?"

"You were off saving the world, remember?"

She chuckles. "If only…but damn, this is out of control. So, Nicholas still bought the gallery?"

"Yes, and thankfully so because it completely dug us out of debt, and then some."

"What about lawyer and court fees for the divorce? Do you have enough stashed away to handle all of this on your own?"

"Ethan and I decided that since we'd mutually fallen out of love and since we'd both had affairs—granted, his had been going on for a whole year without my knowledge—that we'd keep the lawyers out of it. We're splitting everything down the middle for the most part. We used the money from the gallery sale to pay off all of our debt, and—out of guilt I'm assuming—Ethan insisted that I keep the rest."

"Wow, Reluctant Hubs did one right thing, I suppose."

"He's not *my* Reluctant Hubs anymore," I remind her.

We both have a laugh over that—and even though underneath my laugh, I am heartbroken over the irony and the sadness of how it all went down, a huge part of me is relieved. Relieved that I came clean with Ethan, that the devastation of infertility is finally over…and relieved that we have closed the door on something that was only bringing us both pain and grief.

"So, have you been in touch with Nicholas since you left LA?" Liz asks before taking another gulp of wine.

"He's written and called…but I haven't listened to his messages yet, and I haven't read his emails either. The agent handling the sale of the gallery corresponded with him directly, so I didn't have to."

"What about the photos you took of the dance company for his gallery opening? Have you followed through on your promise there?"

"Yes, I sent all of the files directly to his new gallery director…but I haven't had the courage to write to Nicholas personally yet."

"So, let me get this straight. After the single most incredible night of your life, you refuse to communicate with the man, and now you think you might be carrying his baby?"

Sighing, I shake my head. "That about sums it up."

"And when is the gallery opening in LA?"

"In two days. I fly out tomorrow."

"Shit."

"Yeah, shit," I echo.

Liz reaches for the pregnancy test, which has been burning a hole in my kitchen counter for our entire talk. "Let's get this party started then, shall we?"

She's right. It's time.

Taking the test from her, I head to the hallway bathroom in silence. My hands tremble as I close the door and open up the package. The little white stick looks the same as the gazillions of tests I've taken in the past couple of years…but something about this time feels different.

After years of infertility, I feel completely ridiculous even thinking for a second that this time, I might see two pink lines instead of only one.

But as I get down to business, I can't deny the instinct pulling at my gut—the one that's saying *anything is possible.*

After I finish the test and place it on the bathroom counter, I meet my own gaze in the mirror. My bright blue eyes are shining, my skin is clear and rosy, and my lips are curling into a smile.

Violet was right in the Los Angeles airport that day—I am glowing.

Before I allow myself to peek at the results which are surely washing over the little pregnancy test window by now, I recall the psychic's final words to me on the night of the full moon, on the night I came alive in Nicholas' arms.

You must take good care of your health over these next few weeks and months. This is of utmost importance, as you don't have only *yourself to think about.*

Taking a deep breath, I squeeze my eyes closed, lower my face, and peel my eyelids open slowly.

The tears were waiting, ready to be released, ready for the answer I already knew was coming.

A knock comes softly at the door. "Natasha, is everything okay?"

Cradling the test in my hands, I open the door and beam over at Liz.

"It's positive," I say, barely believing the words as they pour from my mouth. "It's positive, Liz."

"Oh, Natasha!" Liz pulls me into her embrace, and there in the hallway of my perfect little Georgetown home that is only half-furnished and is currently up for sale after the demise of my failed marriage, my best friend and I jump up and down, crying and laughing like two jubilant little girls.

I've been picturing this moment for years now, and never once did I imagine it like this.

But that's only because my imagination couldn't stretch that far at the time. I couldn't imagine such boundless joy—the kind of joy only a woman can feel when she has received the best news of her life.

Thirteen

I spend the entire flight to Los Angeles poring over Nicholas' emails. He has sent me one every single day since I last saw him, and only now do I have the courage to read his passionate words.

I start from the beginning. Some of his messages are short and sweet, recounting memories of our amazing night—of the way our bodies melted together so perfectly, of the way we laughed to the point of tears, talked as if we'd known each other for decades, kissed as if the sun would never rise, as if the night would last forever.

Other letters are longer, more detailed confessions of the way he feels about me, how his desire for me is only increasing as the weeks roll by, how he doesn't want to let the best thing that has ever happened to him get away.

But when I reach the end, his very last email sends a sharp pain right to my heart.

> *Dear Natasha,*
>
> *This will be my last email to you. I think I have said everything I can possibly say, and still no response from you. I know you are probably still figuring out your life back home, and my hope in writing you every day has*

simply been to let you know that I haven't forgotten about the way you make me feel or the amazing connection we shared on our one incredible Hollywood night.

That, and I wanted you to know what a beautiful person you are, inside and out.

I won't forget you. But I also know I need to let you go. If things ever change on your end, please do get in touch.

I hope you'll still be at the gallery opening later this week. You created quite the buzz with your photographs of Ava, so I have no doubt that there will be a big turnout at this exhibit. It would be a shame if you missed it.

As for me, I will be there, but I promise to leave you alone. I don't want to confuse or upset you, as I fear I may have already done all these weeks with my letters.

—Nicholas

Tears sting my eyes as I re-read his final words to me. Have I already lost him? Why didn't I read his emails before today, and respond at least once?

What was stopping me?

Well, the divorce drama of course, and the processing I had to do as Ethan was moving out, and—

My hand instinctively runs over my belly, stopping my brain from making one more cowardly excuse for why I have been avoiding Nicholas.

As I listen to the quiet sounds of my breath, to the beating of my own heart, I know.

Fear.

All along, it was fear. Fear of being truly happy. Of letting myself fall for someone who is right for me for a change, someone who sees me for exactly who I am, and who wants to be with me anyway.

As the plane jets across the country, taking me closer to the man I have been avoiding, closer to the life and the city I've feared my whole life, I know that it's time to let it all go.

My heart is ready for love—*a big love*—and it doesn't have any room left for all of that toxic fear.

Suddenly, my fingers are on the keyboard, tapping a response faster than my brain can keep up.

This isn't a typical, "I'm sorry for not getting back to you" email, though.

The words that pour from my heart to my fingers and onto the page stem from that primal instinct the psychic referred to in her candlelit living room, the instinct I have been ignoring for years now.

From: Natasha Taylor
To: Nicholas Reyes
Subject: Natasha's Confession

Did my soul already know?
Had she already planned that magical night?
The night your eyes would take me hostage.
The night chemistry would flow between us, effortlessly.
An electric current of heat.

My soul, she must have known
How important you would become to me.
How happy I would be
Knowing you exist.

She knew...that smart, vibrant, sexy soul.
She totally knew.

You are a gift.
A beautiful, perfectly timed gift.
One I will never take for granted.
One I will love, always, for this.
For where you have taken me.

The world has opened
Now that you have arrived.

After I finish my string of heartfelt words, I close the email with one final sentence.

I will be at the gallery opening, Nicholas—single and bearing news.

xxxx

Natasha

As I hit the "Send" button, I can only hope that Nicholas still wants to see me at this point, and that when I tell him about the child I am carrying—the child that belongs to him, to *us*—he doesn't run for the Hollywood hills.

My hand finds my belly once more, and I smile softly, telling my little baby that no matter what happens, *we* will be okay.

Fourteen

Palm trees, city lights, and wannabe stars paint the streets of downtown Los Angeles as the taxi zips closer to my destination on this warm Saturday night.

I check my phone for the thousandth time since I sent my response off to Nicholas the day before, but still nothing. His gallery director sent me specific instructions *not* to show up until a half hour before the opening. She said they had the exhibit under control and wouldn't need my help setting up.

I couldn't help but worry that it was Nicholas who asked her to keep me away until the big event, so that he wouldn't run into me beforehand. After the intimate night we shared and after the way he poured his heart out to me in his letters, not hearing from me all these weeks must have hurt him immensely. And I'm not sure if my little poem—no matter how genuine—has repaired the damage I've done.

Despite the relaxing night air which wafts in through the taxi window, kissing my cheeks and whispering that it will all be okay, my stomach is still twisted in knots. I'm not sure if it's the beginning of pregnancy symptoms setting in or nerves over the uncertainty of my situation with Nicholas, or both.

Whatever it is, I find myself calling up a memory of me and my mother, riding in the back of a limo, on the way to one of her many film premieres.

Confessions of a City Girl

I was only twelve at the time, an impressionable young girl on the verge of my teenage years, but already way too mature for my age—a mother to my own mother.

Ava had fallen in love with the lead actor in this particular movie, a dashing older man who was married with two children. From what she had shared with me at the time, he'd fallen for her too—a sudden and devastating fall, as it usually went with my mother's lovers—but he wasn't ready to leave his wife, and my mother was beginning to think that he never would be.

He would be arriving at the premiere with his voluptuous Latina wife on his arm, and Ava was an absolute wreck.

Just before we climbed out of the limo to pose for the crowds, a dazzling mother-daughter duo on the red carpet, I remember taking my mother's hand in mine and gazing into her tear-stained emerald eyes.

"It doesn't matter if he chooses you or not, Mom. You're beautiful just the way you are."

Ava had smiled at me, and instead of ordering me not to call her *Mom*, she leaned over and kissed me on the forehead. "So wise you are, my darling Natasha. So wise."

As the taxi pulls up to Nicholas' brand new photography gallery, and I place one shiny silver stiletto on the sidewalk, I have a feeling that if Ava were here tonight, she would take my hand and tell me the exact same thing that I told her, all those years ago.

⸙

Drew Hanover, the dance company director, is waiting for me at the doors of the gallery as I arrive.

"There you are, love," he says, his huge grin and open arms a welcome sight to my frazzled nerves.

"Hey, Drew," I say, allowing him to pull me into his tight embrace.

"Your photos of my dancers are brilliant, Natasha!" He steps back, fanning his teary eyes. "Absolutely stunning, just like the photographer herself." Drew plants a long kiss on my cheek, complete with a lingering smooch sound and all, before attempting to usher me into the gallery's front doors.

I hesitate for a moment, trying to catch my breath.

"What is it, love?" he asks

"Is Nicholas here yet?" I whisper, stealing a glance down the sidewalk.

Drew lifts a curious brow. "Not at the moment. But there's something you need to see inside before you get mauled by the crowds for your spectacular photographs."

"What are you talking about?"

A devious smile peppers his cheeks as he opens the door for me.

"Come see for yourself, love."

Planting a shaky hand on my belly, I step through the doorway into the elegant gallery. The artistic, candid shots I took of Drew's dancers on that life-changing afternoon only one month ago span the gallery's sleek walls, filling up the space with such overwhelming beauty that I am momentarily silenced.

Granted, I must have combed over each of these photographs hundreds of times before sending them off for printing, but experiencing their life-sized versions in this gorgeous gallery is almost too much for my hormonal, emotional heart to handle. Memories of that day rush back to me in waves as I make my way around the room, not believing that these works of art came from my very own camera.

Drew trails behind me, cooing and gasping over each picture. But just as we reach the center of the gallery, he goes quiet.

I shoot a questioning glance in his direction, but he is already spinning my shoulders back around, pointing me toward a massive photograph featured front and center in the exhibit.

It is a picture of me, dancing onstage in complete abandon, totally unaware that I am being photographed. My leg is extended back into a high arabesque, my gaze lifted to the ceiling where a spotlight casts a violet glow over my face and neck.

A single tear rolls down my cheek, but my luminescent blue eyes are sparkling and shimmering with unabashed, pure joy.

Underneath the photograph, a silver plaque reads:

Dancer in Love
Natasha Taylor photographed by Nicholas Reyes

Drew leaves me alone as I run my fingers over the engraving of our names and let my gaze rest on the photograph once more.

The shot is so striking, so real, so raw, that I am having a hard time believing the dancer in the photograph is me. But she *is* me—she is my truth.

I am amazed that after the disastrous way my dance career ended, after the loss of my baby Clara, after a loveless marriage and the ravaging infertility that followed, that after *all of that*, my passion, my pure adoration for dance, for movement, never left me.

And Nicholas has captured it all—my essence—perfectly in this photograph.

Regret over not writing him back all these weeks almost brings me to my knees in the center of the gallery, but before I can go there, a hand covers mine.

"Natasha."

I breathe in his masculine scent, feel his presence close behind me, and afraid of what might happen when I turn around, I find myself wanting to stay here in this moment forever.

But then I remember my resolve to let go of the fear, to move toward love.

And so, I find the courage to turn around.

Nicholas stands before me, his warm smile and those captivating eyes wrapping me up in their sweetness, their honesty, their love.

"Nicholas, I...I don't know what to say. It's beautiful."

He reaches up, tucking a strand of hair behind my ear. "*You're* beautiful, Natasha. I was only photographing what was right in front of me."

I can actually feel myself glowing this time as we beam at each other in the middle of the gallery, two lost lovers who have found each other under the most unlikely of circumstances.

I don't even notice that my hand has once again settled on my belly until Nicholas' hand covers mine there.

He tilts his head to the side, lifting an expectant brow. "The news?"

My smile only grows as I nod, once, twice, three times, tears rolling down my cheeks.

"I just took the test two days ago..." I can see by the excitement in Nicholas' eyes that I don't need to be nervous about what I am going to say next, but this has been such a long journey, with such an unexpected twist, that I can't help but stumble over my words. "I know this is so soon, so crazy, and it's totally fine if you're not up for this—you know I expect nothing of you—but Nicholas, it was positive, and ...*it's yours*."

Nicholas pulls me into his arms, covering my cheeks, forehead, neck, and shoulders with so many kisses, I can't help but let out a delighted laugh. Then he sweeps me off my stilettos and spins me around, laughing and kissing me all the while.

Our lips finally meet in a burst of sweet, unadulterated passion...a passion that runs deeper than anything I have ever experienced.

As I relax into his safe arms, I realize that his kiss is the answer that I needed, the answer I was hoping for ever since I watched those two little pink lines appear.

He is still holding me as we finally give our lips a break and gaze into each other's eyes. "Your poem was the most beautiful thing anyone has ever written to me, Natasha," he says softly. "Thank you."

"I'm sorry I didn't write you sooner. With the divorce—"

"Shhh," he says, placing a finger over my lips. "No apologies tonight, okay?"

He places me back onto my heels ever so gently and rests his hand on my belly—a place that finally, for once, holds so much promise.

Tears rim his eyes as he smiles at me. "Know that I will be by your side every moment of the way, Natasha. *I'm in.*"

"Thank you," I whisper. "Thank you so much."

He slips his comforting hand around to the small of my back as we turn together to face the front of the gallery.

"Ready to see your career fly, beautiful?" he says, shooting me that bold, disarming grin.

I beam back at him, and for the first time in years, I feel confident, *certain* that I am on the right path.

"Yes, let's do this," I say.

Nicholas takes my hand, and we walk, side by side, through the gallery. Just before we reach for the front doors, Ava's voice comes to me in a whisper.

"Keep this one."

I glance back through the gallery, searching for my glamorous mother, for her radiant blonde curls, her mesmerizing emerald eyes, but instead I only find the shining portrait of myself which stands proud and tall in the center of the gallery.

It is in this moment that I finally understand what she meant when she sent me that very same message on the night of the full moon.

Closing my eyes, I make a promise to my mother, wherever she may be.

I won't let him go, Mom. I promise, I will never let this love go.

That night, as Nicholas and I welcome in the crowds, as I am approached by magazine art directors and gallery owners and offered more opportunities than I ever could've dreamed of, I realize that in my mother's dying moments, she finally gave me the gift she was never able to give during her days on this earth, during her days as my mother—a true chance at life, at love, at happiness, and—as unconventional though it may be—a chance to create the loving, beautiful family I have always wished for.

Confessions
of a City Girl

San Diego

One

"Elizabeth Valentine, look at me." My father's impatient voice booms through his Langley office, snapping me back to the days when I was a little girl, staring up at his domineering shadow, inevitably about to take the blame for whatever shenanigans my little sister Julia had just pulled.

My dad's demanding career with the CIA meant that he never had time for us *or* our shenanigans.

But today, the unforgiving Director of the National Clandestine Service is making the time because I am a thirty-three-year-old woman with my own proven track record of over ten years in the CIA—a track record which is now tarnished, and potentially ruined with the grave error I made on my last mission overseas.

Austin's death was my fault.

That reality shoots into my consciousness once again, too painful for me to fully realize, even six months after the fact. Instead, I want to run away from this sterile building, call my best friend Natasha, and tell her everything. But as a covert officer, that isn't an option. Just like all of my other friends, Natasha believes I work for the State Department.

I can't tell her that I watched my partner, Austin Black, die in my arms. I can't tell her that he took a bullet...*for me.*

The memory of Austin's translucent blue eyes as he collapsed against me within seconds of that bullet hit—the bullet he could've been spared if only I wouldn't have confessed—

"Elizabeth."

Finally, I look into my father's stone gray eyes, wishing they were softer. Just for today.

"I know you don't normally report to me, but this can't go on any longer." His knuckles turn white as he clasps his hands together over the desk. "It's been six months since Black was killed, and you're still walking around here in a daze, making mistakes, doing subpar work at best. What happened in Afghanistan that you aren't telling me?"

"You read the report," I say, wishing we could leave it at that. Wishing I could've gotten myself together these past few months so we wouldn't be having this conversation.

"Yes, I did. Straightforward enough. One week in the safe house. An unexpected ambush. Enemy fire. Shot to the chest."

Swallowing the truth—something I am all too good at—I look him in the eye. "Yes, that about covers it."

"What the report didn't mention, though, is that you were in love with the man."

My father catches me off guard. He never uses the word *love* in my presence.

I swallow the knot that has gathered in my throat since last fall when my world was flipped upside down. "I didn't...I mean, what are you talking—"

"Cut the bullshit." He slams his fist against the desk, sending a stack of papers flying to the floor. "No one around here has the balls to say anything to you, to demand that you get your act together, partly because you're my daughter, and partly because the entire team knows you were in love with Black. But I don't give a damn. You knew this line of work carried risks, and you chose it anyway. Now your partner is dead, and life at the Company goes on. But if you can't cut it around here—"

"I'm fine," I snap. "It's been a hard few months, but I'll get it together. You don't need to scold me like a child."

My father ignores me, continuing in his stern tone. "You've always been so sensible, Liz. So focused, smart. I never thought you would let your feelings get in the way of your career, of your purpose at the Company. This not only cost Austin his life, it also cost us the entire operation." He pauses, shaking his head at me. "I know there's more to this incident than what you've reported."

So he knows.

He knows that my love for Austin is ultimately what led to his death.

"Whatever happened between you two over there is in the past. But I *won't* stand here and let you waste your career. You've worked hard for this, Liz. Harder than anyone else on your team. You've never used me to get to the next step—you've done it all on your own. But if you don't get your shit together, you know what will happen."

"Is it too late?" I ask, wondering if after the loss of Austin, I will lose my only other true passion—my career at the CIA. I have sacrificed everything—friendships, relationships, a love life—to make this job work. To follow in my father's footsteps.

And to think, if only I had lied one more time—to myself, to Austin—none of this would be happening.

Austin wouldn't have been killed.

My father shakes his head. "If you can pull your head out of your ass…" He pauses, and for a flicker of a second, I catch a hint of compassion in those hardened eyes. "No, it's not too late."

I clear my throat, straighten my posture. "Okay, understood. I'll get myself together." If only I knew how. If only I could lean on my friends to help me. But my father is right—I chose this career. I knew the risks. I knew about the isolation. As his daughter, I witnessed firsthand the way an undercover career in the CIA can destroy your personal life, bleeding into every relationship until each one is completely unrecognizable, until the only person you can count on is yourself…and even that is questionable.

"I spoke with your sister this morning," my father says. "She wants you to come to San Diego, spend some time at her…*yoga studio.*" My father is pained just saying the words—he's never approved of Julia's escape to the

West Coast, her adoption of such a "ridiculous hippy lifestyle," as he so affectionately calls it.

Truth be told, while I am happy for Julia that she seems to have found her niche, I have to agree with my father on this one thing. I've never understood the whole yoga and meditation craze. Sitting cross-legged to breathe and just be with yourself? Twisting your body into all sorts of painful poses? No, thanks.

I'd rather drink a bottle of red and call it a day.

"Apparently she's running some sort of retreat this week," my father continues. "Says it could be perfect for you."

"You're actually suggesting that I go?" I try to keep the desperation from seeping into my voice, while in my head I am still clinging to the image of that bottle of red wine. "Isn't leaving right now the worst thing I could possibly do?"

"Taking some time off to get your head straight is the *only* thing you can do right now, after this mess. Besides, you're certainly not accomplishing much around here these days."

His words sting, but he's actually being kind to call it a mess. Austin is dead. I am the daughter of the Director of the National Clandestine Service; as such, I am *never* permitted to screw up, not to this magnitude anyway.

This isn't a mess; it's a complete disaster.

"Does Julia know anything?" I ask.

"Your sister knows the rules, Liz. She didn't probe."

"I don't need to do yoga by the beach," I snap at the preposterous notion. "I need to get back into the field."

My father shakes his head. "You're hardly in a state to head overseas."

I clasp my hands together in my lap in an attempt to stop their trembling. "I'm an adult—you can't force me to leave everything behind for some touchy-feely yoga retreat with Julia and her chanting yoga friends. I don't see how that will help me deal with what has happened."

My father's jaw locks as he slides two pieces of paper across his desk. "You don't have a choice in the matter."

A quick scan of the first page reveals a flight itinerary with my name on it.

Departing Washington National for San Diego. 8 a.m. tomorrow.

Flipping to the second page, I find a photograph of a bronzed man twisting himself into some ridiculous, upside-down pretzel pose.

"Who in the hell is this?" I ask.

"Patrick Roberts," my father answers. "Your sister's new husband."

His words have to sink in for a few moments before my brain can come up with a coherent response.

"Julia got married?" I spurt finally. "Without telling me? To *this* guy?"

My father nods, disapproval lining his scrunched-up brows.

"Wait, his last name is Roberts?" I say. "So Julia's name is going to be *Julia Roberts?*"

My father sighs. "You know Julia has always had that silly obsession with the actress—but to take it this far. *My God.*"

Since the first time we watched the movie *Pretty Woman* as little girls, my sister has been obsessed with Julia Roberts. She's watched every single Julia Roberts film too many times to count, and in our college days, she even dyed her hair the exact same shade of red and opted for golden brown contacts in an attempt to capture her look—which was silly because my sister is absolutely gorgeous and has never been short on male admirers.

"You know there's a reason behind her Julia Roberts madness, though, don't you?" I say to my father, wondering if he even remembers.

He draws his lips into a tight line, his gaze darting out the window.

"Mom had her laugh—that same, contagious laugh as Julia Roberts," I say softly. "And once she left—"

"Once your mother disappeared from our lives," my dad cuts in, "I was expected to care for two little girls on my own." For the first time in our conversation—and perhaps the first time in years—I notice my father's emotionless shield lifting, and I see the hurt, the disappointment, the shame in his eyes. "Which is why I need you to go to California and check out your sister's new husband."

"Do you have a reason to believe there's something off with him?" I ask, gazing down at the crazy pretzel photo. "Well, besides the fact that he can twist his body in ways *no one's* body should ever be twisted."

"Apparently, they eloped last month. She just told me on the phone last night. A quick background check left a few unanswered questions. Something isn't quite adding up, and I don't have time to deal with this. I trust you'll be up to the task, though."

"You do realize this is why Julia moved across the country. Why she chose to run off and get married without telling you first," I say, unable to hide my exasperation. "Because of this—your looking up every single guy who has ever come into our lives, right down to our first kisses in junior high school, thinking they *must* be hiding some monumental secret. Not every man is out to sabotage our lives, Dad." I raise up the photo of Patrick, the long-haired yoga pretzel. "Especially not this guy. If this is just some ploy to get me to—"

"Austin was my most skilled agent," my father cuts in. "You were privileged to work alongside him. But you let your feelings get in the way, and now he's dead and your career is on the line. If you want to have any chance at keeping your job, at getting your life back together, you'll go to San Diego and you'll find out who in the hell this Patrick Roberts character is. Do you understand?"

I stand from my father's desk, gripping the flight itinerary in my hands, wondering why I ever believed that following in his footsteps would make him love me more.

"I understand," I say, swallowing my tears, my pride, and my desire for a real parent during one of the hardest years of my life.

Just as I am letting myself out of his office, he calls out to me.

"Elizabeth, wait."

I turn around slowly, dreading whatever words might come out of his mouth next.

But when I catch his gaze, a pained look passes through those stone eyes.

"You may not remember this since it was just after your mother left, and you and Julia were only little girls…but my partner was killed too."

All I remember of those years is hearing my dad cursing behind closed doors, and then leaving us with our grandmother again. Leaving… always leaving.

"I know what it feels like," he says. "Take this week to get your head on straight, then come back here and prove that you can do this."

Slipping out of his office, I walk numbly down the corridor.

One week in San Diego. Do some yoga. Investigate my sister's new husband. If it means keeping my career, keeping some semblance of the life I had before everything turned upside down, I'll do it.

I'll do anything.

But first, since I can't call my girlfriends and vent about any of this, I really need to get home to that bottle of red wine.

Two

My sister's pale blue Beetle convertible zips up to the curb just as I am stepping out of the San Diego airport. Dressed head to toe in black, I am a total fish out of water in this sea of sunshine, swaying palm trees, Botox, and beach babes.

With her movie star blue eyes and the blonde waves that cascade down her perfectly tanned skin, Julia is one of those unbelievably gorgeous California girls. Hers is a natural beauty though, just as my mother's was. With my auburn hair and hazel eyes, you would never know the two of us are sisters... except for our identical laugh—well, it's more of a giggle really, but today, as I am trying to cope with the fact that my own sister didn't even call me to tell me she got married, I don't think there will be much giggling going on.

Julia bounces out of the car, and the minute she gazes into my tired eyes, she wraps me up in a hug. She is the one person in my life who knows what my father and I actually do for a living—it's a privilege that comes only for immediate family—but she doesn't know...*can't know*...the details about my partner's death.

After our long embrace, she squeezes my shoulders, smiling her pearly whites. "Oh, Liz, I'm so glad you're here. This week is going to positively change your life!"

That's Julia—always bouncing, optimistic, excited.

Sometimes I wonder how we grew up in the same home.

I force a smile, my muscles already aching at the thought of stretching my body into those impossible yoga poses I've seen on Julia's website, while still, my heart is the most broken muscle of them all.

I wish I could tell Julia. Just this once, I wish I could tell her everything.

But there is the business of Patrick the yogi which must be dealt with. "So, congratulations on the new husband," I say, eyeing her left ring finger, only to find that it's still bare. Interesting.

She grabs my suitcase and hauls it into the trunk, tossing a nonchalant "Thanks!" over her shoulder, as if I'm congratulating her on a new job or a new car, not a new husband. She clearly doesn't want to deal with the round of questioning that will come next.

As we climb into her little beachmobile and zoom away from the airport, I launch in.

"So, why didn't you call to tell me? I mean, this is huge, Julia, and I've never even heard you mention this guy's name."

She cranks up the radio as we whiz past the sailboats lining the sparkling bay, the runners out for their lunchtime jogs. *California really is a different country,* I think as I push my sunglasses up and take in the spectacular view. How does anyone get any work done around here?

"We only just met a few months ago," she quips. "And besides, if I had called you and Dad and invited you both to our big day, would you have even made it?"

There she goes, that sister of mine, always spouting the truth.

"That's not the point," I say, firmly avoiding it.

"That is *exactly* the point." Julia veers onto the highway, revving the Beetle up to eighty as her hair blows wildly with the top down. "Inviting you only to know for a fact you wouldn't make the time to show up to the single most important day of my life would have only made both me and Patrick feel horrible. I know your career is demanding; we grew up with the same father, always moving, always leaving—I get it. But is there any room for *living your life* in this career path you've chosen, Liz? Any room for friendships, family...for love?"

The mention of love sends a stab of pain straight to my already wounded heart.

Clasping my hands together in my lap, I try to forget about Austin, about the confession I made to him that day, about the tragic way it all ended. But even the blue skies and endless California sunshine aren't doing it for me today.

Julia's hand lands on my knee. "Oh, God. I'm so sorry, Liz."

Her sweet words only make me more upset. I wipe furiously at my eyes, never one to display emotion in public, even if it is in front of my sister. "It's fine. Really, I'll be fine."

We sit in silence for the next few minutes as we head up I-5 to Julia's Del Mar beach home.

Finally, I catch Julia eyeing me warily. "So, for Dad to call me and suggest that you actually come out here to do yoga, I know that whatever is going on must be big."

"Julia, you know I can't—"

"I know, I know. Obviously, *I know*." While Julia fully comprehends the rules, she has never liked them. She's all into sharing our deepest emotions, our *truth*, as she so irritatingly calls it every time we speak on the phone, and the fact that I lie—albeit out of necessity—to all of my friends and family on a regular basis really drives her nuts.

"What I was going to say, though, is that it was a big deal for Dad to be in support of you coming, but an even bigger deal that you got on that plane. You haven't exactly been supportive of my life out here all these years, you know."

Here we go.

"Julia, I—"

"I couldn't tell either of you that I met someone and fell in love because Dad would inevitably find a million reasons why the poor man is plotting to kill me, and you would just be jealous of my happiness, the way you always have been."

She says this last part so matter-of-fact, as if it is an undeniable truth that I have always been jealous of my sister's joy.

I shift in my seat, pretending that she didn't just punch me in the gut while she's just humming along to the radio, another beautiful day in San Diego.

"I understand you not telling Dad," I say finally. "But I'm your sister. We share everything. I would've been happy for you. I *am* happy for you."

"We *used* to share everything, Liz. When we were girls. But once you joined the big bad Company, that changed. *You* changed."

"Fine, I changed. But you can't go into my line of work, deal with the shit I'm dealing with on a daily basis, and not become hardened by it all. That doesn't mean I don't want to hear about what's going on in *your* life. Especially news this big."

Julia veers off at the Del Mar Heights exit, and soon, the endless blue Pacific comes into view. I am momentarily speechless; I still can't believe my sister calls this paradise her home.

"Well, in a few minutes, you're going to meet my husband and then you'll see why I fell in love and tied the knot so quickly."

"Oh, you mean it wasn't just because you wanted to officially become Mrs. *Julia Roberts*?" It's just too good to pass up; I can't help myself.

"It's Julia *Valentine*-Roberts," she snaps. "I'm hyphenating."

"Oh, just drop Valentine," I tease. "You know you want to."

Julia Roberts ignores me and turns in to the driveway of a magnificent beach home sitting atop the cliffs of Del Mar.

"*This* is Patrick's house?" With its colorful array of tropical plants lining the front walkway and the floor-to-ceiling windows overlooking the rolling waves of the Pacific, this place is straight out of a coastal living magazine.

"It's *our* house now," Julia corrects me. "Remember, we're married."

"Well, it happened so quickly, I almost forgot. Plus, you're not wearing a ring."

"Patrick and I don't believe in rings," she says, climbing out of the car. "We don't need material items to prove that we love each other."

I lift a skeptical brow in her direction. "Really? Because the Julia I remember used to pore through bridal magazines and tear out pages of her favorite rings."

My sister ignores me and bounces through her mini rain forest, so in her element amid the cheerful pink flowers tumbling down the lush vines in front of her gorgeous beach pad.

Dragging my suitcase behind her, I decide to let it go for now and try to be supportive. "How about a midday glass of wine before we head to the yoga studio?" I call out.

She turns and levels a serious gaze at me. "You may live a completely secret life, but if I know my sister, I know that you downed at least two of those mini bottles of wine on the flight out here."

"That's preposterous," I say, finally letting a smile slide past my lips. "It was a morning flight!"

"Since when has that ever stopped you?" she asks.

"Fine," I concede. "But it's my understanding that when one's life is falling to pieces, time of day of alcohol consumption is completely irrelevant."

Julia shakes her head at me. "Kale smoothies, meditation, and yoga—that is my prescription for you, young lady. Oh, that and a good dose of Bradley Hunter. Dear Buddha, wait until you see this guy."

Three

"Who's Bradley Hunter?" I ask as we make our way into Julia and Patrick's immaculate home, where every wall, every piece of furniture, wall hanging, lamp—absolutely *everything*—is sparkling, pristine white.

"I met Bradley in the waiting room at my acupuncturist's office—"

"You're seeing an acupuncturist now? What for?" I eye my sister's glowing skin, her shiny hair, her toned legs. "Honestly, I've never seen a healthier human being."

"Patrick set me up with her," she responds. "He said it helps release blockages."

"You look pretty free-flowing to me," I say as I watch her unload bundles of kale, spinach, broccoli, cucumbers, and berries from her refrigerator. I take one look at the colorful pile of fresh produce, drop my suitcase in the middle of her kitchen, and head straight to her wine rack.

Julia smacks my hand as I reach for a bottle.

Really, sometimes you'd think *she* was the older sister here.

"Back to Bradley," she says with the usual edge to her tone that only *I* tend to bring out. "The minute he looked at me, I just knew we had a deeper connection...a soul connection, you know? Obviously we must have known each other in our past lives."

"Obviously," I say, popping a handful of blueberries into my mouth so that I won't say what I'm really thinking.

"And we've clearly reunited souls in this life to bring love, light, and yoga to the community." Julia smiles brightly as she tosses her golden locks over one shoulder and washes the produce.

I stuff more blueberries into my mouth, this time wishing I wasn't so envious of my sister, of the pure simplicity of her life.

Love, light, yoga, and smoothies. Really? God, if she had any clue what I have just lived through.

"So, what does Patrick think about you and Bradley coming back together in this lifetime to spread your love and light around?" I cringe inwardly as my characteristic sarcasm makes a bold appearance. I just can't help myself, though.

"Liz, we're all here to spread our light with the universe." A high-pitched male voice sneaks up behind me.

I flip around to find a man floating down the spiral staircase, a vision of flowing white linen and unbelievably orange skin.

This must be Patrick.

I have the sudden urge to ask him if he is the taller father of the Oompa Loompas—the *enlightened one,* perhaps—but since this is the first time I am meeting my sister's new husband, I bite my tongue.

"So nice to meet you, Patrick," I say.

He immediately goes in for the hug, squeezing me so tightly and for so long that I begin to smell his *scent.* Surely the natural deodorants these days could take it up a notch?

When he finally releases me, I suck in a dramatic breath, to which Patrick replies, "That's right, Liz. *Breathe.* Just keep breathing." He swirls his hands around my face in some wild flowing gesture, and then saunters past me to Julia as if that were a totally normal greeting.

My sister is humming away like a happy little bird as she stuffs loads of kale into her Vitamix. Yes, just a normal day here at the Roberts' beachside smoothie-bar.

"Were you meditating, honey?" Julia asks Patrick. "I hope we didn't disturb you."

Patrick's orange face goes dim. "Yes, I was pretty deep, actually...but it's okay. Life continues to flow, doesn't it?" His tone is a little too patronizing, and Julia's smile a little too tight...making me wonder just how well this bizarre dynamic *flows* behind closed doors.

She flips on the Vitamix, whipping all that green stuff into a frenzy as I lean against the wall, suddenly overcome with exhaustion. Even though they both mean well, Patrick and Julia's yogic view on life isn't really helping me at the moment.

I want to curl up in a ball and go to sleep for another six months—or however long it will take to heal this hole in my heart.

Instead, I take the glass full of green sludge that Julia is forcing into my palm, noticing my gag reflex kicking in just looking at it.

"I know it looks gross now, but trust me," she says. "After one week on these, you'll be so addicted, you'll never know how you lived without them."

"Oh, I'm sure," I say before taking the plunge.

As I force down the thick liquid, a bright idea occurs to me. Maybe if Patrick drinks enough of these, his shoulder-length dirty-blonde hair will turn the same forest green color of the Oompa Loompas, which will complete his Enlightened Oompa Father look.

God, I'm terrible.

Once I have finished my first green smoothie, Julia nods in approval and plucks two yoga mats from the foyer.

"Patrick, love, would you mind taking Liz's suitcase up to the guest room?" Julia's tone takes on a new level of sickening sweetness, as if it's the only way she could get this yoga master husband of hers to lift a bag. "She's had a long trip, and we have to rush off to the opening session of the retreat or we'll be late."

Patrick doesn't look happy about the bag transportation—which I don't find all too enlightened of him—but he takes it up the tall winding staircase all the same. Just before we leave, he calls down to us. "I'll be sitting for the next three hours. My vibrations are rising."

"That's wonderful, honey," Julia replies. "We'll be out all afternoon, so not to worry, we won't interrupt."

Outside, I squeeze my sister's elbow. "His vibrations are rising?"

She sighs, tossing the mats into the back of the Beetle.

"Patrick takes his meditation practice very seriously, Liz. I really admire him. He can sit for hours at a time."

I settle into the passenger seat, contemplating this. "What does he *do*, exactly?"

"You mean when he sits?"

"No, I mean, what does Patrick do for a living?"

"Oh, don't even try to pretend like Dad didn't send you out here with a thorough background investigation on Patrick," Julia quips. "You could probably recite the names of everyone in his family, his blood type, medical records… God, you probably even know how many times he masturbates a day."

"He takes care of it more than once a day? Oh, so *that's* why he only wears white," I tease.

Julia levels a warning look in my direction. "I'm going to act like you didn't just say that." She pulls out of her driveway and speeds down the street. "He was a spiritual counselor, but that can be very taxing. Giving so much of yourself to others. So he's taking some time off for himself."

"And that works, with your lifestyle here?"

"You mean, are we paying the bills?" she asks, getting right to the point.

"Well, yeah. Are you?"

Julia swerves into a tight little parking spot only about three blocks from her home, which makes me wonder why we didn't just walk. But then I remember that in California, everyone drives *everywhere*.

"We're fine, Liz. You don't need to worry," Julia says.

Something in her tone says just the opposite, though. I decide not to press further—not yet anyway. Instead, I stay silent as we make our way to the entrance of Pure Bliss, Julia's new yoga studio, located right in the heart of charming Del Mar on Pacific Coast Highway.

Just as I am about to open the studio's front door, a muscular forearm cuts across my chest.

"Here, let me."

I take a step back to find a set of broad shoulders underneath a fitted white T-shirt and two tanned, chiseled biceps squared in front of me. As my eyes climb higher, the outrageously sexy man holding the door locks his sky blue gaze on me and shoots me a grin so sultry, I'm sure my pupils are melting upon immediate contact.

And I am *not* one to melt in a man's presence. But *this guy*...

"You must be Liz," he says. "Julia's told me so much about you." He extends his free hand. "I'm Bradley; I'll be leading the retreat this week."

Dear God... or should I say, *dear Buddha?*

This is the guy who's going to be molding me into all sorts of crazy poses over the next week?

I'm toast.

Four

"Lifting your hands to heart center, take a few moments to place an intention for today's practice." Bradley's soothing voice travels through my sister's small, beachy yoga studio where five women, myself included, sit cross-legged in a circle, breathing, eyes closed.

Well, *I* don't have my eyes closed because I am sizing up our hot yoga instructor, trying to figure out how in the hell we are supposed to close our eyes and breathe when *that* is sitting in front of us. And as for our *intentions*—well, I can only guess the dirty intentions floating through the minds of the women next to me.

No wonder Julia felt a "soul connection" with this guy upon immediate eye contact. Although, I think she may have been confusing "soul connection" with an "I want to see you take off your shirt every day in my yoga studio and stretch that gorgeous body into all sorts of wild poses" connection.

While Bradley continues instructing us on how to breathe—we are now doing some sort of alternate nostril breathing, which I'm not grasping, not by any stretch of the imagination—I notice that he doesn't have the same intense yoga master look as Patrick. Instead, he looks more like a normal dude, a hot San Diego surfer.

I can already see him walking out of the water, wetsuit stripped down his chest, water dripping from that full head of hair, a sexy gleam in his smiling eyes...and then stopping to put his board down and bend over into downward dog...

Before I know it, my daydream sends me into an uncontrollable burst of laughter. I try my best to stifle the giggles, but instead they erupt in a snort.

Oh, shit.

Bradley opens his eyes and directs his intense gaze right at me.

I bite my bottom lip to make it stop, but when Hot Yoga Man lifts his hands up in prayer to the sky and instructs us all to do the same, my inappropriate spurt only gets worse.

Julia peeks her head into the studio and joins the other women in their death glares.

I pull my hands back to my heart center and close my eyes, trying to get it under control.

"Let's all take Liz's example and smile as we take one more round of breath," Bradley instructs the group.

When I open my eyes, I find all of the women beaming over at him, and with that sex-and-sunshine smile he is flashing right back, these women have already forgotten about how annoyed they were just moments ago for the break in their precious silence.

And I realize that this is the first time since Austin's death that I've actually forgotten about that fateful day for more than five minutes.

"Laughter is one of the best forms of release, and that is exactly what we'll be doing this week—*releasing*," Bradley says. "So anytime you feel the urge to laugh, cry, take child's pose and breathe it out, you are welcome to do that. This is an open space, a safe space, a space for sharing our truth."

Oh, God. Has he drunk the truth Kool-Aid too?

How am I supposed to "share my truth" when I can't even tell my best friend what I do for a living, or tell my sister about losing Austin?

Bradley glances my way once again, and this time I smile back at him and mouth, "thank you."

There's something curious about the way he is eyeing me, but I'm sure he's just not used to seeing my type of girl in here—dressed in black when all of the other women are decked out in blinding shades of pink, blue, green, and yellow; breaking into fits of hysterical laughter for no apparent reason while we're supposed to be meditating; and clearly having no clue what in the hell I am doing here while everyone else appears to have been birthed in a yoga studio.

Over the next half hour, Bradley proceeds to guide us through a basic flow sequence: lifting our hands to the sky, bending over into a forward fold, moving down into a plank position, then lowering down into chata-ra-ga-ga something or other, pushing up into some mermaid looking backbend, and finally ending in down dog, only to begin the whole thing again.

When Hot Yoga Man demonstrates the poses, they look so easy—a perfect flow coming from a perfect man body. The other women don't seem to be having any issues either—well, I suppose if you were born in a yoga studio, this wouldn't be that difficult, would it?

Then there's me.

If we do one more chaturanga dan da da da, or whatever the hell he's calling it, I think my shoulders are actually going to dislocate and fall off my body. I don't have the urge to laugh anymore. I just want to collapse in a pile on my purple mat and go to sleep.

Bradley walks around the room, surveying all of our asses as they point to the sky in our down dogs—which makes me realize what a smart man he is to go into a career as a yoga instructor. When he finally arrives at my ass, he places his hands on the sides of my hips and gently pulls them back. My hamstrings and calves are screaming, and it's all I can do to not let out a scream myself.

Plus, with his hands on my hips like that...

"Holy shit."

Oh no, did I just say that out loud?

I peek up to see if anyone has heard me, but with the tribal music Bradley has pumping in the background, I think I'm in the clear this time.

Bradley's hands are still on my hips as he instructs us to "melt to the floor and find our child's pose."

After I melt—well, more like flop—to the floor, he presses those firm hands down on my hips and butt, rocking me side to side until I actually do feel myself melting.

Oh, this man is *good*.

He holds onto me for what feels like an eternity, but still, that ball of tension, worry, and fear that has been locked in my gut ever since I made my love confession to Austin six months ago—it won't release.

The confession, the smoldering kiss, the ambush...and those piercing gunshots.

There it is again—Austin's blood. Everywhere—on my hands, on my chest, on my face. I can't make it stop.

Please, make it stop. Please let him be okay.

Please let him live.

"Liz? Liz? Liz, it's okay. I'm here."

A deep voice—not Austin's—snaps me back to the present. A hand is on my back, my cheeks are wet, and a puddle of tears is gathering on my mat. I lift my face to find Bradley kneeling next to me, concern swept all over his chiseled features.

I don't even glance around to see if all of the other women are staring at me—I'm sure they are, and I am completely mortified. I fly up from my mat and out the back door of the studio to a balcony that faces the rolling ocean, only blocks away.

I want to dive into those crashing waves and never come out. Pretend that the last six months of my life never happened. Pretend that I didn't just have a terrifying flashback from the day Austin was killed, and an embarrassing meltdown in a yoga class in front of all of those perfect California women who don't even know me.

The tears are really flowing now, and I can't stop them.

Damn.

I bury my face in my hands, telling myself to pull it together. I can do this. It's just one week and then I'll go back to DC and get my life—*my career*—back on track.

"Liz, are you okay?"

It's Bradley again, his soothing hand on my back, his voice calm amid my hysterical storm.

I lift my tear-stained face to his and try to stop the flood, but something about the way he is looking at me, as if he is genuinely concerned, as if on some deeper level he understands this kind of pain, makes me cry even harder.

Bradley doesn't ask again if I'm okay. Instead he pulls me into his chest and holds me, until finally the sobs subside and I can breathe again.

Taking a step back, I wipe at my eyes so I can look up at him—I didn't realize how tall he is until now, with him standing so close to me.

"I'm so sorry," I say. "I don't normally do this. I *never* do this, actually."

Bradley keeps a hand on my shoulder and smiles warmly at me. "No worries. This is actually pretty common in yoga classes."

"Women breaking down into hysterics and making a dramatic exit out of the studio? Really?"

He chuckles. "Well, maybe not the dramatic exit part, but the tears, yes. Quite common."

"I bet you didn't expect all of this ridiculous female drama when you became a yoga teacher. You were probably just hoping for the good parts—girls in tight yoga clothes, hands on hips, nice views—all of that. And instead you're getting sobs and runny noses."

"That's not why I became a yoga teacher," Bradley says, his accent making an abrupt switch from Chill California Surfer Dude to something more posh, sophisticated, and edgy.

"*Oh, come on.*" The sarcasm shoots from my tongue before I can stop it.

But Bradley doesn't back down. He stays planted right in front of me, intense and solid.

"It's okay if you're not buying it, Liz. Me, yoga, the whole scene here. I get it. All I ask is that you give it a chance. Try to stay open and see what might happen."

"The last time I was open, things didn't work out so well." An image of Austin's shocked face as I confessed my love to him flashes through my mind. I bite the inside of my cheek so I won't cry all over Bradley's T-shirt again.

Bradley runs a hand through his full head of hair, letting out a sigh. "I know how that goes."

"You do?" I say, shivering as a gust of cool wind travels over the waves and swirls around us on the balcony.

"You've got goose bumps. Sometimes it's surprisingly cool outside in San Diego. We need to get you a jumper."

"A jumper?" My mind immediately goes back to the hideous plaid jumpers Julia and I were forced to wear in Catholic grade school.

But as Bradley shifts awkwardly before me, clearing his throat, I realize that he meant "jumper" as in the British word for "sweater."

What the—?

"We all have a past." Bradley is back to his calm, wisdom-filled voice, a quick turnaround from that strange British slip. "But today, you're here. And you have an opportunity to do some work on yourself. You can either make the most of it, and let yourself go through whatever process you need to go through, or you can spend the week closed off, resisting everything, and leave exactly the way you came. It's up to you."

Bradley turns abruptly and heads back into the yoga studio, leaving me alone with his words echoing against the crashing waves.

I should be reflecting on what he just said to me, but instead, I am wondering what happened in *his* past that led him here, to this little slice of beach paradise.

While I'm no yoga expert, one thing I do know is how to read people, how to know when they're hiding something. And I've got an inkling that it isn't Patrick, my sister's oh-so-enlightened Oompa Loompa husband I need to be looking into. It's *Bradley*.

He can spout off about openness, honesty, and truth all he wants—but I know when someone is hiding something.

And this Hot Yoga Man has a secret.

Five

A spicy salsa tune blasts through En Fuego, the trendy Mexican restaurant where I'm meeting the yoga crew after our long day of sobbing, pulling muscles, and watching Bradley demonstrate one impossible pose after the next—oh wait, that was *my* day.

The other four women didn't have quite the traumatic experience on day one of our yoga adventure as I did. This is evidenced by the breezy looks on their tanned faces when I join them at their high-top table downstairs near the bar.

Jasmine, a blonde, big-busted mom of two who is not-so-happily married to a billionaire, throws back a massive sip of her margarita before flashing me a devious smile. "Liz, we were just talking about what it would be like to get Bradley in bed. I mean, did you see how flexible he is? I didn't know it was possible for a man to get his legs back that far..."

"And those arms." Anabel, a dark-haired beauty with a pair of those imposing cat eyes that only models have, gazes longingly into space. "Did you see his side cock pose?"

"Mmm. Beautiful. Haunting." This comes from Rain, a petite hipster girl with thick black glasses and the softest, clearest skin I've ever seen.

"Side cock pose?" I echo, willing the corners of my mouth to stay level. "Is that the one that my sister's husband is doing on the website?"

Callie, the youngest yogi of the group, answers promptly. "No, that's sideways upward lotus in headstand."

"Oh, right. Of course," I say, turning toward the waiter to avoid breaking into another inappropriate laughter fit. "I'll take a margarita. Rocks and salt please," I tell him, wondering if this sexy young surfer boy can sense how badly I need a drink right now.

Rain pipes up. "I bet Bradley knows how to get really creative with the props. Can you imagine what he could do with a bolster?"

All four of the women gaze aimlessly past the vines of tropical flowers overhead as they lose themselves in their own private Bradley Hunter yoga sex fantasies.

I can't help but let my mind do a little pondering over Bradley's skills in the bedroom as well. It has been a *long, long* time for me. Longer than I'm willing to admit.

"Or a block?" says Anabel, crunching on a tortilla chip.

"Or a strap?" adds Callie.

Jasmine's dark emerald eyes go devilish. "He probably uses the strap to swing over you like a wild yogi trapeze artist." She fans at her flushed cheeks. "Dear God, how are we going to make it through this week without jumping his bones?"

Skinny little Rain is looking at the menu. "Do you think Bradley is dairy free?"

"Good evening, ladies." Bradley's deep voice sneaks up on all of us, and there is no trace of the posh, slightly British accent that slipped out earlier. By the knowing gleam in his big baby blues, I can only guess that he heard the trapeze comment, but Jasmine doesn't seem the least bit fazed as she tugs her tight yellow tank top down another inch and shoots him a sultry grin.

"You don't mind if I crash the girl party?" Bradley asks, though he is already taking a seat next to me.

"Of course not!" Anabel says a little too excitedly.

"We were hoping you'd make it," Callie adds.

Rain places a hand on his arm. "Honestly, after today, I feel like the course of my life is forever altered."

"I'm so happy to hear that," Bradley responds with only sincerity in his voice, making me wonder how he can take all of this so seriously. I want to tell him that after today, I feel like a stretched-out rubber band that might snap in half at any second.

Just then, my margarita arrives. *Oh, thank God.*

Bradley eyes me as I throw back a few long sips without taking a breath in between. I don't care if he's judging me. Instead, as the amazing mixture of lime and salt washes down my throat, I am reminded that sex and romantic relationships aren't the *only* pleasures that have been missing from my life as of late. There has been a big black hole where tequila should've been, too.

Our sun-kissed waiter stays to take our order, and in all my life, I have never heard so many requests to hold the cheese, the meat, the dressing, the beans, the tortilla, the corn, the sauce—basically the entire freaking meal—as I do tonight. But our giddy California dude jots it all down as if this is totally normal.

When it's Bradley's turn, I am fully expecting him to order a piece of lettuce and nothing more. But, to my surprise, Hot Yoga Man orders his fish tacos without a single extra request. Then he turns to Rain and Jasmine. "To answer your question, ladies, I'm *not* dairy free. I need the animal protein to help with my trapeze exercises."

Jasmine chokes on her margarita, and Rain's pale cheeks take on a shade of red I've never before witnessed. Bradley is quite pleased with himself and turns to me with a grin so bold, I feel my own flush creeping up my neck.

Damn this guy.

Before he can get to me too much, I spot Patrick and Julia Roberts across the bar. Patrick is still sporting his billowing white linen uniform, orange skin aglow, but Julia's usual perky smile is turned downward into a frown.

Patrick's calm, yogic expression molds into one of impatience as my sister grips his shoulders and spins him around to face her. She then proceeds to go off on some heated tangent, which I unfortunately cannot hear from my vantage point all the way across the bustling bar.

But, that's about to change.

"Just going to head to the ladies'," I announce to the group as I slide out of my seat and weave through the crowd toward the happy Roberts couple. I squeeze into a free crevice just one person behind Patrick and Julia, right in their blind spot, and I tune in.

"I don't understand why you have to keep going to Mexico for these retreats, Patrick. There are plenty of mindfulness retreats right here in San Diego. I mean, I'm having one at my own studio this week if you need it that badly. We just got married, and you've already been gone almost every single weekend," Julia scolds.

"Julia, *luva*, I don't expect you to understand seeing as how I have reached a *much* higher level in my spiritual work than you have." Patrick's all-knowing, condescending tone makes me want to smack the glass of water-no-ice right out of his hands, but I force myself to stay planted.

"These weekends in Mexico connect me to the swirling, twirling energy of life all around me! You can't possibly deny me that," he finishes triumphantly.

Swirling, twirling energy of life?

Who in the hell has my sister married?

"It's not that I want to deny you of anything," Julia says, a bit softer now. "I just want to spend my weekends with my husband. I've dreamt of being married my whole life, and now that it's here, I feel like your spiritual work, your meditation practice—all of it—comes before me."

I lean just enough to the left to get a picture of Patrick's profile as he looks at my beautiful sister with his beady eyes. "Oh my sweet, naïve, dear Julia. We are partners now, in this unfolding blossom that is life. Do you really want to deny me the sweet honey?"

At this line, I have to stop myself from visibly gagging. This guy is a trip, and whether or not he's going to Mexico to meditate for ten hours a day or sleep with prostitutes, I don't like the way he's talking to my sister.

The crowd shifts slightly, and I move with them to stay hidden, but someone else catches me in the act.

Bradley.

"Already heading to the bar for round two?" he asks, shooting a quick glance toward my sister and her husband. They are now taking their argument about meditation, marriage, and the sweet nectar of life to the table with the other yoga girls.

"Is that judgment I detect in your tone?" I ask.

"I'm not the judgmental type," he says. "I was hoping I could buy your next drink, that's all. After today, I figured you could use another."

"Oh, well...thanks," I say, mentally scolding myself for being such a pill. He did come to my rescue today during that ungodly meltdown.

And...he *is* outrageously handsome.

Or is that just the margarita talking?

As Bradley slides a warm hand onto the small of my back and walks me up to the bar, I realize that one margarita has never had the power to make me feel so...*hot*.

I really like this guy.

The thought shoots into my head before I have time to stop it. Thankfully, though, Hot Yoga Man is not a mind reader. Or at least I don't think he is until he gazes down at me with the most curious look in his eyes.

"Margarita, rocks, salt?" he asks.

"Mmhmm," I mumble, feeling suddenly off balance by how close he is standing to me, by the sweet scents of sunscreen and cologne on his skin. Around us, the San Diego beach crowd is drinking, laughing, and swaying their hips to the booming salsa tune, but I am stuck in some sort of Bradley haze, unable to take my eyes off him.

He hands me my second margarita of the night and clinks his glass with mine. "To surviving your first day of yoga."

"A miracle indeed," I reply before taking a big sip.

"And according to your sister, it's a miracle you made it out here at all. She says you don't take much vacation," Bradley says.

"What was that last word you said? Vacation?" I joke. "Not familiar with it. Can you define, please?"

Bradley leans against the bar, his sexy grin almost unbearable. "I used to be like you, you know. Worked to death, exhausted, not even sure how to relax when the opportunity was presented."

"During your days in England?" I say in my own spotless British accent—one of the many I've perfected for my undercover work.

Bradley doesn't even flinch. "You caught my jumper reference earlier, eh?"

"What? Oh, I just thought you wanted to dress me up like a Catholic schoolgirl."

He laughs, bright and endearing. "Well...I wouldn't be opposed to it, of course. But that's not what I meant. My mom is British, so occasionally her vocabulary slips out."

I eye him, knowing instinctively that there is more to it than that, but with my second drink on its way down and my body finally, *finally* relaxing after my torturously long day of yoga, I decide now isn't the time to push it. I'll simply run a history on him later and see what comes up.

"So, Julia tells me you work for the State Department. That you travel a lot for work," Bradley says. "It must get tiring."

"Yeah, it's definitely not glamorous," I say.

"What happened today in class...it was work related?" he asks.

I shift away from Bradley, not at all wanting to think about my embarrassing breakdown today, let alone talk about it in the middle of this carefree bar. And even if I did, it's not like I can tell this near stranger about the atrocities that happened during my last trip overseas. I can't tell anyone.

His hand lands on my shoulder. "I'm sorry. I shouldn't have—"

"It's fine," I say, though the knot forming in my throat is telling me otherwise.

"Listen," he says, running his hand down my back, a gesture that is too intimate for the short time we've known each other. But for some reason I find myself loving it. "I know we just met, but I'm here, if you need anything."

Bradley gives me that look again, the same one he gave me earlier outside the yoga studio, like he knows *exactly* how I feel. Like he gets it.

Which isn't possible, yet the empathy and concern in his eyes is unmistakable.

"Thank you," I tell him. "But I think I need to get some sleep. It's been a long day."

"Do you want me to walk you back to your sister's?"

The thought of walking down the beach alone with Bradley is too much for my wounded heart and sex-deprived body to handle right now.

I can't get too close to this guy. I can't get close to anyone.

"No, I'll be fine," I say firmly. "See you in the morning."

And with that, I jet out of the bar and away from what could have been the most relaxing, fun night I've had in a long time.

But who am I to let loose?

I have a job to do. And with my sister and her yogi spouse out of the house for the evening, there couldn't be a better time to get started.

Six

Back at the Roberts' glowing white beach pad, I take a quick sweep through the house, but when I don't find anything too out of the ordinary—well, except for the closet stocked full of purple sex wedges in various sizes... *ugh*—I decide to dig a little deeper.

Patrick's initial history didn't reveal any "holes" as my father had indicated—this was clearly only a ploy to get me to agree to the trip. But the whole Mexico thing didn't sit well with me. Patrick may very well be crossing the border every weekend to chant and om and raise his vibrations...*or* he could be up to something sketchy.

My first stop is Patrick's "office," which looks more like a disorganized meditation cave with all sorts of curtains, candles, pillows, and blankets thrown around. Upon immediate glance, there aren't any obvious places where he might be hiding something, except for the large corner desk. After a quick riffle through the drawers produces nothing of interest, I pull the desk away from the wall and slide beneath it to check for any hollowed-out holes hiding beneath the desk or duct tape on the back sides of the drawers—both prime spots to hide passports, money, SIM cards, that sort of thing.

But just when I decide it's all clear down here, the front door slams shut downstairs and a series of high-pitched moans echo through the house.

Oh no. That is definitely *not* my sister's voice.

More moans and breathy growls emanate from Patrick's mouth before I hear Julia. "Oh, master. Take me, master. Take me!"

Hearing my sister call Patrick her *master* is almost just as traumatic as a bad day in the field. I am tempted to give myself earmuffs and curl into the fetal position underneath the desk until their horrifying yoga sex experiment concludes, but then I hear them bounding up the stairs.

"I think tonight calls for the biggest wedge we have, my *luva*," Patrick says in his breathiest, most feminine voice.

Oh, shit. The sex wedge closet is just outside Patrick's office door. I really cannot handle having a run-in with these two in their state. Nor do I want them to know I was snooping in Patrick's meditation cave.

I smash my back against the wall nearest the door so I am out of sight as they scour the sex wedge closet for the largest piece of sex furniture they own. Just the thought of this makes me want to dive out the window, but the oceanfront cliffs of Del Mar below wouldn't make for the softest landing.

"Mmmm, this one is best for deep pelvic thrusts. Do you agree, *luva?*" Patrick says.

"The deeper the better," Julia says with a giggle.

I have to bite my tongue not to curse at the sky. *Really?*

The Sex Wedge Pelvic Team takes off to their bedroom—*thank God*—and I decide it's high time for me to get the hell out of this house. With all the "sitting" Patrick does, I'm sure he has more than enough energy saved up to last all night, and I'm not about to stick around for that debacle.

After I fly down the stairs and out the front door, I make my way to the walking path that lines the cliffs and overlooks the moonlit Pacific, which is hauntingly beautiful tonight. The sound of the waves crashing against the shore and the fresh scent of salt water soon take away the PTSD I'm feeling from Patrick and Julia Roberts' sexcapades back at the house.

Another few minutes down the path, and I spot one of the most stunning beachfront homes I've seen yet. Like Julia's house, this one has floor-to-ceiling windows, but its shining jewel is one of those magical infinity pools that appears to end where the horizon meets the ocean.

When I take a few steps up the hill to get a better look, the well-lit living room reveals a pair of upside-down legs...*what the—?*

It's Bradley, in all his muscular glory, doing a handstand and wearing only a pair of tight black boxer briefs.

Dear Buddha.

He lives here?

And he does nearly-naked handstands in the windows for all the world to see?

This is just too much.

Despite the reasonable side of my brain telling me to *walk away*, I find myself creeping toward his windows to get a better look. Bradley's body is like a perfectly sculpted lightning rod shooting straight up into the heavens—not your everyday finding on a nighttime stroll. At least not on the East Coast anyway. I'm learning pretty quickly that things are different out here in the land of sunshine and sex wedges.

Over three minutes go by with Bradley poised in perfect, complete stillness in this impressive handstand. As I sneak around the edge of the pool, mesmerized by his chiseled back muscles, I am beginning to believe Jasmine's prediction that Bradley would, in fact, be quite good at trapeze sex...whatever that means. I think he'd be pretty damn good at anything in that department, really.

Butterflies swirl through my abdomen as I tiptoe even closer, watching him spin around on his hands to face the other direction.

Now I can see his entire beautiful face. Even upside down this guy is magnificent.

Damn, it's been so long. Too long.

At this thought, I feel my left foot submerging in warm water, and without warning, the rest of my body takes a plunge.

I swim up for air, noticing the obscenely bright motion light that has been activated at my clumsy crash into Bradley's infinity pool.

Shit, shit, shit.

I have to get out of here before he sees me. Staying as low as I can, I swim to the edge, but just as I peek my face up out of the pool, I am met with a pair of feet.

I can't quite read Bradley's expression as he checks out his intruder, but I *can* see that the package inside those black boxer briefs is significant.

"I was just thinking about taking a midnight swim. Great idea, Liz," Bradley says before diving right over my head and into the pool.

This was so *not* how I saw the night unfolding.

Seven

Bradley pops up to the surface, smooths back his full head of chestnut brown hair, and swims toward me, his teasing grin unbearably handsome.

"So, do you do this often?" he asks. "Creep around people's houses at night and dive into their pools fully clothed?"

"Well, I'm certainly not going to strip naked before trespassing," I say, trying to hide the smile that wants to slide across my lips. "That would be ridiculous."

Bradley swims closer and dives under the water, circling me like a hungry shark. When he emerges, his face is only an inch from mine. Water drips off his long lashes, rolling down the freckles on his nose, the dimple in his left cheek—the dimple I wish I could kiss right now.

I have to get out of this pool.

"Those jeans can't be comfortable in here," he says, closing in on me. His hands find my shoulders. "And this schoolteacher cardigan. It's got to go."

I tell myself to turn around, swim away from this yoga sex hypnotist, but I am transfixed on his piercing blue eyes, on the way they're watching me as he peels my sleeves down and slips off my sweater. He tosses it to the patio above without breaking my gaze, and his smooth hands quickly find their way back to my bare shoulders.

"That's better," he says. "Unless you want me to keep going?"

"Do you do *this* often?" I ask. "Naked handstands in your window, followed by routine strip-downs for all of your intruders?"

But Bradley doesn't answer me. Instead, his lips are on mine before I can say another word. And even though the pool is warm and his lips are even hotter, my entire body shivers beneath his kiss.

Bradley cups my face in his hands and presses his bare chest up against mine until I feel my back reach the wall of the pool. As soon as his hands begin roaming, our kisses growing more intense, more passionate each second, I realize I still have a choice.

I can pull away, tell him I can't be here with him like this. I can climb out of the pool. I can walk back to Julia's, go to bed, and pretend this never happened.

I can stop myself, yet again, from getting close to someone. Someone I actually like.

But when Bradley's hand runs down the front of my soaking wet tank and reaches the top button of my jeans, the lightning I feel in my abdomen and chest tell me that I don't have a choice at all.

And so, in the most uncharacteristic Liz moment of my life, I pull Bradley even closer and whisper in his ear. "Get these jeans off me. *Now*."

I swear I hear him growl as he works his magic underwater, unbuttoning like a pro. Then he dips his head beneath the surface and goes down, down, down...until my jeans are a distant memory. He is just as swift with my tank top, leaving me swirling in this whirlpool of lust and wearing only the most boring white cotton bra and underwear set I own, although Bradley certainly doesn't seem concerned with my choice in fabric.

The most liberating feeling washes over me as I wrap my legs around his waist and let him run his lips down my neck, collarbone, and finally over the tops of my breasts. Tilting my head back in pure ecstasy, I catch a stunning glimpse of the stars blanketing the sky, and for this brief moment in time, I feel completely removed from the restricting life I have so thoroughly and completely folded myself into for years.

My new reality—the one where my body is entwined with the most gorgeous man I've ever laid eyes upon in his infinity pool overlooking the beautiful beaches of Del Mar—feels like a dream that is happening to someone else, someone more carefree, someone who does things like this.

And I, Liz Valentine, simply do not do things like this.

But as Bradley scoops me into his arms and carries me up the stairs and out of our warm bath, I decide that just for tonight, I will let go of the girl who's been stifled and suppressed, afraid to let loose, afraid to break free, and worst of all, afraid to *live*.

It's about damn time I cut her loose.

Bradley lays me down on a cushy white poolside chaise, and instead of jumping right on top of me as I expect him to do, he stands over me for a few moments, watching me, breathing me in. His broad silhouette moves closer, and as he runs his smooth hands over my feet and all the way up my shivering legs, I close my eyes, relaxing into his touch.

Soon I feel his hands molding around my waist, his lips caressing the skin around my belly button, tracing a path up to my breasts. He climbs over me, and I pull him close, unable to wait another second to feel his warm, slippery body on mine. We kiss beneath the stars, my legs wrapped around his waist; the pressure, the force of him arouses a part of me that I haven't let out in years.

I reach for his boxer briefs, tugging at them as he removes my bra. It doesn't take long for us to become a perfectly naked fit, our hungry bodies melding together in a way that could only be described as sublime. Before we take things any further, Bradley catches the moonlight in my eyes, runs a soft hand down my cheek, and smiles at me.

"I'm so glad you fell into my pool, Liz Valentine."

I smile up at him, surprised by the tenderness I see in his blue eyes, the affectionate way he is holding me, the pause he is taking to show me that even though this is a rash act of passion, it still means something.

"I am too," I tell him. And I mean it.

At this, his hips press closer and firmer into mine until the feeling of him inside of me takes the breath from my lungs. He wraps his arms around my shoulders, not breaking eye contact as he moves over top of me, making this intimate connection we share more intense, more powerful by the second. Our lips find each other in the darkness and our bodies play to a beat all their own as the rest of the world fades away…so far away it is now that all I know, all I see in this moment is Bradley.

And damn is he beautiful.

Running my hands down his back, I feel my entire body, my entire being embracing him, releasing into him, so relieved to finally feel someone so close, so connected to me. But I know that it's not just anyone who could make me feel this way—there is something unique about *him*, about the way he gazes at me, holds me, wants me, as if somehow he actually understands me.

He barely knows me, but something in those deep blue eyes says that he gets it.

"You feel perfect," Bradley says, his sensual whisper tickling my ear, making me want more of him, all of him. He must sense my hunger because he rolls to his side and pulls me over with him until I am sitting on top of his glistening body, watching the way the moonlight reflects in his lustful gaze. He reaches for my hips, and our bodies rock together in such perfect unison that I lose myself fully and completely to this moment, to this man.

His hands grip me firmer and tighter until we experience the most incredible, blissful release right alongside each other. I am unable to hold myself up for another second as toe-curling pleasure shoots through my entire body, so I lay my chest atop his, my head on his heart.

Bradley holds me so sweetly and for so long that my eyelids soon begin to close. Before I drift off in his arms, I realize that for the first time in ages, I am smiling. I am happy. I am safe.

"Thank you," I whisper.

He kisses my forehead, pulls me closer, and we drift peacefully into the night together.

Eight

A beam of early morning sunlight breaks through my heavy lids as I bat my eyes open. The wispy white drapes framing the floor-to-ceiling windows billow softly in the breeze, and the sound of ocean waves crashing against the cliffs below urges me to close my eyes again, to revel for at least a few more minutes in this deep, satisfying sleep.

I haven't felt this rested in months. No, *years*.

But why? Where am I?

This is when I notice the heavy arm draped around my waist, the firm body breathing heavily behind me.

Oh no.

It all comes rushing back to me in an instant.

My clumsy plunge into Hot Yoga Man's infinity pool. Our heated kiss in those crystal blue waters before I let him undress me, and then handed myself over to him on a poolside platter, complete with multiple orgasms and moans loud enough to wake up the entire beachside community.

My entire life outside of the CIA is all about staying under the radar. Not being the one to stir up trouble. And certainly not being the one to sleep with an obscenely handsome, sweet, passionate yoga instructor *outside* his house on my first night in San Diego!

What the hell was I thinking?

A panicked glance down at my body reveals one of Bradley's oversized T-shirts covering my top half, but nothing at all concealing the rest.

I have to get the hell out of here.

Slowly removing his hand from my waist—God, even his hand is smooth and gorgeous just like the rest of him—I roll softly out of bed and scour the room for a pair of boxers, shorts, anything to make me decent before I bolt out of his beach pad and pretend like this never happened.

Inside his walk-in closet, I find a small wooden dresser and begin opening and closing drawers until I locate one filled with swim trunks. I take the top pair off the stack—lemon yellow with streaks of blue and black—and step into them as quickly and quietly as I can, my hands shaking all the while.

My hands don't even shake like this when I'm overseas, holding a gun, defending my life. But sneaking to steal a pair of Bradley's swim trunks, I'm trembling like a scared little girl? Really?

Just before I close the drawer, the corner of a photograph peeking out from beneath Bradley's stack of swim trunks catches my eye. I glance back into the bedroom to make sure he is still sleeping soundly before pulling the picture out for a brief examination. The photo is worn around the edges, like he's been carrying it for a while, but not yellowed. Taken in the last five years, I would say.

The picture is of a striking woman in her late twenties with long, disheveled honey brown locks. A revealing black dress hugs her voluptuous frame, and the tiny table where she smokes her cigarette, coupled with the small cup of espresso she's about to sip, tell me she's likely at a café somewhere in Paris. Her gaze is troubled, forlorn.

She does not know she's being photographed.

A rustle in the bed behind me urges me to tuck the picture back into its hiding spot and stop snooping, for God's sake. Bradley has probably had more women than I could count. Of course he would have photos of his conquests lying around the house.

But as I creep back into his bedroom, I notice that there isn't a single photograph anywhere to be found. And as I make my way out of his beach pad unannounced, I don't find any pictures of friends or family lining his white walls.

The house is beautiful, but besides the clothes in his closet, nothing else appears to be personalized. It is sterile—a vacation home for visitors. And even though I've known Bradley for less than a day, last night gave me a pretty good feel for the kind of person he is underneath his Zen façade—strong, passionate, spontaneous.

This house is none of those things.

I consider conducting a more *thorough* investigation while he is sleeping, but the idea of Bradley waking up only to discover me snooping around his house like a crazy woman stops me.

It doesn't matter why Bradley chose not to hang pictures on his walls or make this house his own. It doesn't matter because I'm not going to let what happened last night happen ever again.

Nine

"Liz Valentine? Where have you been all my life?" The sound of my best friend Natasha's voice over the line is like a shot of chamomile to my hyped-up nerves.

"You're exceptionally cheery considering the sun has barely risen," I point out, noticing that I am the only person who is jetting down the beach in full-on stress mode. The thought that there probably isn't another agitated person within a twenty-five-mile radius of this beach paradise only serves to make me more anxious.

"Just on my way to my morning prenatal yoga class on the beach," Natasha says, her tone all blissed out and lovely.

"Are you going to stop at the farmers' market after? Or perhaps an open-air brunch on the Pacific followed by a shot of Botox and a boob job?"

Natasha giggles. "Don't hate me because I moved to LA."

"I thought it would take at least a full year for you to convert, but it's happened. You're one of *them* now," I say. Natasha recently made the move from DC to Los Angeles to start a family with the love of her life, and she's never sounded happier. Still, I can't help but make a few sarcastic remarks about her rapid transformation.

"One of who?" she says, playing dumb.

"You've become a Californian. Buying fresh avocados at the local market, making batches of green sludge in your Vitamix, rising with the sun to twist your body into inconceivable, horrifying poses. You know what I'm talking about."

Natasha laughs. "What's so wrong with embracing the lifestyle out here?" she says, and I can hear the smile on her face. "Besides, it's good for the baby."

"You're only one month away from birthing another human being. Shouldn't you be soaking up all the sleep you can get before you're terrorized by late-night screams and exploding diapers?"

"And shouldn't you be working?" she counters. "Soaking up that workaholic lifestyle you love so much on the East Coast?"

"I *should* be working...but instead I'm doing the walk of shame on the beaches of Del Mar."

There is a long pause before Natasha grasps what I've just said.

"What? You're in San Diego and you didn't tell me? And more importantly, *you had sex?*" She is screeching now.

"Well, don't say it like I'm a virgin or something," I hiss.

"With as long as it's been, technically, maybe you are," she teases.

"Virginity doesn't have a reset button, Natasha."

"I'm sorry. You know I'm kidding. Tell me everything!"

And while I can't tell Natasha *everything,* I can at least tell her about my thrilling night with Bradley, aka Yoga Sex God.

"So what's the problem?" Natasha asks after I've spilled the beans.

"The problem, my dear friend, is that I'm leaving California in less than a week to go back to my crazy-ass job, and I'll never see this guy again." Natasha, like the rest of my friends, believes I have an insanely demanding career working for the State Department. After Austin's death six months ago, it took all of my strength not to tell her the truth about what I do.

"Yeah, got that part. So, what's the problem?" Natasha reiterates, this time with a giggle.

"I can't get close to him, Natasha! I barely know him, and I'll never see him again. Besides, something isn't adding up. The British accent he slipped into yesterday—"

"He told you his mom is British!" Natasha reminds me.

"It's still suspect," I say. "Between that and the lack of anything personal in his huge beach house and the photo of that Paris girl hidden in his drawer, who knows what this man is hiding from me." The tide washes over my feet, but I barely notice the frigid waters. I am thinking of Bradley's hot hands on my skin and trying to come up with a million more reasons why I should never let him touch me again.

"Even in college, you never did understand the meaning of the word *fling*," Natasha says. "You don't need to know why he didn't decorate his house or who the girl in the photo is. All you need to know is that the man gave you multiple orgasms and made you forget about work for one whole night. One whole night, Liz! A total and complete miracle."

"I can't go to that yoga studio today. He'll be adjusting my down dog while I'll be thinking of what happened between us and why it can never happen again."

"It *can* happen again," Natasha says, exasperation seeping through her voice. "Dear God, for one week, let yourself have some fun and stop putting this man under a microscope. Not every man is a bastard, you know."

"But—"

"No buts," Natasha scolds. "It's time to pull that stick out of your ass and live a little."

"You've gotten a lot bossier since you got knocked up, you know that?" I say to my friend in jest, because for as much as she's giving me a hard time, I like this new version of her. She's stronger, more confident. She knows what she wants and isn't afraid to go for it. I used to be able to say as much in my work… but as for my personal life, well, that's always been a different story.

"I may be bossier, but I'm your best friend. If I'm not going to give it to you straight, then who is? Certainly not all of those wishy-washy yogis you're hanging out with this week. Now if you'll excuse me, I have to go roll around on a mat in the sand and visualize my Zen baby birth."

"Don't tell me you're skipping the epidural to do a natural birth," I say, cringing at the mere thought of squeezing an entire baby out of my lower half, drugs or no drugs.

"Oh, there *will* be drugs. Don't you worry."

"Whew! So you haven't gone totally Californian on me, after all."

"I'll always be an East Coast girl at heart. You know that. But I do love myself a green smoothie," she admits. "And I've started wearing these leggings that are made out of recycled bottles. They're so comfortable! You have to try them."

"*All right.* Go do your baby yoga."

"And you go do that Hot Yoga Man."

"We'll see."

As I hang up and walk the path back to my sister's home, I wonder if Natasha doesn't have a point. I never allow myself to have the kind of fun I had last night. Never. My dad sent me here to take the week off, to get my head on straight, and if sleeping with my yoga instructor was part of that plan, then so be it. I also shouldn't assume that Bradley is hiding some deep-dark secret from me.

At the same time, what if he *is* hiding something?

It certainly doesn't hurt to check up on him, if anything for my sister's well-being. She's hired the man to run retreats at her brand new yoga studio. My father would want me to do my due diligence for Julia's sake, at the very least.

This is my justification as I send Bradley's name and address off to Martin, one of my most trustworthy colleagues. If there's anything off with this Hot Yoga Man, Martin will find it and let me know.

Until then, I will do my best—as Natasha ordered—to pull the stick out of my ass and live a little.

Unfortunately, the sound of my sister's screeching voice flying out her kitchen window doesn't bode well for my mission to let loose and have fun.

Ten

"If you chant that mantra at me one more time, I swear I am going to rip that white scarf from around your bony neck, and I am going to strangle you with it!"

That's my Julia.

From my super-secret spy position crouching beneath Patrick and Julia's kitchen window, I am beyond relieved to hear my sister talking—or shouting, rather—some sense into her bizarre yogi husband.

"Calm, my *luva*. Anger is not a productive emotion. You of all people should know this. *Shanti*, Julia. Shanti, shanti, shanti…peace." As Patrick chants this last part in his characteristic falsetto voice, I have to stop myself from diving through the open window and taking hold of that damn white scarf myself. How could she have married this nut job?

"*Stop! Chanting! At! Me!*" Julia's screams garner the attention of an innocent silver-haired couple walking a brood of tiny dogs down the nearby bluffs. They spot me huddled in a ball, eavesdropping, so I smile and wave, not sure what else to do. They shrug and smile back, continuing on their leisurely stroll. Maybe the neighbors are accustomed to these morning scream-chant yoga duels emanating from Patrick and Julia Roberts' peaceful beachfront abode.

"Ooooooommmmmm..." Patrick's chanting vibration goes on and on...and on, not even taking a brief pause when glass shatters against the walls.

The sound of violence tells me it's time to make my entrance. When I open the back door, I find Julia hurling wine glasses past Patrick's head as he stands poised in tree pose, white linen abounding, eyes closed, hands clasped at heart center.

And he is *still* chanting the sound of om.

"Can't you have a normal response to the biggest news of your life? I just told you I'm pregnant, you yogic asshole, and all you can do is stand there like a fucking tree and om at me?"

Holy shit. Julia is pregnant?

Patrick finally speaks, but he doesn't dare open his eyes or break his tree pose. "My dear one, when we entered into this marital agreement, I was quite clear that I have not incarnated in this lifetime to reproduce."

And there goes another glass. This one grazes his right ear, but the tree that is Patrick still doesn't sway.

Damn, he's got some serious balancing skills.

Julia growls and stomps her feet the way she used to do whenever she didn't get her way as a little girl. Just as she is reaching for another glass from the cupboard, I place a hand on her arm.

She sucks in a sharp breath as we make eye contact, and immediately, a look of complete mortification washes over her beautiful features. Tears well up in her big blue eyes.

"How long have you been standing here?" she asks.

"Long enough." I wrap an arm around her trembling shoulders, pulling her away from the glassware. "Let's get out of here, okay?"

She nods, tears spilling down her flushed cheeks. Meanwhile, Patrick is still a pillar of calm amid a floor of broken glass and an onslaught of pregnant sobs.

And he is *still* chanting.

I usher Julia toward the back door and tell her to wait for me outside. But she hesitates, looking first to Patrick, and then back at me with wariness in her eyes. She doesn't know exactly *how much* physical damage I am capable of, but she knows I'm much stronger than my petite body would let on. "Liz, don't—"

I place a finger on her lips to shush her, and before she can stop me, I walk over to this maddening husband of hers, push a forceful finger into his chest, and tip him right over onto his skinny little yoga ass.

The contempt in Patrick's eyes is priceless as he removes a shard of glass from his backside and glares up at me.

In response, I bring my hands to heart center and bow my head. "Namaste," I tell him in my calmest, most compassionate, yogic tone.

"I can't believe you chopped down his tree!" Julia crows, wiping at her eyes.

My sister and I have spent the past hour taking refuge at her yoga studio. In between her hysterical sobbing and laughing fits, she is gorging on organic dark chocolate and chugging chocolate goat's milk.

This is how they do crisis in the California yoga community, I realize, wishing it were a little more like this in my line of work.

But work is the furthest thing from my mind as I realize that for the first time in so long, I have the opportunity to be here for Julia like a normal sister. Like a friend. It's a role I have missed out on so often—too often—because of my career.

"Why goat's milk?" I ask, once she's dried up the carton.

"Cow's milk bloats me like you wouldn't believe," she says, breaking off another square of dark chocolate.

I take a gander down at Julia's unbelievably flat tummy and think about the fact that in a few short months, she'll have one of those adorable baby bumps...but I won't be here to see it.

Once I go back to my clandestine career with the CIA, it's doubtful I'll even make it back out to California for the birth, let alone play any significant role in her child's life.

Julia squeezes my knee. "What is it, Lizzy?"

I bite my lip, willing the tears not to fall. "I just don't want to miss this, you know."

"Would you ever consider leaving the CIA? Moving out here to live near me?"

Julia's question catches me off guard, but for the first time in forever, the idea of leaving my career behind and starting over doesn't sound so awful. Especially if it means supporting her through what is bound to be a trying time in her life.

"You might need me if Patrick doesn't stop chanting at you."

"Oh, God. Don't remind me." Julia is still straddling that thin line between laughter and total and complete meltdown. By the way her bottom lip is quivering, I can see we are heading toward the latter. "What if Patrick really doesn't want this baby? Would you stay, Liz? Would you help me?"

Before I can answer, the front door to the studio swings open, and there stands Bradley Hunter, a shirtless vision of wet hair and sunshine that immediately brightens Julia's mood.

"Dear Buddha," she mumbles through a mouthful of chocolate.

"Morning, ladies," Bradley says, his gaze lingering about ten seconds too long on me. Even in Julia's newly pregnant, husband-hating state, she is quick to pick up on the awkwardness in the air and raises a questioning brow in my direction.

I ignore her, instead glancing nervously at my watch. "Oh, is it already that time?"

"No, it's not," Julia says. "Retreat doesn't start until noon today."

"Just finished surfing and thought I'd come in early to practice before day two of retreat begins," Bradley says, rolling out his yoga mat.

Julia is still studying me intently. "Wait a second…" She trails off as she leans into my ear, hissing. "Where were you last night?"

Again, I pretend to ignore her. This time, I begin cleaning up her mess of chocolate wrappers from the floor. Bradley is already in full headstand nearby, also pretending to ignore the exchange going on between me and Julia.

I need to get out of here.

"You know, I'm really tired," I say with an overdramatized yawn. "I might skip retreat today and spend the day with you, Julia."

Now she is pointing to Bradley and back at me, covering her mouth like a sixteen-year-old girl who's just received the best bit of gossip imaginable.

Bradley descends ever so gracefully from his headstand and walks up to us, placing a firm hand on my shoulder.

"I think you should stay, Liz." The scents of sunscreen and surf wax emanate from Bradley's bronzed skin, immediately taking me back to last night, when that smooth, warm skin of his was all over me.

"You should *definitely* stay," Julia echoes. "Besides, I have glass to clean up at home and an unresponsive husband to fight with. You don't need to be bothered with all of that when you have Bradley here to teach you some...*yoga*."

Subtlety has never been my sister's strong suit.

Before I can protest, she is kissing me on the cheek and jetting out the door.

As soon as we're alone, Bradley takes a step closer. "Is everything okay?"

"Oh, just some trouble in paradise for the newlyweds." I dodge his piercing gaze and glance toward the door. "I really think I should spend the day with my sister. I'm sorry I can't stay."

Bradley reaches for my hand. "No, I meant, is everything okay with you? When I woke up this morning, you had already left."

Our hands linger there, melded together, before I finally turn to him.

"I'm sorry, Bradley...I just...I can't do this. Last night was...it was incredible. The best night I've had in...God, forever. But I barely know you, and I'm leaving soon, and you work for my sister, and—"

"If you're not comfortable with this, it never has to happen again," Bradley cuts in.

I should be relieved when he says this, but instead, my heart is sinking.

"I'm glad you understand," I say, still not able to pull my hand away from his.

"Of course," he says, tugging me toward him.

"Good," I say with a firm nod.

"Good," he says, nodding right back.

"Glad you agree," I say, biting my lip.

"Absolutely," he says, the corners of his mouth sliding up into that disarming grin of his.

Oh, God.

"So happy we have that settled," I say, telling myself to *let go of his hand. Stop looking at his gorgeous smile.*

"Me too," he says, stepping so close now that I can practically feel his pulse beating in his neck, faster, faster, and faster still.

"Never again," I whisper.

"Never…" He trails off as his fingers lace around the back of my neck and his lips find mine.

Within seconds, we have toppled onto his mat, and I am reveling in the warmth of his kisses, begging him to rip off my clothes.

So much for self-control.

Eleven

The rest of the week passes by in a haze of down dogs, green smoothies, sore muscles, beach walks, pregnancy planning with Julia, and the best part of all...*Bradley*.

Just as the girls in my yoga retreat predicted, Bradley can do things with yoga blocks and straps that I never dreamt possible. But even better than his yogi trapeze skills in the bedroom are the talks we've had lying on the beach at night, gazing up at the stars; the way my head fits snugly into that perfect spot between his shoulder and his chest when we fall asleep together; and the way he looks at me like there isn't another woman around for miles.

The vivid nightmares I've experienced incessantly since the day Austin was killed have vanished, and I am beginning to enjoy things I never, *ever*, thought I could enjoy with such ease—eating kale salad, gossiping with the girls, making out like a teenager, meditating for more than five minutes, and even drinking chocolate goat's milk with Julia.

For the past few days, I have let go of my obsession with investigating every single person who comes into my life or Julia's. I've stopped searching through Patrick's personal belongings, accepting that he is simply a yogi who has taken things too far, and one who my sister loves, despite the fact that he is still not keen on carving time out of his rigorous meditation schedule to be a father.

I have refrained from snooping any further through Bradley's house, slowly coming to terms with the fact that everyone has a past. I don't ask him about his, and he doesn't ask me about mine. Instead, we're enjoying the present moment—I know, how truly Zen of me—and despite all odds, I am beginning to feel...*normal*.

And so, it is in this abnormally normal state of mind that I am trotting to the last day of retreat carrying the following: a bundle of sage, a stack of lifestyle magazines, and a fluorescent pink poster board. I'm also delightfully sore and a little tired from my romp under the covers—and let's not forget on the mat, in the pool, on the sand, *and* in the shower—with Bradley last night.

When I reach the front door of Pure Bliss, I catch a glimpse of my reflection in the window.

My auburn hair is loose and wavy, my cheeks are full of color, and I'm smiling.

No, I'm *beaming*.

The sight of myself looking so utterly jubilant and carefree catches me off guard, and for a moment, I can do nothing but stand here and stare at my reflection like an idiot. The thoughts I have been pushing to the back of my mind all week—*this is temporary, I'm leaving soon,* and worst of all, *I'm going to miss Bradley*—threaten to wipe the radiant smile from my face.

But I force those thoughts away, along with the realization that my flight leaves tomorrow morning, and as soon as I return to life in the field, I may never have a week this lovely, this romantic, or this peaceful ever again.

"Sage and Vision Board Day!" It's Jasmine, the mother of two who is unhappily married to a billionaire and whose absurdly high cheekbones seem to have become more Botoxed by the day.

She pinches my side. "Are you ready to clear out all that bad energy and create the life of your dreams, Lizzy?"

Before I can tell Jasmine that I desperately want time to slow down on this last day, or that in fact I want time to *freeze* right here, right now, she leans into my ear and whispers, "I know what's going on *my* vision board—Bradley Hunter's hot, naked body in my bed."

"Ladies, allow me." It's Bradley, of course, always making his entrance right when the girls have voiced their latest sexual fantasy involving him as the star.

Jasmine only shrugs as we walk into the studio together. "I hope he heard me," she whispers loudly.

"I'm sure he did," I reply, sneaking a peek at Bradley, who winks at me in response.

I take a mental snapshot of his flirtatious glance, the affection in his eyes.

And again, more than ever, I wish that I could freeze time.

"Thank you for sharing your practice with me. Namaste." Bradley bows his head, and we all bow in return as we wrap up our final practice together.

I keep my eyes closed for an extra minute, noticing how invigorated my body feels, how clear my mind is, how refreshing it feels to breathe—*really breathe*—and how there is hope in my heart.

When I first walked into this studio less than a week ago, I was a guilt-ridden, fear-plagued, exhausted ball of stress.

Damn, there really is something to this yoga stuff.

"Take fifteen minutes, and we'll reconvene to finish our retreat with sage cleansing and the creation of your vision boards," Bradley instructs.

Excited chatter fills up the studio as we all roll up our mats. The fact that I am just as thrilled as the others at the idea of waving a bundle of energy-clearing sage around my body and filling up a poster board full of visions for my ideal future is still a bit shocking to me, but I tell myself to be present. To enjoy it.

After all, I'll be stepping on a plane tomorrow.

Jasmine, Rain, Anabel, and Callie gather around Bradley, asking him to spend the break demonstrating some wild inverted pose which I have yet to brave. I decide to leave them to it and instead grab my purse and head for the ladies' room.

Inside the bathroom, I check my phone to find a text message from Martin, my colleague at the CIA who I contacted earlier in the week to check out Bradley.

I open the message, fully expecting a clean report. So much so that the words on the screen don't compute in my calm, clear mind.

Bradley Hunter doesn't exist. Real name: Oliver Anderson. Former British operative. Got burned. Careful, Valentine.

No.

I force myself to read the words over and over...and over again, until *finally*, I believe them.

Bradley used to work for the British government. And he was burned—which likely means that he screwed up so badly that he was forced to leave behind not only his clandestine career, but also his entire life—friends, family, home, *everything*—and take on an entirely new identity.

How could I have been so careless as to get involved with a foreign operative, for God's sake?

Have I completely lost my mind?

My emotions go numb and my instincts kick in as I walk out of the bathroom and slip quietly out the back door of the studio. Taking off into a jog down the palm tree-lined street, I run until I reach Bradley's immaculate, depersonalized, beachfront home.

My colleague wouldn't lead me astray, but still, I have to see for myself.

Twelve

Bradley's sliding back door is unlocked, which is quite the careless move for someone who has taken on a false identity and who most definitely has at least one piece of proof from his past hidden *somewhere* in this house.

As I sweep through the bright, airy rooms—each one containing a memory of me and Bradley kissing or stripping off clothes or making love—I think back to that first day we met, when he slipped into his British accent.

I knew then. I knew he was hiding something.

And yet, I spent the week frolicking beneath the sheets with the man. Ignoring my gut instincts—the instincts that have never led me astray in the field, except for the *one time* I let love get in the way.

I push the absurd thought from my mind that I have come even remotely close to *falling in love* with Bradley, and instead, I search for uncategorized books on shelves, paint missing from screws in light fixtures, gaps in dust patterns on tables, and hidden SIM cards taped to the bottoms of drawers or nightstands.

Finally, on the back of a large desk pressed firmly into the wall, I find it.

A hole patched up with duct tape.

Inside, a burgundy colored passport.

Holding the passport in my hands, I am no longer able to stave off my storm of emotions. My fingers tremble. My heart hurts. My eyes well up.

This was the first good thing that has happened to me in so long.

Why does it have to be a lie?

I shake my head, tell myself to pull it together. I've watched my colleagues—my friends—die. I've pulled the trigger to save my own life. I've seen innocent families lose children, all in the name of war.

I've held the man I loved as he died in my arms.

I've been through so much worse than *this*. I know the way the world works.

So, as I open the passport, what I find shouldn't come as a surprise.

Surname: Anderson
Given Name: Oliver
Nationality: British Citizen

And yet, as I read and re-read Bradley's real name, my heart is broken. Shattered. Torn apart.

Before I have time to pick up the pieces, I am on my feet, running down the stairs.

At the bottom of the staircase, I smack straight into a hard, warm body.

It's Bradley.

Or should I say, *Oliver.*

⁂

"Liz, what are you doing—?"

But his voice drowns in his throat when he spots his own British passport in my hands. For someone who lies for a living, he doesn't do a great job of hiding the panic flickering through his eyes.

"You've been lying to me this whole time," I say, somehow keeping my tone calm even though I want to scream at him, pummel his chest with my fists, anything to show him how much this hurts.

"And so have you," he says.

His statement only catches me slightly off guard. With Bradley being a former operative, he would have done his due diligence in checking out *everyone* he came into contact with here in San Diego. That would include my sister *and* her family, which means he would be well aware of my father's position as the Director of the National Clandestine Service. And between the meltdown I had on our first day of retreat and how tight-lipped I've been about my work at the "State Department," it wouldn't have taken much for him to put the pieces together that I, too, work for the CIA.

I try to sidestep him, but this British operative turned yoga master is quick. He blocks me and scoops me up, throwing me over his shoulder like a rag doll.

Now I know that it certainly wasn't years of handstands and surfing that gave Bradley this beautiful body.

It was years of government training. Training just like I've had.

"Put. Me. Down," I growl.

But instead, Bradley carries me upstairs and deposits me in his master bathroom. I know he'll be ready for any move I make, so instead I stay planted in the center of the room and watch in amusement as he locks the door behind us, turns on all of the faucets to steaming hot, and stuffs a towel underneath the door.

The steam will absorb the sound in the case that I—or someone else—bugged the house.

I cross my arms over my chest and lift a brow at him as if to say, *is this all you've got?*

A maddening grin peppers his cheeks as he walks toward me. "Let's cut the bullshit, shall we?" He is fully in his British accent now.

If I weren't so angry at him, I'd say he sounded sexy.

"Yes, why don't we, *Oliver*."

"Brilliant. Ask me anything."

Wispy layers of steam billow up around us as Bradley leans back against the shower door all nonchalant, as if he is actually enjoying this.

The bastard.

"How long have you been Bradley?" I drill.

"Five years."

"And how long were you a British operative?"

Bradley shakes his head at me. "That's not how this works, love. I answer a question, then it's your turn. Got it?"

I am about to tell him that *no*, I will not be answering any of his questions, but being the smartass he is, he launches in anyway.

"How long have you worked undercover for the CIA?" he asks.

"I work for the State Department," I shoot back.

"That's bollocks and we both know it."

"The woman in the photo. In Paris. Who is she?" I ask.

The mischievous smirk disappears from his face. "Why are you holding onto a career that only makes you miserable?"

I cross my arms over my chest, not breaking eye contact. Not for a second.

"How badly did you fuck up that you were forced to leave and take on a new identity?" I quip.

Bradley pushes off the shower door and closes in on me, pressing my back up against the wall. "Do you really want to know all of this *truth*, Liz? We've already spent our entire lives dishing out lies to everyone we know. Why stop now?"

"Wouldn't it feel good to tell one person? Just one?" Even as I say this to Bradley, I know that I am aiming the question just as much to myself as I am to him.

Bradley's chest is against mine now, our breath rising, fast and in sync. Despite the betrayal I feel, my body still craves him. My mouth still thirsts for his taste.

And my heart, it aches for him. In a way it's never ached before.

As much as this overwhelming desire is making me want to run away and never look back, I won't leave here until I know who this man really is, what he has done, and what he knows about me.

"Tell me," I say.

Thick layers of steam swirl around Bradley's face, but I can still see the regret in his eyes—in fact, I can taste that nauseating regret, as if it's my own.

"The woman in the photo..." he starts. "I was using her to gather intel."

Bradley looks to the floor before lifting his deadpanned gaze to me.

Using her could mean any number of things, but by the way the words slip so guiltily from his tongue, I assume he meant he was sleeping with her. In our line of work, almost nothing is off-limits if it means getting our job done.

There is one thing, however, which we are *never* supposed to do: become emotionally attached to our subjects. We are highly trained robots acting a part; human emotions mustn't enter the equation, even if sex is involved.

As such, love is *always* off-limits.

Because when we let our emotions cloud our vision—as I did with Austin only six short months ago—missions are botched. Careers are ruined. Lives are lost.

I step toward Bradley, taking his hand.

"You fell in love with her."

He blinks, slowly, and finally...a nod.

"And she's gone now," I say, knowing this story all too well.

The light I've seen in his eyes all week vanishes, if only for an instant. In its place are the same guilt-ridden, hollowed-out shells I've seen in my own mirror every day since Austin's death.

He shakes it off, though, the way we have to. The way we are trained to do.

"The same thing happened to me," I admit, not believing that I am actually letting this pass through my lips, but not able to stop myself all the same. "Well, he was my partner. But if I wouldn't have told him how I felt about him right at that moment, he wouldn't have been caught off guard during the ambush, and..."

"He wouldn't have been killed," Bradley finishes for me.

For a moment, Bradley and I stand in silence, holding hands while our secrets sizzle in the cloud of steam around us.

He understands me.

Soon, Bradley's hands find my face, the smile returns to his beautiful eyes, and those soft lips of his come closer, hovering over mine.

"Stay, Liz," he says. "Stay in San Diego. Start a new life here...*with me.*"

A rush of warmth shoots through my chest as soon as he says the words.
I want to say yes.
I want to have a life.
I want to fall in love.

"But...how?" I demand. "How did you do it? My career—it's been my entire life."

"It's an empty life," he says. "Bleak. Full of lies, disappointment, and death. It's not living, Liz." He runs a hand down my cheek, giving me that honest gaze that pierces right through me. It's the same way he looked at me on the first day of retreat when I broke down outside the yoga studio.

As if he understood me. As if he knew *exactly* how I felt.

And as it turns out, he does.

"I wasn't forced to leave," he says. "The mistakes I made...they covered it all up. I could have stayed, but nothing would have changed. So I left. I chose this life, this identity. I wanted a fresh start. I wanted to leave it all behind and have the chance to be someone completely new. Someone who chooses life. It's a choice you can make, too. They don't own you."

"I feel like they do," I whisper.

"You're not living, Liz," he says firmly. "If you stay in this career, you will die alone."

"I know," I admit. And truly, to the heart of me, I *know* that I have not been living. I have been hiding behind a career that is rapidly sucking the life right out of me.

This time, I don't fight the tears. I let them fall. They roll down my cheeks in waves, but Bradley doesn't run. He doesn't turn away.

Instead, he wraps his strong arms around my waist, pulls me into his chest, and holds me until I can't cry any more.

"I'm sorry you lost your partner," he says, kissing the side of my head, squeezing me even closer.

"I'm sorry you lost the woman you loved."

He reaches up, dries my tears. "It was a long time ago," he says. "I had to let it go and move on. The funny thing is, I don't think I realized just how much guilt I've been hanging onto until I saw it in your eyes, the first day you arrived. I knew instantly that you'd been through something similar."

"And I knew that you knew," I tell him.

"So...what next?" he asks.

Finally, I break the slightest smile. "Don't you have to kill me now that you've admitted who you really are?"

Bradley's ridiculously sexy grin returns in full force. "Don't *you* have to kill *me* now that you've admitted who you work for?"

I shrug. "I guess we're screwed, huh?"

At this, Bradley grabs me and kisses me.

I don't fight his kiss either.

I fall into it, like a girl who has been waiting, longing, and ready to fall for so long that it is the most natural thing in the world.

But I wouldn't fall for just anyone. Only a super-secret spy who can do five-minute handstands would do it for me at this point.

When we come up for air, I ask him, "So, should I call you Bradley or Oliver?"

"Does this mean you're staying?" he asks.

I take a deep breath and respond with the only answer that is in my heart.

"*Yes.*"

Epilogue

Three Months Later

"Liz Valentine, you are quite possibly the best private investigator the scandalous town of Del Mar has ever seen." It's Bradley, my partner in crime, lifting his champagne glass to me as we celebrate the close of our first big case.

After the day that we steamed up Bradley's bathroom with our darkest confessions, I flew back to DC, marched into my father's office, and promptly turned in my resignation.

My father's expression went blank as he glanced up from the piece of paper that marked the official end of my career with the CIA and the beginning of my new life.

"You're sure?" he asked.

I smiled at him. "I'm sure." And I'd never meant anything more in my life.

My father didn't offer any words of encouragement that day. Instead, he stood from his desk, walked over to me, and wrapped me up in a hug.

All those years, I never realized that the one thing my father wanted was for me to be happy. He was never more proud of me than the day I resigned from the CIA, and I have never felt more loved by him.

Before I left his office, my dad called out to me. "Elizabeth, I trust you won't run off and marry some whacked-out drug lord living a secret life as a yoga master, like your sister did. Damn that girl."

As it turned out, my sister's husband wasn't twirling on down to Mexico every weekend to meditate for hours on end—instead, Patrick was smuggling drugs back across the border. The day before I left San Diego, I discovered him unloading a massive stash of marijuana from underneath the floorboards in the sex wedge closet in their house.

Poor Julia had to come to terms with the fact that her marriage was built on a purple sex wedge of drugs and lies, and with her husband in prison, wearing a jumpsuit as orange as his overly-tanned skin, she would soon be facing motherhood on her own.

But...not *completely* on her own, because as soon as I resigned and packed up my DC apartment, I was on the first flight back out to San Diego. And with Julia's scandalous marriage debacle on the forefront of everyone's minds in the gossipy beach town of Del Mar, Bradley and I realized we wouldn't have to give up our spy careers forever.

And that's how Valentine-Hunter Investigatory Services was born.

Bradley and I had just uncovered our first cheating spouse—Jasmine's billionaire husband, who, as it turned out, was keeping an entire second family in a mansion in Northern California, where he frequently traveled for "business." The day we delivered the news, Jasmine planted her cherry-red Botoxed lips on both Bradley's cheeks and mine before looking to the sky and shouting "Hallelujah!"

Never had I seen a woman happier to hear the news that her husband had been cheating. Then again, never before had I known a woman who was about to potentially receive *billions* of dollars in a divorce settlement.

But, we *are* in Southern California. And as I've learned, beyond the mansions and the money, the smoothies and the surfing, the meditating and the upward facing dogs, the bleached-out blondes and the bouncing boobs, there are more lies, drugs, and scandals in this part of the country than I ever could have imagined.

Thankfully so, for the sake of my and Bradley's new business.

Today, as Bradley congratulates me on my first private investigator victory, I smile back at him, reveling in the simplicity and beauty of my new life at the beach.

"Thank you," I tell him. "But it really was a team effort. If you wouldn't have traced his *other* wife's tummy tuck back to his credit card, we may not have cracked the case."

Bradley chuckles and slips an arm around my waist before kissing me on the lips. I lean into him, loving the feel of his mouth on mine more than I can ever remember loving anything in my life.

After our delectable kiss, I rest my head on his shoulder and gaze out at the Pacific, watching the waves roll in as the sunset dips below the horizon.

"I don't think champagne should be our only reward for solving the great mystery of Jasmine's cheating husband," I say.

"Oh?" Bradley responds, intrigued.

"I'm thinking a dip in your infinity pool, to relive our first night together."

"I like the way your mind works, Valentine. Except this time, I think we should take off our clothes *before* we jump in."

I slide my hand into Bradley's, glancing up at this man who knows my secrets and wants me anyway. This man who makes my heart leap and my skin sizzle upon immediate contact. This man who has turned my life upside down and who makes me smile every single day.

"What are we waiting for?" I ask him.

He grins, sly and sexy, before we take off down the bluffs together.

With darkness settling in over our lovely beach town and a fresh blanket of stars twinkling up above, we strip off each other's clothes and stand at the edge of the pool, hand in hand.

And without so much as a thought about what comes next, *we jump*.

Confessions
of a City Girl

Washington D.C.

Prologue

"Mrs. Bell, are you absolutely sure there are no further steps you and Mr. Bell can take to reconcile this marriage?"

In my thirty-two years on this earth, I've never been caught speechless. I was born a New Yorker; as such, from the moment I took my first breath, I've had an opinion to share.

A loud one.

Which is why I became a novelist. I simply had so much to say that I had to begin writing it all down, otherwise my vocal chords may have snapped in half.

But today, as Judge Bailey's million-dollar question echoes through the courtroom, all I can do is stare blankly at his silver hair, at the tired lines around his eyes, and pretend he is talking to someone else.

"Mrs. Bell?" The judge's stern voice rattles my insides. I feel like I might be sick.

How am I supposed to answer this question? With the truth? That yes, of course Mr. Bell and I could have done more to save our dying marriage! Should I swing from the rafters, yelling and crying about how much I still love my husband with every ounce of my being, but that despite all of our futile efforts to stop the bleeding, here we are.

In divorce court.

Violet and Josh.

Josh and Violet.

A pair of artists who used to go together like chocolate and strawberries, Paris and romance, satin sheets and steamy sex.

But today, as we sit alone at our separate tables, dismantling the life we've built together, the only thing we have in common is the shattering of our exhausted hearts on this dirty courtroom floor.

"Mrs. Bell, please answer the question."

Now I am flat-out ignoring the old bastard, my eyes darting anywhere but into that truth-seeking gaze of his.

In my avoidance, by accident, I catch a glimpse of Josh.

As an actor, Josh could always laugh or cry harder than anyone I knew. He delivers emotion with so much punch that it is nearly impossible not to join him in his elation or collapse with him in his misery.

But today, slumped in his chair, the man I've loved for more than a decade is a ghostly, ragged shell of the vibrant person he used to be. He doesn't move or make a sound as a steady stream of tears rolls down his cheeks.

Just when I have the urge to flail my broken-hearted body across this courtroom, wrap my arms around my husband, and call the whole damn thing off, Josh turns his tear-stained face to me.

He is defeated. Worn down. Finished.

He doesn't speak, but I can hear him all the same.

Go ahead, Violet. This is what you wanted, isn't it?

I nod, ever so slightly.

Because somewhere, deep inside of me, I still feel the remnants of the confident, independent, sassy girl I used to be. And that girl is clawing, scratching, *screaming* to get the hell out of this dead marriage.

As much as this decision is tearing apart my insides, the pages in *our* romance novel have burned, and all that is left are ashes of a relationship I once thought—*we* once thought—would last forever.

No, Josh, the death of our love story is *not* what I wanted.

But despite the very real tears he is shedding, my husband has already moved on. From our love, from our bed, from the life we built.

So, what other choice do I have?

The judge clears his throat. "Mrs. Bell. We don't have all day."

I turn my face away from Josh. From his tears. From our life together.

And with one breath of stale courtroom air, I finally find the strength to speak.

"Yes, Your Honor. I'm sure."

One

Eight Months Later

"Introducing Violet Bell, New York Times bestselling romance novelist and author of the acclaimed novel *The Magic of Us*, which was released as a major motion picture last year starring Ryan Gosling and Rachel McAdams. And while, unfortunately, I cannot take any credit for inspiring the romance in Violet's spicy novels, I am proud to say that this lovely woman is one of my closest friends from our days at Georgetown. Give it up for the talented Ms. Bell, everyone!"

After eight years of being called *Mrs.* Violet Bell, the sound of my close friend Aaron introducing me as *Ms.* Bell makes me wish I had taken the other half of my Xanax before strutting onto this stage. Rattled and newly divorced though I am, I smile dutifully at the crowds of Georgetown University students who have gathered to listen to a panel of alumni talk about how successful and thrilling and cool our lives are ten years after graduation.

If successful and thrilling and cool means rolling my depressed ass out of bed before noon and putting at least one piece of food in my mouth in any given twenty-four-hour period, then bam! I have arrived!

As I take my seat in between a lawyer, a doctor, and an investment banker—a typical line-up of Georgetown grads who have their shit together—I'm reminded that *I* am here to add a touch of spice to this otherwise bland group. But *only* a touch, because as my ever-practical friend Aaron warned me only moments ago, in his oh-so-proper British accent, "Let's keep it PG-13, Vi."

Aaron sits next to me, rounding out the Georgetown alumni crew as the token speech writer working on Capitol Hill. As the students' applause dies down, I tap my water glass and whisper in his ear, "Is there any vodka in here?"

After all five of us have given the students a quick description of what we've been up to these past ten years—mostly on the career front—Aaron takes the microphone.

"I know you've all been dying to ask our accomplished group of panelists some questions, so let's open up it up. And remember, it doesn't have to be all about career paths. Questions on life, love, relationships, and family are fair game too."

This is the part where I have to actually grip my chair so I won't bolt out of the auditorium. *Why isn't that damn Xanax kicking in?*

A tiny little blonde thing sitting in the front row raises her hand.

"Yes, the young woman in the front," Aaron calls on her. "Could you please stand and tell us your name?"

"I'm Anastasia, and my question is for Violet." Anastasia pins her big baby blues right on me and takes a bold step toward the stage. "I know you've been super successful with your books and everything, but your personal life seems to be falling apart. Can you tell us more about your divorce with Josh Bell?"

Just as I am reaching for the microphone from Aaron—who is suddenly holding on to it with a death grip—a voluptuous red-head next to Anastasia pops up. "Has it been difficult watching him score the biggest role of his career after your split? Seeing his face in the tabloids with a different woman every week? I mean, he's *so* hot and so successful now; I can only imagine the regret you must be feeling."

Before I can answer, a curly-haired brunette joins the college paparazzi. "Do you think you made a mistake leaving him? Are you going to write a book about it?"

Anastasia rounds it out with one final question. "What happens when a romance novelist's life falls apart? That's the story we really want to hear."

"I'm not quite sure this is the direction we want to—" Aaron starts, but I snatch the microphone from him.

I stand, taking my own bold step toward the front of the stage. "Aaron, I think this is *exactly* the direction this talk needs to take. When we were in their shoes, don't you wish someone would've told us what life is really like once you leave the perfect little Georgetown bubble?"

Cheers erupt from the students, and even though Aaron looks as though he may murder me, I know the time has come for me to let it loose. Even if I wanted to keep this imminent outburst under control, there is something inside me that feels for these kids. They're so naïve. They have no clue what atrocities are waiting for them after they take that gold-plated diploma and leave the pearly gates of Georgetown.

And I think it's my duty to tell them.

That, and my Xanax hasn't kicked in.

"Let's take Rob, our investment banker, for example," I launch in. "Rob works eighty hour weeks and has already been divorced twice. He makes an obscene amount of money, lives in a baller apartment in Manhattan, and when he's not pretending to give a shit about his spoiled kids, he can regularly be found snorting cocaine off a prostitute's tits." I walk over to Rob, who is looking at me with the most horrified expression on his normally smug face, and I pat him on the back. "I mean, can we blame the guy? He has to do something to deal with his miserable life."

"Then we've got Sarah, our Wall Street lawyer. This girl is kicking some serious ass at work. Mergers and acquisitions and deals so massive she can hardly see straight through all the money they're throwing at her. She's definitely on her way to making partner at the firm, but, tell me Sarah, when was the last time you had a meaningful, *real* relationship with a man?" I point the microphone at her perfectly-lined lips, but she is speechless. "Okay, forget a real relationship; clearly you don't have time for that. How about the last time you got laid?"

"That is none of your business, Violet," she hisses into the microphone.

"Maybe not, but my guess is that you're not answering the question because you can't even remember the last time you had a man in those 1500 thread count Egyptian cotton sheets you sleep in for three hours a night. Am I right?"

Aaron stands up, grabs my shoulder.

"Violet, that's enough," he snaps, unable to hide the sheer mortification in his voice.

I pull away from his grasp, too high from all this truth-telling to stop now. "What, Aaron? Are you afraid I'm going to tell these kids that you've been so damn busy climbing ladders on the Hill that you haven't had a real date in over two years?"

I barely have time to register the pain that flashes through Aaron's big blue eyes as I continue on my rampage.

"What about you, Violet?" It's our friend, Anastasia, yelling from the front of the stunned student crowd. She—along with every other student in the audience—has her iPhone pointed straight at me, no doubt taking video of the downfall of Violet Bell.

"Yes, go ahead, snap your photos and take your videos, because guess what divorce has done to me, kids? For the first time in my life, I give no fucks! Not a single one! I've been hiding in the shadows for too damn long while my ex-husband is screwing every twenty-year-old actress he can get his hands on and prancing around with these plastic bitches on the cover of every fucking magazine I see in the grocery store. Which is why I barely eat anymore! I have to take a handful of Xanax just to leave the house to buy a box of Pop Tarts! I mean how fucked up is that?"

I stalk to the edge of the stage and send a boiling gaze down at these budding little journalists. They look only slightly frightened behind the shield of their iPhones, but mostly, they look hungry. Hungry for the truth.

"You want to know what life is *really* like ten years after graduation? Is that what you want? Well, I was invited here as the *creative one* in the group to encourage all of you that it's okay to be different. It's okay to follow your instincts and let your creativity flow, guys! Even if it means screwing up your life! Go for it! Live your mother-fucking dreams! Look at me! Look how fabulous my life is now that I've followed my shattered, broken heart. It's a fucking mess. I am so tired of plastering on a fake smile and telling the world that I'm fine, that life is fabulous, that my career is blossoming, and that I just love my new single life! Because you know what? It blows. Divorce is a monstrosity. The institution of marriage is fucked. Totally and completely fucked. I've been writing romance novels for years, and I don't believe a single word of what I've written. It's all a huge load of crap. Romance—*true romance*—does not exist, kids. Well, if romance is spending years falling asleep on opposite sides of the bed from your husband, pretending like it's fine when you notice him staring at every other ass that walks past him on the street when he never looks at yours anymore, but realizing at the same time that you don't even care because *you're* staring at other guys' asses wishing one of them—*any of them*—would take you to bed because your husband hasn't wanted to have sex with you for months. If that's romance, then kids, I found it."

Aaron's hand wraps firmly around my arm, but I shrug him off. I'm not finished yet.

"Yeah, that's right, a romance novelist who wasn't having sex with her own husband. I've been living a lie, writing the sex scenes I only wished were happening in my own bedroom."

I point my gaze at the voluptuous redhead and the curly-haired brunette who are raising their hands—such patient little students.

"Ah, yes, the question about regret, right?" I ask them.

They nod eagerly.

"Do I regret leaving my husband?"

I pause, soaking in the silence that has settled over the auditorium.

And finally, I answer the million-dollar question. The question that I know everyone in my life has been dying to ask since the day I walked away from my marriage for good.

"Even though the marriage was dead, even though my husband barely looked at me anymore, even though I knew he was already sleeping with someone else before I told him I had to go…I'm ashamed to say that yes, I do regret leaving him. Because as horrible as life was at the end of our marriage, it's still worse without him. It's been absolute hell. I have a book due in a month, and I haven't been able to write a page. Not one single page. I'm running out of money because my slack-ass, out-of-work actor husband was awarded an obscene amount of alimony when we divorced…and only after I began paying him more money than I'm making did he go on to score the biggest role of his life, and now he's making so much money he's turning work away! But you know what? Fuck money. What does it matter? I'm falling apart. I have to take Xanax just to survive the day. I've never been more depressed in my life. I mean, the love of my life fell out of love with me. I based every single hero in my romance novels on my husband—a husband who never even read a page of one of my books. But no matter how much I loved him, no matter how many ways I showed him that love, he couldn't love me back, not in the way I needed him to. And I'm so pathetic that I miss him. I miss a man who didn't even love me anymore! I miss him so much that I cry myself to sleep every night wishing it could've been different. Wondering what I could've done…what I could've done to keep him."

I barely notice the tears rolling down my cheeks as I turn my back from my captivated audience, hand the microphone back to a horrified Aaron, and stalk offstage. Somewhere, in the back of my mind, I hear a faint voice of reason telling me that I've just ruined everything—well, everything that wasn't already ruined. But I am too numb, too shattered to care.

Two

I don't find the courage to show up at Aaron's house until eleven o'clock that night. He lives alone in a beautiful brownstone just a few blocks off Dupont Circle, and even though this is one of my favorite neighborhoods in DC, and Aaron is my absolute favorite friend in the whole world, it took me over twelve hours of walking aimlessly through the city to make my way to his doorstep.

I haven't eaten, I haven't looked at my phone, and I haven't looked in a mirror all day. I'm sure if I did, I would find a haggard, shattered shell of the happy, glamorous woman I once was.

When I ring the doorbell, I'm certain Aaron isn't going to want to look at me either.

I stand there for what feels like hours, forcing my feet to stay planted on his welcome mat, even though I just want to turn and run. I want to be someone else. Someone who hasn't turned their life to total and complete shit.

But before I can do that, I have to sleep. And even if Aaron doesn't want me at his house, I have to at least pick up my bag and check my sorry ass into a hotel. Considering my credit cards are maxed out and I've either spent or given Josh almost every penny of my latest book advance, I'm not sure how

I'll manage even one night in a hotel, but thankfully Aaron opens his door before I have time to further ponder my grim financial outlook.

And there stands Aaron. The one man who has always accepted me for exactly who I am. But tonight, as my shame-filled gaze creeps up his tall body, lingering on the buttons of his black collared shirt, I have a feeling I won't find acceptance in his eyes the way I usually do.

And I'm right. In those normally sweet blue eyes of his, I find contempt. Anger. Pain.

And I can't handle it. I can't handle any of it anymore.

"Aaron, I—"

The tears come faster than my words, and I collapse into my friend. Thankfully, he catches me. And despite how much he must hate me right now, he picks me up, carries me to the couch, and lets me rest my head on his chest until I have no tears left to cry.

"Where have you been, Vi?" Aaron asks. "You just disappeared. I've been calling you all day."

"How can you even still care after what I did?"

"I don't want to talk about what happened today, Vi. Suffice it to say that you've created a shit storm of epic proportions not only for yourself but also for me, and now is not the hour to clean it up." Aaron takes my hands in his, holds them tightly.

"You're shaking. You're a mess. Have you eaten?"

"I'm not hungry."

"I don't care. You need to eat something." Aaron walks into the kitchen and as I hear him fumbling around in his empty fridge, I realize—I *know*—that Aaron is the best friend I've ever had.

"How did you not throw my suitcase out the window?" I call into the kitchen. "How are you being so nice right now?"

Aaron peeks his head around the doorway and graces me with the slightest of grins. "Not my style to kick you while you're down, love."

I pull my knees to my chest, starting to feel a little hungry after all. "What are you making?"

Aaron presents a frozen pizza that has probably been in his freezer for at least a decade. "Burnt pizza okay with you? And by burnt, I'm clearly referencing the severe freezer burn."

Somehow, I find it in myself to smile. "You're such a bachelor."

"According to you, a quite pathetic bachelor who hasn't had a real date in over two years."

"I didn't call you pathetic."

"You may as well have." Aaron disappears into the kitchen, and his comment has made me remember all of the other mortifying things that flew out of my mouth at the panel today.

"Aaron, I—"

"Don't want to hear it," he calls out. "We'll be even after I force-feed you this atrocious excuse for a pizza. Deal?"

But before I can answer him, I am compelled to turn my phone back on. It's been buried in my purse all day, a ticking time bomb waiting to destroy any last shred of hope I may have had that somehow, after my public meltdown today, my life might still be intact.

And why I have chosen this particular moment to detonate that bomb, I'm not entirely sure. All I know as I cringe at the multitude of voicemails and text messages from my literary agent, my publisher, my girlfriends, my ex-mother-in-law, my own mother, my nosy New York family, and of course, from Aaron, is that my little outburst did *not* go unnoticed. The only person I don't yet see a message from is my ex-husband, Josh. Maybe, by some miracle, he doesn't know yet?

The first text message I open is from Kathryn, my most loud-mouthed cousin—which is saying a lot in a family full of blunt, tactless New Yorkers. Kathryn sent me a YouTube link followed by a text saying: *WTF???*

I click on the link, knowing I shouldn't.

But it's too late.

Ex-wife of Actor Josh Bell Loses Her Shit at Georgetown Alumni Panel.

There I am on YouTube—a voluptuous 5'6" madwoman, storming around the stage like I own it. My long espresso locks are an absolute mess— *did I even shower this morning?*—and the circles beneath my heavily-lined jade-green eyes are epic. I am the definition of a reckless divorcée, hurling F-bombs and insulting my classmates with talk of cocaine and prostitutes and Egyptian cotton sheets. Telling the whole damn world about Josh's affair and my sexless marriage. And admitting that I don't believe in love or romance or happily ever after when I am a romance novelist for God's sake.

But it's not even the fact that my anti-love diatribes are on YouTube that is making me hyperventilate. It's the fact that those diatribes have gone viral.

"*Nine-hundred thousand, three-hundred and thirty-seven views?* In twelve hours? How is that even possible?"

Aaron walks through the doorway and plucks my phone from my hands. "For fuck's sake, Vi, why would you look at that right now?"

"You knew this was on here when I walked in the door tonight?"

"Yeah, me and nearly one million other people knew it, Vi. Your ex-husband is the hottest craze among women ages fifteen to seventy-four. Of course all those hussies want to watch his ex-wife go bat-shit crazy on YouTube. What did you expect?"

I snatch my phone back and watch the horror show once more, this time with Aaron sighing over my shoulder.

"I think the bit about the prostitutes and the cocaine was perhaps the strongest moment of the speech. And look at that wanker's face! Priceless."

"Aaron!" I smack him in the arm. "This isn't funny!"

"Of course it's not, Vi. But when you've lost everything, when you've become a YouTube sensation—and *not* a good one—in less than twelve hours, you have two choices: you can either laugh or you can cry. And I'm sure you've done enough pissing and moaning about for one day."

"For one lifetime," I correct him. "For *ten* lifetimes."

"Quite right." Aaron takes a step closer to me and places a finger under my chin. "And look on the bright side, love. Even though you've denounced romance for good, I still believe your novels are going to be flying off the shelves. Everyone loves a scandal. Now, are you ready for a slice of that dreadful pizza?"

"How can you be so...?" I trail off, admiring the shine in his bright blue eyes and wondering why I've never seen Aaron in this light before.

"How can I be so what?" he asks. "Charming? Sexy? Desirable? A dream come true for the growing population of cougars in DC?"

"Yes, all of the above."

Aaron flips a dishtowel over his shoulder and takes my hand. "It's as natural as breathing for me, love. Now come and eat."

And then my friend leads me into his bare-bones kitchen, where he feeds me the worst pizza that has ever been made. But as he continues trying his best to make me laugh, I realize that nothing has tasted this good in years.

Three

It's the middle of the night and I'm lying on my back, watching the ceiling fan in Aaron's guest bedroom spin endlessly, wishing the damn thing would just fall on my head and put me out of my misery. My phone is lying on my chest, buzzing, dinging, ringing, and vibrating with a fury I didn't know an iPhone could possess. The constant barrage of calls, messages, e-mails, and Facebook posts are all there to remind me that the *entire world* witnessed the biggest meltdown of my life.

And since I know there's no way I'm going to sleep tonight, I decide that I will answer the next call that comes through, no matter who it is. I'm already drowning; I might as well face the music.

As if on cue, my phone rings. It's Janine Maxwell, my hard-core New York literary agent. It's probably the fifteenth call I've received from her today. This one isn't going to be easy, but screw it. I answer anyway.

"Janine, I—" I begin, but I stop when I can hear her breathing fire on the other line.

"Violet, really? After three missed deadlines, you *still* haven't written a word of the fucking book? Are you aware that I pretty much had to sell my body *and* my soul to your editor at St. Martin's to get this final extension for you? And instead of just *writing the damn book*, you are blasting your personal shit all over YouTube and telling the world how romance is a load of crap? Dear God, Violet. You are not making my job easy."

"It was a momentary lapse in judgement," I say, knowing full well that explanation is bullshit.

"That lapse lasted more than a moment, honey." An angry sigh travels over the line. "It's three a.m., and I need to take my sleeping pill to try to get at least two hours in before those five-year-old twin monsters of mine wake up and ruin my life the way they do every morning. So, I'm going to get straight to the point. I spoke with your editor at St. Martin's, and they want the book in two weeks or else they're dropping the contract. You've already violated it with *three* extensions, so they're being nice by even giving you two more weeks."

"But they know I haven't written any of the book," I protest.

"Exactly, Violet. They know you can't turn in an entire book in two weeks, not when you're recovering from this shit storm. They *want* to drop you. And when they do, you'll be required to pay back the amount you've already received for your book advance within thirty days or you'll have yet another unpleasant court date on your hands."

I shoot up from the bed, my panic level taken to new heights. "Thirty days? But they've already given me half of the advance, and that was over one-hundred grand. One-hundred grand that I don't have any more."

"How on earth have you gone through that money in—you know what? That's not my problem. I'm not your fucking mother. I'm your agent, and I need to sleep. You will turn that book in in two weeks, or you will not only be losing your book deal, your publisher, and your money, you'll be losing your agent too."

"Janine, there must be a way—"

But Janine isn't going to trouble shoot with me tonight, or any night, because she's already hung up the phone.

"Two weeks? Two weeks??" I say aloud.

"Two weeks until what, love?"

It's a shirtless Aaron, standing in my doorway in his gray boxer briefs, all sleepy-eyed and yawning.

"Why are you up?" I ask, completely unfazed by his nearly naked body coming to sit beside me on the bed. Aaron's an extremely good looking guy—tall, toned, and muscular with a full head of dirty blonde hair; the most innocent blue eyes I've ever seen on a man; and the smoothest, sweetest complexion. The girls always went wild over him in college, but he never had a clue what to do with all that feminine energy they were hurling at him. Sure, he had his fair share of one-night stands, but dating and relationships? Forget it. That boy just didn't get it. In our twenties, when most of our friends were coupling up, getting married, and later having babies, Aaron was so immersed in his career on the Hill that he barely noticed. He truly is the eternal bachelor—something which I have actually always appreciated about him because it has meant that no other woman was going waltz in and steal him away from me.

Aaron wraps an arm around my shoulders. "I knew you wouldn't be sleeping…just wanted to be sure you were okay."

"I'm not."

"Figured as much. So, two weeks to what?" he says.

"I have two weeks to write this damn romance novel or both my agent and my publisher are going to drop me. Not only that, but I'll have to pay back the half of my book advance that I've already received within thirty days."

"It was a big advance, then?"

"Ummm…yeah. Massive. Having my first book turned into a movie really upped the ante."

"And you don't have the money anymore?" he asks.

"Barely a penny."

Aaron runs a hand through his hair and lets out the sigh to top all sighs. "Well, fuck."

"Yeah, fuck."

"Do you know what the new book's going to be about?" Aaron asks.

"No clue."

"No inspiration, no ideas, nothing?"

"Nada," I say as I collapse on my back, my head sinking into the feathery pillow. Aaron follows suit, and we lay side by side staring at the ceiling fan spinning over our heads. Once again, I wish it would fall. Only on me, though. I would never want it to mangle Aaron's beautiful face.

A long silence passes before Aaron squeezes my hand. "Well, there's only one solution, love."

"And that would be...?"

"Let's make a romance novel."

And, for the second time in my life, I'm speechless.

In my nervous silence, I think about how many times Aaron and I have laid side by side like this—in our tiny college beds, on Copley lawn at Georgetown, in Aaron's massive King-sized adult bed, and even in the bed I used to share with Josh—staring up at the ceiling or the sky, laughing and talking for hours. And never once in those moments has Aaron made a move on me. We have always kept each other firmly in the friend zone, and my stomach is quivering a bit at the thought that he might, after all these years, be trying to change that.

Finally, with a cautious turn of my head, I look to my friend. "Are you suggesting that we...?"

He turns to me, an amused grin spreading over his face. "Oh fuck, Vi. Do you think I'm trying to sleep with you?"

"Well, what the hell else to you mean by, *let's make a romance novel?*" I imitate his British accent, horribly I might add, which gets him laughing.

"If I was going to try to sleep with you, don't you think I would've done it by now?"

I flip onto my side, turning to face him. "No, actually, I don't think you would've tried even if you secretly wanted to all these years. We both know you've never had any game."

Now Aaron flips onto his side, and we are at a face off.

"Well excuse me, Miss Fancy Pants Romance Novelist, for not whisking women off in horse-drawn carriages or trotting around shirtless in a Scottish kilt like the heroes in your epic love stories, but I *do* have game, and you just don't know it because I've never thrown any your way."

At this, I can't help but burst into laughter. "And is that what you're doing now? Throwing game my way?"

"No, my lovely friend, I'm not. What I'm suggesting is that we'll spend the next twenty-four hours going to all the most romantic spots in DC, with the sole purpose of gathering inspiration for your story, and then you'll lock yourself away for the next thirteen days and do nothing but eat, sleep, and write that book."

"So, you actually *know* all of the most romantic spots in DC?" I tease.

"I resent your tone and your lack of faith in my romantic abilities. I can be *quite* romantic."

"Aaron, I'm sorry sweetie, but you are the least romantic man I've ever known."

"Lies you spin. All lies. How would you know about my romance skills?"

"Or lack thereof? Umm…remember when you tried to date me in college before we became friends?"

"Darling, do not hold me responsible for the mistakes I made as an ignorant eighteen-year-old who couldn't see past the end of his own knob."

"Your knob is so long you couldn't see past the end of it?" I joke.

"Longer," he says with a grin.

"See, like I said, the *least* romantic man in the world."

Before I know what is happening, Aaron stands up, sweeps me into his arms, whisks me out of the guest bedroom, and down the hallway to his room.

"What are you doing?" I squeal.

He throws me onto his bed, climbs over top of me, and hovers above me with his lips so close to mine that, for a moment, I actually think my best friend is going to kiss me.

But he doesn't kiss me. Instead he stays there, his breath warming my cheeks, his eyes piercing into mine for what feels like years…And while I would never admit it to him, I realize that somewhere deep down, I like having him this close to me.

Aaron takes my hands and pins them over my head. "You want inspiration?" he says.

I'm out of words, yet again. I don't know who is lying on top of me, but it is certainly not Aaron, the man I have friend-zoned for eons.

"You want romance?" he says with a sexy grin. "Give me twenty-four hours, love, and I promise you, we will plot the shit out of your next novel."

I smile up at him, realizing that perhaps there's much more to Aaron than I ever saw...or wanted to see.

"Okay Casanova, it's a deal."

At this, he smiles the biggest, sweetest smile I think I've ever seen, rolls over onto his side, kisses me on the cheek, and wraps me up in his arms.

"We better get some sleep then, love. It's going to be a very busy day tomorrow."

"I can't wait to see what you have up your sleeve," I say.

"Oh don't lie. You couldn't give a shit what I've got up my sleeve. I know what a sex fiend you are—you really just want to get a good peek inside my pants."

"You're right. I'm only interested in your huge knob."

"Story of my life," he says.

As I drift off to sleep, I know that Aaron and I have suddenly entered into some strange new territory—one I don't think either of us has a clue how to navigate, but I'm too exhausted, and too comfortable in Aaron's arms to care.

Four

It's ten o'clock on Saturday morning, and although I absolutely would have preferred to stay in Aaron's cozy bed for the entire day—hell, the entire year—so as not to have to face the absolute horror of what I did yesterday, Aaron has woken me up, forced me into the shower, and is now dragging me onto the street to wait for our Uber ride which is taking us to an undisclosed location.

"Where are we going?" I ask him as I stifle a yawn and squint at the sunlight beaming through the wispy clouds overhead.

"Well, if I told you, it wouldn't be very romantic, now would it?"

"Romance isn't all about secrets, you know," I say.

Aaron turns to me, sighing. "Would you please just let me do my job for the day?"

I put my hands up. "Okay, okay. I'll shut up."

"Violet Bell shutting her mouth? Never thought I'd see the day."

Just as I'm smacking him, a little gray Prius buzzes up to the curb.

"Allow me," Aaron says, opening my door.

"What the hell are you doing?" It's the driver, a stubby little dude with the angriest, bushiest black eyebrows I've ever seen.

"Sorry," Aaron says. "Are you not Mark, our Uber driver?"

"Fuck no," Eyebrows says as he peeks through the window at me. "Wait, you're that girl on YouTube who lost her shit yesterday—Josh Bell's wife, right?"

At this Aaron slams the car door shut and taps the top of the car. Hard. "Move along, move along."

As the car speeds away, my friend looks to me apologetically. "Well, that was a strong start to our romantic day in the nation's capital. Wouldn't you agree?"

But I am already turning around and walking—no, *sprinting*—back to Aaron's house.

"Oh, no you don't." Aaron grabs my shoulders, spins me around.

"If some random dude in a Prius with the bushiest eyebrows I've ever seen—"

"Did he even *have* eyes under those monstrous blobs of hair?" Aaron says.

"Okay, the eyebrows are beside the point. What I'm trying to say is that if *he* recognized me, I don't think it's a good idea for me to be running around DC all day. It's going to be a shit show."

"It could be a fun shit show, though, don't you reckon?"

I cross my arms and level my best glare at Aaron. "No, I don't reckon. I'm going back inside and I'm just going to do my best to brainstorm the book."

Right as I say this, my phone rings. I make the mistake of pulling it out of my purse, only to see Josh's number flash across the screen.

Aaron snatches the phone from my hands and presses *"Decline."*

"Doubtful you're going to get a lot of brainstorming done with this happening," he says, waving the phone in the air.

He's right. I know he's right. I just don't want to admit it.

I don't have to, though, because *another* gray Prius pulls up to the curb, and before I can protest, Aaron has opened the door and ushered me into the backseat.

The driver is a nice-looking blonde dude, probably in his mid-twenties.

"G'morning," Aaron greets him. "Mark, right?"

"That's me," he says, zooming around Dupont Circle like a madman with his gangsta rap blaring.

Aaron nudges my side, whispers in my ear. "See, *he* didn't recognize you."

But as we come to our first stop light, Mark, our blonde, green-eyed gangster in a Prius, takes a peek in the rear-view mirror and smiles brightly. "Hey, you're that chick on YouTube—Josh Bell's wife. I've never had a celebrity in my car before!"

"Ex-wife," I correct him. "And I'm hardly a celebrity."

"Well, you're hot enough to be famous," he says.

"Oh, dear God," I mumble.

Aaron is smiling, though. "Just take the compliment, love."

Fifteen minutes later, Aaron is opening the door for me at Café Bonaparte, my absolute favorite spot to eat in Georgetown. It's on Wisconsin Avenue, not far from campus, and while I'm hardly thrilled to be so close to the scene of the crime only one day after said crime has occurred, the cuisine at this place is so delicious that I decide it will be worth the risk.

The décor inside the café is exactly the way I remember it from my days as a college student. Cute little wooden tables are situated close together like they would be in a true Parisian café. Framed black-and-white photos of the iconic sites of Paris line the sunshine-yellow wall, and a sleek bar lines the opposite wall which is painted a bold red.

When we take our seats, I go straight for the cocktail menu, obviously.

"I'll have the St. Germain cocktail and the Bastille crêpe, please," I tell the petite waitress who visits our table.

Aaron glances at his watch. "Ten a.m. Starting early...I'm impressed."

"It's not very romantic of you to question my alcoholic tendencies on a day like today," I point out.

The waitress snickers. But she stops laughing abruptly, and when I meet her gaze, I find a surprised look of recognition in her pretty hazel eyes. And now she's just staring. I can tell she can't help herself, so I give her what she wants.

"Yes, I'm Josh Bell's wife. *Ex-wife.*"

"I wasn't—" she starts, but I wave a hand.

"It's fine. I better get used to it, right?"

"I'm really sorry you've had to go through all of that," she says. "And I wasn't going to call you his wife…I just wanted to tell you how much I love your books."

"Oh, well, thank you," I say, pleasantly surprised. "That's sweet of you to say."

She shrugs, her cheeks blushing just the slightest bit. "We could all use a little romance in our lives, right?"

"Quite right," Aaron chimes in as our sweet little waitress leaves the table.

"Now that went pretty well," he says.

"It'll be going even better when I have that champagne cocktail in my hands."

"I didn't realize I'd have a drunk morning date, but I can roll with it, you know," Aaron says. "I'm flexible like that."

"Umm…you…flexible? Hardly."

"I'm sad that you have such little faith in my abilities to woo a woman."

"What does being flexible have to do with wooing a woman?" I say.

He leans over the table, a devious grin spreading across his face. "I can stretch my legs in ways you can't imagine, love."

"Aaron! When did you get so…so…?"

"Sexual?" he says, over-exaggerating his already strong British accent.

"Oh, God. You're too much."

My cocktail arrives just in time, and as the bubbly alcohol washes down my throat, I feel Aaron watching me intently. "What?"

"Nothing," he says, not breaking my gaze.

"What? Why are you looking at me like that?"

"You know, you had the day from hell yesterday, and still, you look absolutely stunning this morning."

I pause, thinking he's serious until I remember the point of our day out on the town. "You don't need to throw corny lines out just to get this romance thing going, Aaron."

"I'm not trying to get any romance thing going. Just calling it like I see it. You look beautiful this morning, and I wanted you to know that."

"Oh...well...thank you," I say, hoping he can't see my cheeks blushing, because I feel them lighting on fire.

"You're welcome."

I take a gander at my friend—at his sweet grin; his light, rosy complexion; and those huge, lovely blue eyes. "You're looking pretty nice, yourself," I say. And I mean it.

He shrugs his shoulders. "I know."

"And you're *so* humble."

"Humble is my middle name, baby," he says in his best Austin Powers voice.

Just then, our food arrives, and I am no longer concerned with my best friend's smashing looks or with the fact that he is embarrassing me with his talk of how beautiful I am apparently looking this morning when I know for a fact that I look as if I just rolled out of a twenty-four-hour factory shift. I am not concerned with any of this because I am overwhelmed with delight at the sight of this decadent ham and cheese crêpe on my plate.

After my first bite, I feel my body relaxing. "This is *so* good."

"I thought you'd enjoy coming back here," Aaron says.

"It's my favorite," I say through a mouthful of cheesy, buttery crêpe. "I'm surprised you remembered."

"I know all of your favorites, Vi."

"*All* of them?" I say.

"Yeah, pretty sure I know them all."

"Okay, let's see what you've got."

Aaron dabs the corner of his mouth with his napkin, then straightens himself up in his seat. "Favorite movie: It's a tie between *French Kiss* with Meg Ryan and Kevin Kline and *Serendipity* with John Cusak and Kate Beckinsale."

"Well, that's easy because we've watched those together like a million times. And you love them too."

He cocks an eyebrow at me.

"What? You don't like them?" I ask.

"Darling, please. *French Kiss* and *Serendipity*? I am an actual man, you know. Loads of testosterone, big knob, deep voice."

"But you've watched each of those movies with me at least ten times."

"Because I know you love them."

"But I thought you loved them too."

He shakes his head, chuckling. "Had you fooled, didn't I?"

As Aaron goes on to list my favorite TV shows, books, romance novelists, ice cream flavor, pizza place, French town, Italian town, beach, wine, vineyard, and even my favorite brand of French lingerie, I realize that while Josh knew all of these things too, he didn't like to partake in most of them with me. He only wanted to watch *his* shows, discuss *his* favorite movies, eat at *his* favorite places, and he'd throw a toddler-worthy temper tantrum if he didn't get his way. I was so used to giving him what he wanted that for years I'd completely let go of what *I* wanted—except for when I was with Aaron. Aaron has always said a firm and loud *yes* to anything I want to do. And he's always done it with a smile on his face. Watching *French Kiss* and *Serendipity* ad nauseum is just one example. He used to ice skate with me at the National Gallery of Art every winter when it opened just because it was my favorite way to mark the change from fall to winter. He used to listen to me read passages from my favorite romance novels, and now I'm realizing it wasn't because he's a huge fan of romance novels. Hell, he's read every single one of my books cover to cover while Josh couldn't even bother himself to read the back cover.

When Aaron finishes his exhaustive list of all of my favorites, he reaches across the table, grabs my strawberry champagne cocktail and throws back the last few sips.

"I think I deserved that," he says with a proud grin on his face.

Instead of getting mad at him the way I usually do when he finishes my drinks without asking, I smile back at this man who knows me better than anyone in the world and who loves me anyway, and I say, "You deserve a lot more than that."

When we leave Café Bonaparte, I stop Aaron on the crowded Georgetown sidewalk, take his hands in mine, and kiss him softly on the cheek. "Thank you," I tell him.

His eyes light up, and he wraps his strong arms around me, squeezing me so tightly that my feet lift off the ground. When he puts me down, he kisses me back, on the forehead this time. "Always, love."

"Where to next?" I ask.

He takes my hand in his. "I have just the place."

But just as we turn around to head down Wisconsin Avenue, we are met with a barrage of flashes and shouts. A black sea of photographers rushes toward us.

"What the—?" Aaron mumbles under his breath.

And before we have a second to brace ourselves, the intrusive line of questioning begins...

"Violet! Is Aaron Wright your new man?"

"Were you sleeping with him while you were with Josh?"

"Does Josh know you were having an affair?"

"Have you spoken to Josh since your YouTube diatribes went viral?"

"How does it feel being the estranged ex-wife of the hottest star to hit the big screen since Brad Pitt?"

I'm blinded by the flashes, the questions, the blatant attack. So blinded I can't move. I can't speak. I just stand there numbly, a dumb deer in headlights.

Aaron steps in front of me and places a hand up as he maneuvers us through the crowd of vultures who now have us completely circled. "Enough!" he shouts as he gets me to the street and slides me into a cab.

"Go!" he orders the driver.

"Where?" the driver says.

"Just get us out of here," Aaron says as the paparazzi storm toward the cab, banging on the windows, shouting, and clicking away like total and complete Neanderthals.

I don't even realize that tears are rolling down my cheeks until Aaron pulls me into his chest and wipes them away.

"Fucking maniacs," he mumbles. "I'm so sorry, Vi."

"I did this to myself," I say, watching my tears soak through Aaron's T-shirt.

Aaron doesn't reply, because we both know I'm right. But he holds me anyway. And I am overwhelmed with gratitude to have him by my side.

Five

"Pull over right here," Aaron instructs the cab driver before handing him a wad of cash.

We step onto a bustling Constitution Avenue and gaze out at the endless grassy lawn that makes up the National Mall. The Washington Monument towers over the fresh green landscape, and even though it's an absolutely gorgeous spring day in the city, this tourist hub is the last place I want to be.

Aaron takes my hand as he rushes down the sidewalk.

"Don't you think it would be best to lay low after what just happened?" I ask him.

"Oh, we will be laying low, all right. Follow me, love."

Aaron leads me into one of those dreadful tourist shops stocked full of cheesy patriotic T-shirts covered in American flags that say things like: *I Heart Washington D.C.*. He grabs an American flag ball cap off the wall and fits it snugly onto my head.

I take a peek in a nearby mirror and shoot a look back at Aaron. "Dude, seriously?"

"I'm only getting started." He chuckles before whisking me around the store and covering us both head-to-toe in the most embarrassing tourist garb. When his work is finished, he drags me to the mirror to assess the damage.

Confessions of a City Girl

I am sporting an oversized pair of red, white, and blue sunglasses; an *I Heart Obama* T-shirt; the American flag ball cap; and perhaps the best part—a fanny pack that says *DC Moms Kick Ass*.

Aaron is a male replica of me with an equally awful patriotic hat, sunglasses, and T-shirt, except his fanny pack says *DC Dads Kick Ass*.

"Brilliant," he says as he twirls me around, admiring his work. "Just brilliant."

"And hideous. Horrifying. Mortifying."

"Which is why it's so brilliant, of course."

I take a look at the pair of us in the mirror, and it's just so ridiculous I can't help but laugh. "I wouldn't be caught dead walking the streets of DC like this."

"Exactly. A picture of fashion you always are. Which is why no one will recognize you in this god-awful tourist outfit."

"Now all we need is a Segway and we'll fit right in with the tourists," I joke.

Aaron's eyes light up. "Oh, I like where you're going with this..."

"No," I say. "I am not riding on one of those things."

Aaron lifts a mischievous brow in my direction.

"Aaron, *no*."

Twenty minutes later, my worst nightmare has come true. I am zooming down the National Mall on a Segway with a DC Mom fanny pack dangling around my waist, and the rest of my body clothed like an American flag. Aaron zooms right along ahead of me, smiling and whistling away, as if this is the most natural thing in the world.

"This is by far the most unromantic thing I could ever think of doing in DC!" I call up to him. "The absolute worst!"

As I'm shouting, I nearly crash into a small Asian family. They dodge me just before I can flatten them to the ground with this ridiculous vehicle—or chariot or whatever the hell it is—that I am riding upon.

"Sorry!" I yell as they dive off the sidewalk in a panic.

"Whoa, whoa, whoa, watch where you're going Miss Violet!" Aaron shouts back at me. He slows down so we are riding side by side. "The last thing we need after what happened yesterday is a charge of Segway manslaughter on our hands."

"Aren't you mortified riding on this thing?" I hiss.

"Normally I might be, yes, but seeing as how we are disguised as tacky tourists and no one has a clue that I'm a prominent speech writer on the Hill or you're that crazy chick from YouTube, I could hardly give a fuck, love. Now, follow me. I'm taking you somewhere beautiful."

Aaron zooms off ahead of me, seeming to be quite skilled at this Segway business, while I struggle along behind, trying my best not to smash into families, strollers, and small children along the way. Part of the reason this is so tricky is because I keep reaching into my fanny pack to see who is calling me.

My phone, of course, has been buzzing non-stop all day, but with Aaron keeping me on the move, I haven't had time to answer it. I think that's partly *why* he's keeping me on the move, smart man that he is. As we're crossing the National Mall, my phone buzzes again, and this time, when I take a peek, I see that it is, for the third time today, Josh.

Josh Bell.

My ex-husband.

It's so strange calling him my *ex* after so many years together. After so many years of loving him. But there he is, *the ex*, calling again, surely after witnessing the downfall of his ex-wife on YouTube yesterday.

I try to press *"Decline"* but the Segway hits a big bump and I hit *"Accept"* instead.

Shit.

Steering the Segway with one hand, I lift the phone to my ear with the other, hoping Aaron will keep speeding right along ahead of me so he doesn't see me doing this ridiculous juggling act. And so he doesn't know that I'm talking to Josh.

"Hi, Josh," I say, my voice coming out all cheery and unnatural, while inside, my stomach is tied in a fit of knots. I might have to jump off this damn thing to be sick.

"Umm....hey..." he says, not at all sounding cheery. "You're sounding a little too happy considering the stunt you pulled yesterday. What on earth possessed you to do something like that, Violet?"

"It wasn't like I planned it," I snap, all that fake cheeriness gone in a flash.

"Could've fooled me."

"You think I did that on purpose?" Now I'm weaving through a sea of high school kids and teachers, realizing that somehow, in this crowd, I have lost Aaron.

"I don't know, Violet. I don't know what to think. I know that ever since I made it big, you've wanted to tell the world that I cheated on you. So, you got your chance and you took it."

"Oh I'm *so* sorry that all of your adoring female fans now know the truth—that you're the kind of guy who sleeps around when he's unhappy in a relationship. Are you afraid your perfect image is tarnished now? Because I have news for you, buddy, when you become such a huge star and let it go to your head the way you have, that bubble is bound to pop sooner or later, and I just opted to pop it for you a little sooner."

"Well, thanks for that. Thanks for looking out for me, Vi. You're a gem of an ex-wife. Really, couldn't ask for more."

"No, really you couldn't. You're already taking all of my money."

"Is that what this is about? The alimony?"

"Honestly, Josh, it's ridiculous that I am paying you over $6,000 a month in alimony when you've just made millions—*millions!*—from your latest movie. How can you even continue to accept my money and feel like a man?"

Josh proceeds to go off on me, the way he always did in those last few fighting years of our marriage. And I'm shaking too hard and feeling too nauseous to listen. The phone slips from my hands—or maybe I threw it...I'm not entirely sure—and then I do what I've been trying not to do the whole time I've been riding on this damn Segway...I crash.

Straight into a telephone pole, of all things. Like a drunk driver.

"Violet? Violet, what the hell is going on?"

It's Josh's voice. All shrill and panicky, screeching through the phone, which is lying next to my head. My head that has just smacked into a fucking telephone pole and now has warm liquid oozing over it, down onto the concrete. Blood. It's my blood.

As if I haven't shed enough blood for that man.

I have just enough energy left in me to reach for the phone and end the call. And then I close my eyes and drift away.

"Well, that's not exactly what I had in mind when I dressed you like a flag and put you on a Segway, but it seems nothing is going to plan for us these days, so we might as well roll with it, right love?"

Aaron and I are lying in the grass near the Tidal Basin, beneath a beautiful cherry blossom tree which is in full bloom. Aaron is holding his brand new *I Love Obama* T-shirt up to the gash on my forehead to stop the bleeding. And I am still feeling nauseous and dizzy.

"I think I might have a concussion," I say, closing my eyes.

"The day just keeps getting better, doesn't it?" Aaron says.

I feel too sick to respond, so instead I just keep my eyes sealed shut and try not to replay the conversation I just had with Josh in my head.

"Why did you pick up the call, Vi?" Aaron asks softly. "You knew it wouldn't be good, not to mention the fact that you were operating heavy machinery."

My temples are throbbing and my stomach is queasy, but I still find it in me to retort. "I would hardly call a Segway heavy machinery."

"Well, however it should be classified, I know one thing: You are not to be trusted on a Segway ever again. Especially not when you are dressed like a flag and have a cell phone ringing in your fanny pack. Thankfully the phone pole survived the impact."

I manage to squint up at him, shaking my head. "I think I need to eat something."

Aaron takes a peek around. "Ice cream sound good?"

"Yeah, actually. Vanilla chocolate—"

"Vanilla chocolate swirl in a cup, not a cone," Aaron finishes for me. "Did your impact with the telephone pole make you forget my brilliant listing of all of your favorites while we were at Café Bonaparte not more than two hours ago?"

"No, haven't forgotten," I say.

"Good. Here, keep this on your head, and I'll be right back." Aaron leaves the bloody T-shirt with me while he runs off.

Overhead, the cherry blossoms are swishing with the wind, and I am left alone for a few moments with my thoughts and a throbbing head. Even though that was a total disaster, lying here on this beautiful spring day beneath these gorgeous pink blossoms while Aaron takes care of me is actually quite romantic. Granted, I don't think I'll be adding the fight with the ex and the telephone pole crash to my novel, but still, Aaron has found a way to make this day lovely.

A few minutes later, my knight in shining armor returns with some delectable vanilla chocolate swirl ice cream. He helps me sit up, and we devour our soft serve together in silence, watching the trees and the water until finally our eyes land on each other.

"I think I owe you an apology, Mr. Wright."

"Oh?"

"Yeah...apparently you do have some game after all."

"Well, well, well. Didn't think I'd hear you say those words after your rant last night."

I glance down at our ridiculous fanny packs, which we both still have fastened tightly around our waists. "It's not the most conventional romance, but it's sweet. And funny. And real. Very real."

"I'm glad you're enjoying the day...well, as much as you can given the paparazzi attack and the unfortunate incident with the Segway. At least I'm giving you some ideas, I hope."

"Yeah, about that, I think it's time we did some brainstorming."

"You have energy for that?" he asks. "With that busted-up head of yours?" Aaron dabs around the cut on my head with his thumb.

I let him fix me up a bit more and then I give him a thankful smile. "It's actually feeling a lot better."

"Ice cream cures a concussion every time."

"Totally," I say. But what I don't say is that it isn't the ice cream that's making me feel better. It's Aaron.

Six

A few hours later, I am sitting outside at Sequoia, my favorite restaurant on the Georgetown Waterfront—which, of course, Aaron remembered—drinking a glass of rosé and plotting out my next ultra-steamy romance novel with my friend who normally spends his days writing dry speeches for politicians on Capitol Hill.

"I have to say, I'm impressed with how well you're picking up this whole romance novel plotting thing. Especially given your day job. And your lack of knowledge on romance in general."

But Aaron is still too wrapped up in the story we are coming up with to respond to my jab. Instead, he steers me back to the task at hand.

"So, let's recap," he says. "We have Dex—the badass, sexy, muscular, tattooed biker from the wrong side of the tracks—who visits the strip club one fateful night and meets Katrina—the legs-for-miles ballerina who moonlights as a stripper to pay back some bad debt she owes someone. The reason for said debt and who this particular 'someone' might be are yet to be determined. The minute Katrina straddles Dex and her huge knockers are square in the wanker's face, it's love at first sight and they live happily ever after."

"Katrina is a ballet dancer, so she doesn't have huge knockers," I point out. "Perhaps I spoke too soon. Not sure you're grasping the complexity of novel writing after all."

"But she works at a strip club," Aaron protests. "She must have at least a bit of a rack."

"There can be flat-chested girls at strip clubs," I argue.

Aaron nods down at my chest, which isn't even close to flat, and he grins. "How would you know, Boobs McGee?"

"Well, of course Katrina's won't be as…as…"

"Bouncy, beautiful, and full as yours?" Aaron suggests.

I feel my cheeks flushing. "Why…thank you," I finally manage to spit out.

"You're quite welcome, love. Your girls really are quite…. well, they're perfect." He holds my gaze for a moment until we both burst into a nervous laughter.

"Okay, back to the task at hand," I say before taking a sip of my wine.

"Right, right," he says, diverting his gaze out to the rowers paddling down the Potomac River. "Time to get serious. So, I believe the love at first sight thing really takes hold when Katrina leads Dex to a private room for a lap dance, and instead of taking off her clothes, she puts on an over-sized *I Love Obama* T-shirt—with nothing on the bottom, obviously—then rides around on a Segway shaking her bare buttocks to a Beyoncé tune—*All the Single Ladies* perhaps?—and it's when she crashes the Segway into her stripper pole that Dex knows, without a shadow of a doubt: *this* is the woman I've been waiting for. *This* is the woman of my life. A patriotic, bare-bottomed ballerina who can shake it while operating heavy machinery, but who still crashes so that I can be the man and save her."

"Yes, that's exactly what I was thinking," I say through a fit of giggles. "You're ridiculous, you know that?"

"Just trying to help with the plot, love. Which leads me to another question about our hero, Dex. Why are girls always choosing the bad guy? What is it about a man who does bad things and treats people like total and absolute shit that makes you want to be with these wankers?"

"*I* don't choose the bad guys," I say defensively.

"What would you call Josh, then? A *good* guy?" Aaron stares at me point blank. His question is a serious one; he never liked Josh.

"Josh isn't...wasn't...well, okay, perhaps he had a bit of a wild streak, but that was still so much better than all of those boring, collar-popping, preppy little pretty boys at Georgetown."

"For the record, I've only popped my collar once in my life, and it was not of my own doing. Alicia popped it for me."

"Alicia the White Witch of Narnia?" I say, not able to help myself. Alicia was Aaron's on-again off-again girlfriend while we were in our twenties, and from my vantage point, she had zero personality and was as boring as the telephone pole I crashed into earlier today, except for when she would interact with me and be icier than the White Witch of Narnia. She also looked like the actress who played the White Witch, which didn't help her case.

"Not sure if you could've disapproved of Alicia any further, Vi, but if you had, she probably would have actually died from it. She really just wanted you to like her."

"Which is why she never—and I literally mean *not once*—smiled in my presence? There's a reason I called her the White Witch. I was afraid she was going to load me up in her horse-drawn carriage, offer me some Turkish Delight, whisk me away to her secret castle in the mountains, and turn me into an ice sculpture."

"Now you're just being cruel," he says, but I can tell he's holding back a snicker. "Back to the original question, which you did not answer by the way— why do girls choose the bad guy? Why did *you* choose Josh? Why not someone more stable, more down to earth, less of a wild card? I mean, *dating* the wild card makes sense. Shagging him makes sense. But marrying him?"

I open my mouth to respond, but then I stop to actually think about this one. Why did I choose Josh? He was, as Aaron pointed out, a total wild card— disorganized, artsy, an absolute creative storm. Not at all the man mothers envision their daughters marrying one day, but I married him anyway. Why?

"So, why did you do it?" Aaron prods.

"We were both so creative and artistic—he related to that side of me more than..." I trail off, about to say, *more than you did*, but I stop myself when I remember that Aaron didn't ask why I chose Josh *over him*. Even though for some reason I feel like that is actually the question he is asking.

"More than...?"

"More than all of the other guys I dated," I finish. "He understood me. He knew that when I needed to disappear into my writing cave for days on end to finish a book that he needed to just let me do that. He let me create. And I let him create. There was beauty in that. But there was also a madness having two artists in the house. Even though *my* art was the one that eventually supported us, it always felt to me like he thought his was more important. A bigger deal. And the fights that came out of that were just...epic. So dramatic. So unnecessary. So exhausting...but you already know our sad story."

"Why did you stay so long then? When it got that bad?" Aaron asks.

I don't have to think about the answer to this question. I know it, immediately.

"Because I loved him," I say. "I was in love. I didn't care that he was a mess, that we were a mess together. I just loved him. Nothing else mattered."

A silence settles between us as we both sip our wine.

"It was really that simple?" Aaron asks finally. "Love...just love."

"It *was* that simple...well, until it wasn't. Until that underlying, strong love we'd shared from the very beginning began to crack. And eventually it just couldn't hold the weight of our arguments any longer. When the foundation goes, the relationship goes. The marriage dies. And that's what happened to us. The marriage, our connection, our bond...it just died."

I suddenly want to be anywhere but at this beautiful river-front restaurant, surrounded by so many happy people drinking their sugary cocktails in the late afternoon sun. I don't want to be telling Aaron about the death of my marriage. I want to curl up in a ball and wish it all away. Go back to a simpler time when I loved Josh and he loved me and that was enough. I thought it always would be enough. Why couldn't it have been?

The feeling of Aaron's warm hand squeezing mine takes me out of my sad trance and makes me realize that there are hot tears falling down my cheeks.

Aaron doesn't reach across and dry them, though. Instead he watches those tears fall and squeezes my hand a little harder. "So, love..." he says. "It all comes down to love."

"It's crazy how the most wonderful, beautiful feeling in the whole world can turn you into a blubbering mess," I say, wiping at my face, wishing I could turn off this damned divorce faucet of tears.

Aaron hands me a napkin. "You're the prettiest blubbering mess I've ever seen. Especially when your eye makeup smears like that and gives you that hot raccoon look. Smoldering."

"You're such a brat," I say, taking the napkin and dabbing at my eyes.

"I'm only kidding, love," he says with a sheepish grin. "You know that."

"I know," I say, feeling grateful for his comic relief. The tears are subsiding. I'm okay. Well, maybe not yet, but when I'm with Aaron, something about him makes me feel like I'm *going* to be okay.

"Did you love Alicia?" I ask.

"God, no," he says swiftly.

"Then why did you stay with her all those years? You're getting on me for choosing the bad guy...so why did you choose the boring, bland witch?"

"You really hated her, Vi, didn't you?"

"It wasn't that I hated her—I just hated her for you. You never had any fun with her. You seemed miserable. And despite what you always said about the sex—"

"At the time, it was the best sex of my life," he cuts in.

"Yes, I know, you've told me," I say, shuddering at the thought of Aaron actually sleeping with her. "Wait...what do you mean, *at the time*? Has there been someone else since who's topped The White Witch?"

Aaron's big blue eyes suddenly shine with a devious twinkle. "I'm not one to kiss and tell, love."

"Are you seeing someone that you haven't told me about?"

"I don't tell you everything, Vi. You've had a lot going on these past years. I've done more listening than talking, if you haven't noticed."

"Well, spill," I order. But immediately after the words leave my mouth, I regret them. For the first time in our long friendship, I realize that I don't want to know the details about who Aaron has been sleeping with or why it's been the best sex of his life.

He takes a big sip of his wine, eyeing me curiously. "Are you jealous?"

"What? No!" I say, a little too loudly.

He taps his fingers on his wine glass, sits back in his seat all smug.

"Never thought I'd see the day," he says. "You're jealous that I've been having insanely hot sex with an insanely hot woman."

"Is she as demanding and icy as the White Witch? Is that what makes it so hot—that she's so damn hard to please?"

"No, this one is not hard to please. Not at all. Orgasms all day, all night, and every moment in between."

"Well, I've been having my fair share of insanely hot sex since the divorce as well," I tell him, crossing my arms.

"I would expect nothing less of you," he says, his feathers not ruffled, not one bit.

Humph. Why is this bothering me so much?

"This really isn't helping me with my novel," I say.

"Right. Back to the epic love story of Dex, Katrina, strip clubs, and motorcycles. Back to the eternal obsession with the bad boy."

"At least Katrina is going to be sexy and fun and kind and sweet. Not an icy bone in that ballerina's body."

"The new one isn't an ice queen, Vi. For the record."

"This new girl—do you love her?"

"Oh, you know me better than that," he says.

"So that's a no?"

"It's not love…it's great, but it's definitely not love."

"Have you ever been in love, Aaron?"

His eyes make a quick diversion away from mine to…well, to anywhere but me. He takes a few moments to reply.

"The million-dollar question—have I ever been in love…?" He trails off as if he has no intention of answering the question, but for some reason, I feel that *this* is the most important question of our entire conversation.

"Have you?" I prod.

Finally, Aaron turns to me. Looks me straight in the eye. But he's not smiling. Instead, I notice a strange look lurking in there. Pain? Regret? I can't quite place it but whatever he's feeling right now, I can sense that it's strong.

Moments pass before he replies.

"Yes," he says. "Yes, Vi, I have been in love."

And just as I'm about to ask him who this mystery love of his life is, or *was*, I bite my tongue and change the subject.

"But with the new girl, it's just sex?"

"Well, not just sex. Explosive sex."

"Okay, okay, I get it. This bitch is amazing in bed. Can we get back to Katrina and Dex, please?"

I throw back the rest of my wine and feel an unpleasant twinge in my stomach. It's not the alcohol, though. It's nerves. It's unexpected emotion. It's something brewing. It's something I've known, maybe forever, but haven't wanted to see. Haven't wanted to acknowledge.

Even now, I can't let myself think it. Because *it* would change everything.

But there it is all the same...

Am *I* the girl that Aaron was—or *is*—in love with?

Is it me?

Seven

After spending the entire afternoon plotting my novel with Aaron, the two of us are now lounging on his rooftop, watching the sun take its nightly plunge down the sky. A bottle of chilled Chardonnay sits in a bucket of ice between us, and we are both tapping away on our laptops. I'm outlining the Dex and Katrina novel, and Aaron is working on his next speech. We are silent as we work, but it's a thick silence. A silence full of unspoken words and unexpressed emotions—emotions that until today, I honestly hadn't realized I'd been stifling.

I know I'm the girl he's been in love with. I've always known this, but I've never wanted to see it. Aaron is my best friend, and I've never wanted anything to put that in jeopardy. As soon as love enters into the equation, everything changes.

If we admitted this love to each other, would we even be friends anymore? Could we be?

I take another sip of wine. A few sips. I don't know the answers to any of these questions. What do I really know anymore? I'm a mess. More of a mess than Josh was throughout our entire marriage. What would Aaron see in me anyway?

Just as this thought crosses my mind, Aaron glances over at my unmoving hands on the keyboard, then up into my eyes. And he smiles. He smiles brighter than the magnificent sun that is shooting swirls of pink and orange all over our DC skyline.

And I remember what I said earlier.

The mess doesn't matter. None of it does.

It's love.

Love is simple, really. When you love someone, you just know. You just feel it. It's not rational. To the contrary, it usually makes zero sense.

I feel the emotions boiling up so strongly inside of me right now that I can barely hold them in. I want to tell Aaron that I know it's me. And I'm bursting to tell him that I feel it too. I really do. Maybe I always have, but Aaron just didn't fit into the picture I had envisioned for my life. He was—is—so straight-laced. Yes, he's funny and sexy and brilliant. But he's a speech writer on Capitol Hill. He's preppy. He's clean-cut. Not the kind of guy the wild, scandalous Violet Bell would choose.

But I feel a shift happening inside of me. Sitting here by Aaron's side as I outline my steamy romance novel and he writes his smart political speech, I realize there is a commonality. A connection. It's strong. It always has been. We work well together. We complement each other.

Opposites do really attract.

"You seem terribly lost in thought over there," Aaron says. "Dex giving you problems?"

When I look over to him and smile, I register in his expression that he knows it isn't Dex I'm thinking about. I'm not thinking about the bad boy this time. I don't want the bad boy...*I want Aaron.*

"What is it, love?" Aaron asks again.

I reach over and place my hand on his. He responds by smiling softly, sweetly, and threading his fingers through mine.

"Thank you," I say, "For today and..." Before I can stop them, warm tears are springing to my eyes.

Aaron squeezes my hand. "It's simple," he says. "It's love."

And then he reaches over, wipes the tears from my eyes, and he kisses me.

My best friend—the one man who knows everything about me and loves me anyway— wraps me up in the warmest, sweetest summer kiss, and I am quite simply in heaven.

I am lost in his lips, his hands threading around the back of my neck, through my hair, over my shoulders…but he stops there. He doesn't take it any further. He just kisses me, again and again, like this is something he's waited a very long time to do.

That night, instead of ripping each other's clothes off and going at it like rabbits, we lie in bed together laughing and kissing, telling stories and remembering all the fun times. We don't talk about how this transition from best friends to lovers or something in between is happening so naturally. We don't analyze it. We don't ask each other why it took so long. We just enjoy it, live it, breathe it.

And finally, fully clothed and feeling so much love, I fall asleep wrapped in Aaron's warm arms.

Eight

Aaron invites me to stay at his place for the next two weeks while I write my novel. I say yes, of course, and I enjoy the bliss of falling asleep next to him every night. We don't make love. We don't discuss what is happening between us. We simply let it happen.

And during the day, while I am supposed to be writing this sexy romance novel about Dex and Katrina, my mind could not be further from their story. My mind is focused firmly on a story I know much better—a true story.

My story.

Anastasia's nosy question at the panel keeps replaying in my head. *"What happens when a romance novelist's life falls apart? That's the story we really want to hear."*

Something about letting loose that day in front of those students and shedding all of that messy truth really got to me. It's all I want to do now—*tell the truth*. I have no interest in making up a story about two lovers who met in a strip club. I only want to tell my own love stories. The story of Josh and Violet, the story of our love and how beautiful it once was, how it all fell apart, and how sad I still am over the demise of our marriage. And I want to tell a new story too—the one that is unfolding right now. The story of Aaron and Violet, of two best friends who are complete opposites. Two friends who, years after meeting, find comfort and love in each other's arms…without the one thing I've always given away so quickly, so freely—sex. It's not that I think Aaron doesn't want to have sex with me. To the contrary, the sexual chemistry building between us is practically setting his DC townhome on fire. But I think he senses that I'm not completely finished with my marriage, with my divorce, with Josh. I think he senses that my mind is not totally, one-hundred percent here, with him.

And he's right. I still have grief and sadness lingering inside me over the loss of my marriage. That much is certainly clear from the YouTube blast—which now has well over one million views. And I think Aaron wants to give me time. Perhaps he's being cautious too. I'm sure he doesn't want to get his heart broken. I don't either. Nor do I want to break his.

And so I sit here in his bedroom, laptop before me, a blank curser on the screen. I haven't written one word of the novel and it's due in ten days.

Ten days.

But I don't want to write the novel. I have no interest in making up a love story and tying it up in a perfect little bow.

Real life isn't like that. Real life is messy and exhausting. Beautiful and chaotic. Romantic and passionate. Devastating and raw.

And so I give myself permission to write the thing I want to write.

The truth.

My novel is due in one day, and I have been holed up in Aaron's apartment writing like a madwoman for the past week and a half—not writing the novel, but instead bleeding my truth onto the page. I'm writing in a way I've never written before. Giving myself permission to tell the truth has opened up some sort of magical writing portal and the story of my marriage, my love with Josh, and the demise of that love, has flown out of me in a way no other book I've ever written has done. I now have close to two hundred pages, and while I'm nowhere near finished telling the story, I feel as if I have relived the love we once had, and I have lost it again. It has been a beautiful process, and a devastating one. But I know it is something I needed to do. And something I must finish.

I will not have a romance novel to turn in to my publisher tomorrow. I will have to pay back my book advance with money I do not currently have.

I know I should be freaking out about all of that. But this truth valve that has opened inside me has made me not care about the contract, the money, my career, my reputation. Telling the truth has made me a bit reckless—more reckless than I already was—and strangely, I feel really damn good about that.

I feel better than I've felt in years.

I feel like myself.

I think Aaron notices this glow on my face when he gets home from work late that night.

He smiles brightly at me as he pours me my nightly glass of wine.

"So, are we finished?" he asks. "Is Dex and Katrina's sordid affair tying up in a beautiful bow that you'll be e-mailing to your demanding publisher tomorrow?"

I haven't told Aaron what I've been up to. He thinks I've been writing the novel all this time. I just didn't want him to talk me out of it. Not that I think he would've necessarily, but I wanted this truth story to be mine. All mine.

Tonight, that's going to change, though. I'm going to share my story with Aaron.

I slide the unfinished, two-hundred page manuscript I printed just moments ago across the table to my friend, my love.

He grins widely as he picks up my pages, but his expression morphs to one of confusion as he reads the title aloud. "*Confessions of a Romance Novelist: A Memoir* by Violet Bell."

He flips to the first page, sitting down as he reads in silence. Minutes and pages pass before his gaze finally meets mine.

"Wow. Vi. I...I don't know what to say. It's brilliant. But it's not a romance novel. It's not the book that's due tomorrow. What are you going to—?"

"I'm not writing the novel. I'll deal with the consequences. I'll make more money. I'll pay them back. *This* is the story I want to write. It's the only one I *could* write."

Aaron sits in a stunned silence for a few moments before asking, "Am I in the book?"

I reach across the table, taking his hand. "Of course you are. I still have a little ways to go before I reach the end, though."

"Well, you don't quite know the ending yet, do you?" He says this with a mischievous gleam in his eye.

"No, I—" But just as I begin to speak, the doorbell rings. Loudly.

Once, twice, three times.

"What the…" Aaron glances at his watch. "It's after ten. Be right back, love."

Aaron leaves me alone in the kitchen as the doorbell continues to buzz, desperately, frantically. And with each shrill ring, my stomach tightens a little more. I don't have a good feeling about this.

Once the ringing stops and I hear Aaron open the door, I make my way into the living room to see who it is.

My stomach drops. My heart goes right along with it. Smashing into the floor.

It's Josh.

Nine

It's pouring rain outside, and Josh is completely soaked. Big drops are falling from his full head of dark hair, streaking over his sad eyes, his tired face. The rain could've been the reason he was ringing the doorbell incessantly, but as soon as I make it to the doorway and find that urgent, lost look in his eyes—a look I grew quite accustomed to seeing in those last years of our marriage—I know that his urgency has nothing to do with the rain. He probably hasn't even noticed how drenched he is. When Josh is in one of his dramatic states, *everything* becomes urgent. His whole being becomes consumed with despair, anger, and fear. Every emotion under the sun sweeps in and takes over until he is powerless against their strength. He is merely a puppet, doing what they tell him. Screaming, crying, yelling, drinking—he is at their disposal. Which is what makes him such a damn good actor. But a husband? Not so much.

"What are you doing here?" I ask, noticing how Aaron isn't backing away from the door. He isn't giving us privacy. Instead, he is standing here, tall and solid, a protective force clearly not wanting to let the storm that is Josh sweep me away.

"I've been calling you all week. You haven't answered. I have to talk to you, Violet." He ignores Aaron and takes a bold step toward me. "I need to talk to you in private."

I sigh, already feeling exhausted at where this might lead. I want to tell him to leave. But whatever it is that Josh needs—closure, perhaps—I know that I need it too. I'm not totally finished with him, with our marriage, with our divorce. Writing our story this week has shown me that much. I haven't quite processed it all, and by the way Josh is looking at me, his face all twisted in anguish and regret, I can tell he hasn't either.

"I'm so sorry about this," I say to Aaron. "I won't be long." I don't grab a jacket or an umbrella or anything to shield myself from the heavy rain that continues to pour as I join my ex-husband on the front stoop and leave Aaron alone, in the doorway, watching us walk away.

I feel torn between these two worlds—my old one with Josh and the new one I have only just begun to create with Aaron, but I know that I need to walk with Josh right now.

We don't speak for a block or two. We pace side by side, in silence, letting the hot rain wash over us. And finally, when we reach Dupont Circle, we make our way under a tree where there is just a little less rain coming down, and we turn to face each other.

I stifle my instinct to talk. To always have something to say. And instead, I let him speak.

"Violet, what you said in that video about missing me, about life being worse without me, about loving me...I miss you too. Life *is* worse without you. So much worse. It's a fucking mess. All those girls—they're nothing like you. They're empty and shallow. They don't have the depth, the beauty, the intelligence you have. Not even close. I still love you, Violet. I'm so sorry I couldn't love you the way you needed me to when we were together. I'm so sorry I fucked up. I fucked up so much, Vi. So many times. In so many ways."

I don't stop Josh to tell him that it's okay that he hurt me the way he did. Instead something inside me tells me to stay quiet for once. To let him lay his heart on the line, the way I so embarrassingly did on stage the other day.

"I'm so sorry I hurt you, Vi," he says, running a hand through his soaked head of hair. Even in his distraught state, Josh is so sickeningly handsome. Those striking cheekbones I used to love to kiss when we'd curl up in bed together. The rugged scruff on his face that I used to tell him not to shave because he always looked so damn sexy with a five o'clock shadow. At an earlier time in our marriage, those looks could get him out of anything...but those days are long gone.

"It's the last thing I ever wanted to do," Josh continues. "I just...I just didn't see you anymore. I didn't see *us* anymore. We—the *we* that we used to be—disappeared, and as soon as we were gone, I just...I don't know. I went off the deep end. I made mistakes. But seeing you being so vulnerable like that on that stage, just letting it all go and not even caring who heard you, it just got to me, Vi. And I remembered. I remembered why we fell in love. I remember how good that felt. And I want it back. I want you back. I love you, Violet Bell."

And there, beneath the rain-soaked branches, my ex-husband grabs me and kisses me.

After hearing Josh say the words I'd wanted to hear for so long, I expect to feel swept away with his lips on mine.

But although I kiss him back, although I give this kiss all I've got, I don't feel swept away. I don't feel the love I used to feel for him. I don't feel any of that.

And I know, when I pull my lips from his, that *this* was our last kiss.

Still, I say nothing, and by the way Aaron is looking at me, by the way the tears begin to pour down his face, I know that he knows. He knows I'm finished. He knows that was the last time our lips will ever meet.

I wrap my arms around him, and we hold each other tight.

"I'm so sorry, Josh," I tell him.

"Please don't apologize, Vi," he whispers into my hair.

I pull away from him just a bit so I can look into his eyes. "It took two to fall in love the way we did, and it took two to break that love. I played just as much of a role in the end of us as you did."

"The end of us..." Josh echoes, trailing off. "Sounds so sad."

"It is so sad," I say.

And it is. The loss of a marriage is devastating. Nothing in my life has hurt me more than losing this man.

And still, as we hold each other beneath the rain, I know that I don't want him back in my life. Even though I still have a long way to go, I have moved forward. I have begun to embrace my truth, to see the good in my new life. And to see what has been staring me in the face for years—the feelings I have for Aaron.

I know there is only one thing left to do.

Let Josh go.

And so I do. I let go of the man I have loved for so long. I kiss him on the cheek, and I turn and walk away.

It's not easy. Walking away never is.

But I'm strong enough to take one step, and then another. I don't know where I'm going or where I'll land. I don't know what this new life holds for me, but *this* is the path I have chosen.

And I must keep walking.

Ten

Aaron is still sitting at the kitchen table when I return. He's reading my book, my memoir, the story of Violet and Josh. The story that is, as of tonight, officially over.

He doesn't get up to hug me or comfort me or ask me if I'm okay. Instead he watches me sit down next to him, studies me intently, asking me silently what has just happened. When I don't answer, he speaks.

"It's beautiful, Vi. Your writing. It's poignant. Real. Raw."

"Thank you," I say.

"You okay?" he asks.

I nod. "I will be."

"And Josh?"

"He will be too...or not. I don't know. But it's not my job to know."

"It's done then?"

"Yes," I say firmly. "It's done."

Aaron nods and lays my book down on the table before standing and walking over to me.

He runs his hands over my wet shoulders, pulls me up from the chair. "You're shivering, love. Let's get these wet clothes off of you, shall we?"

"We shall," I say with a tired smile.

Aaron slips my tank top over my head, letting it drop to the floor. He runs his hands over my shoulders, pulls me close as he runs his lips down my neck, over my collarbone, and over the tops of my breasts. I'm shivering even more now, but not from the cold or the rain.

I'm shivering from how good it feels to have Aaron's lips on my skin.

I pull his T-shirt over his head and admire his firm, beautiful body, kissing his neck and shoulders as his hands roam down to the button of my jeans. He unfastens them in a flash, but as he tugs, my wet jeans just will not budge.

"Looks like this is going to take a bit more elbow grease than I thought," he says with a grin before he sweeps me off my feet—both literally and figuratively—and carries me upstairs to his bedroom.

He lays me down on his big, cozy bed, and as he kneels above me and works my tight jeans down my hips and thighs, kissing every spare inch of my skin along the way, he peeks up and smiles. "You said you hadn't written the end of the story, yet, right? That you don't know how it ends?"

"That's right," I say, loving where he's going with this.

After he peels my jeans off, he lays the weight of his body on me, burying me in his warmth. Nothing has ever felt so good.

"I would love to give you some inspiration for the ending, if you'll let me."

I wrap my legs around his waist, pull his face closer to mine and kiss him.

"I would love nothing more than for you to inspire me, Mr. Wright," I whisper in his ear.

And so, my best friend turned lover does just that. He spends the entire night inspiring me in ways I've never quite been inspired before. And over the coming weeks and months, he gives me the sweetest, happiest ending I ever could have hoped for in my story.

Except it doesn't feel like an ending at all.

To the contrary, it's only the beginning…

Confessions
of a City Girl

Paris

One

"Olivia Banks, it's about time we saw that pretty face of yours around these parts." Genie Robertson, my parents' long-time neighbor, barrels across the lawn toward me, almost running straight into the movers I've hired to clear out my childhood home.

"Hi, Mrs. Robertson." Hoping she isn't planning to embark on one of her two-hour neighborhood gossip sessions, I pull my ever-buzzing work cell from my purse to find the eighteenth desperate text that hour from Miranda, the host of one of the most popular talk shows on television, and also my obscenely needy boss back in New York.

Did you see what a cow I looked like in that frumpy blue dress this morning? This stylist is an absolute catastrophe! Give her the ax! When are you coming back to the Center of the Universe???

I don't have time to respond, though, because Mrs. Robertson is in front of me now, all floral prints and perfume, tears streaming down her puffy, rouge cheeks.

"Genie, really, there's no need to get upset—"

"Oh, dear. Just seeing those big blue eyes of yours makes me think of your mother," she cuts in, her voice quivering. "God bless her soul. And your father only a month later. I knew he couldn't live without her for much longer."

They were so in love; I've never seen a happier pair." She is sobbing now as she reaches for me, pulling me tightly into her chest where her massive bust swallows me up. "To think you'd lose them both after the loss of beautiful Jules all those years ago. And now the house. You poor, poor girl."

I try to pull away—not to be rude, but only because she is suffocating me. Mrs. Robertson's breasts are famous in the small town of Wooster, Ohio, and once she traps you in that endless abyss, there's no telling if you'll make it out still breathing. As children, my little sister Jules and I had many near-death experiences in that bust.

Finally, after her tears have sufficiently soaked my short head of dark brown hair, I manage to release myself from her stronghold.

"Thank you, Genie. But really, I'm okay," I assure her. "Just finishing things up with the sale of the house, then back to Manhattan."

I smile warmly at her as she wipes at her tears; I'm used to being the strong one amid unimaginable loss. There is no other way to be, really, if you want to survive the loss of a home, the loss of an entire family.

She sniffles as she grabs my hand. "You've always been such a busy bee, with your fancy talk-show job in Manhattan. So glamorous. If only Jules could be here to see all of the amazing things you've done with your life..."

As Mrs. Robertson continues gushing and babbling, the way she has been doing since I was a child, my gaze drifts out to the "For Sale" sign I have just taken down in our little front lawn—the same lawn my sister and I used to run around in as little girls. The same lawn where, seventeen years ago, I watched my mother collapse when a policeman pulled up and broke the news that Jules had been killed in a car accident at the young age of sixteen. And the very same lawn where my father keeled over from a fatal heart attack only three months ago, shortly after my mother passed from pancreatic cancer.

I need to get back to New York, I think as the familiar sound of Mrs. Robertson's voice makes me remember a time when my entire family was together, when we were happy.

Now, it's just me. And I need to get out of here.

"Olivia, dear, are you listening?"

"Of course, Genie," I say, placing a hand on her arm. "And I'm so thankful for your concern, but I need to wrap things up with the movers, sign some papers, and catch my flight back to the city tonight."

"Oh, I hope I haven't upset you. You know not to pay any attention to me. I just can't stop chattering!"

I can't help but laugh a little. "I know, and that's why we love you. But I really do have to run. I'm sorry I can't stay and talk more."

She nods, reaching for my hand. "You're still so much like your mother, you know—always so strong, so put together. You will stay in touch, won't you?"

"Of course," I say, knowing that my demanding job catering to Miranda makes it next to impossible for me to stay in touch with anyone these days, but what else can I tell her?

She hugs me one last time, and just for a moment, instead of fighting Genie's embrace, I allow myself to enjoy the feeling of someone else holding me up for a change.

She kisses me on the cheek, then whispers in my ear. "It's okay to be vulnerable once in a while, dear, especially after all that you've been through." With a squeeze of the hand, Mrs. Robertson sets off to her little brick home across the street, and I am left alone on the front porch, swallowing the knot in my throat, knowing that *vulnerable* is not an option.

After the movers pull away, I turn to lock the front door for the last time, but instead find myself pushing through the doorway and stepping into the empty living room. The sun has set outside, leaving the house almost completely dark, but I don't need anything to light my way.

I have my memories.

My feet carry me over the soft white carpet, down the long hallway and up the stairs to the bedroom I shared with Jules until the day she was taken from me. I sit on the floor in the middle of our old room, close my eyes, and immediately her beautiful face lights up the darkness. I can see the freckles that covered her nose, the way her strawberry-blonde hair curled at the ends, and the dimples that popped in her rosy cheeks every time she flashed her glowing, sweet smile. She was an exact replica—well, a much prettier, more feminine replica—of my jovial, red-headed father.

"It's just me now, Jules." My voice is shaking, and I hope that wherever she is, she can hear me. "Mom and Dad...they're gone too now. But I suppose you already know that. I miss them so much. I should've come home more often when mom was sick...I should've been here for both of them. But my job and my life in New York—it's all just so crazy. I barely have time to eat lunch these days, let alone sneak away from the city for a weekend."

I can almost see Jules' sparkling green eyes narrowing, telling me to be honest with her.

"I suppose the truth, though, is that I just hated being here, in this house, without you. And now...it's too late."

The silence that greets me in this shell of a house—a home that once carried so much love—is deafening tonight. So loud, I think it may actually break my heart in half.

But then, just when I feel myself crumbling, my body curling into a ball of sorrow on the carpet, Jules' unmistakable voice flitters into my mind.

"Paris."

I lift my tear-stained face from the floor, looking around the darkened bedroom, but she isn't here.

Of course she isn't. God, am I losing my mind?

I peel myself off the floor, but just as I make it to my feet, I hear her again.

"Paris."

This time the hairs on the back of my neck are standing on end, and goose bumps are slithering up my arms.

My eye catches the open closet door, and suddenly I remember.

The Paris journal.

I run to the closet and switch on the light inside. There is nothing left in here, though, except for a couple of dust bunnies floating around on the floor. The shelf above appears to be empty as well, but as I stand on my tiptoes and reach a hand up there, just in case, my fingers brush against what feels like the spine of a book.

Confessions of a City Girl

My heart beats a little faster as I pull it down to find the journal my sister and I started when we were only little girls, the one we wrote in together until she was killed.

On the cover is a picture of the Eiffel Tower, and tucked inside are all the beautiful post cards we collected of the city we always dreamed of visiting together one day, and the city our French-teacher mother always gushed about: *Paris*.

I slide down the closet wall, lost in a memory of me and Jules lying on our stomachs on her bed, giggling and scribbling away—crushes, girlfriend gossip, break-ups, plans for the future—it's all here in our Paris journal.

I flip to the last entry, my teary eyes skimming Jules' dainty handwriting.

> *I, Julia Banks, and my big sister Olivia Banks, swear to each other that in the next year, we will go to Paris together and accomplish the following:*
>
> *1 – Eat the best chocolate croissant in the city.*
> *2 – Buy a pretty French bra on the Champs Élysées (ooh la la!).*
> *3 – Make and devour a Nutella crêpe in Montmartre.*
> *4 – Dance in the Tuileries Gardens underneath a full moon.*
> *5 – French kiss a French boy at the top of the Eiffel Tower.*

At the bottom of the page, we signed our own little Paris contract to each other, dating it *February 18, 1997*.

That was one week before we lost her.

I never did make that trip to Paris. And despite her love affair with France, my mother never traveled there again either.

We were both too devastated to do anything that may have reminded us of Jules—of the chances that were stolen from her, of the dreams she never realized.

My phone buzzes, startling me from my daze. Of course, it's a text from Miranda.

> *Have you left Ohio yet? Please don't fall in love with an old high school fling or some bibs-sporting country boy while you're home. I need you here. My "stand-in" Olivia*

is a complete moron, not to mention I can barely concentrate on anything she's saying with that frizzy nest of hair on her head. Your absence is an epic disaster. EPIC.

Sighing, I return my gaze back to the list, to the promise I made to my sister all those years ago. And as I think about Miranda's screeching voice narrating that text message, suddenly I know there is only one thing left to do.

Go to Paris.

Two

The next morning, after an overnight flight and a long talk with Miranda, promising her that I would only be gone for one more day, I arrive for the first time ever...*in Paris.*

With only the purse on my shoulder, the passport I carry with me at all times (just in case Miranda decides she needs to jet off to an exotic location at a moment's notice), and the Paris journal in hand, I walk out of the bustling Charles de Gaulle airport. The fresh spring air holds a hint of promise as I feel the sorrow and the stress of my life back home leaving my body. A bright yellow taxi pulls up to the curb, and I step inside, excited to finally deliver on the promises I made to my sister all those years ago.

The French my mother spoke to us throughout our childhood and teen years flows easily from my mouth as I ask the driver to take me to the eighteenth arrondissement so that I can begin by accomplishing the third item on our list:

Make and devour a Nutella crêpe in Montmartre.

I couldn't imagine a better way to start off my one day in the City of Lights.

The cab whisks me toward the city, and all the while, I am poring over the pages of our Paris Journal, laughing and tearing up over the memories—the good and the bad. I have almost reached the end of the thick, weathered notebook when I lift my gaze to find the majestic Basilique du Sacré-Coeur towering up on a hillside in the distance.

The massive white dome atop the basilica shoots high into the backdrop of the deep blue sky above, reminding me of one of the postcards our mother had given to us, which is still tucked inside the journal on my lap.

As we wind closer, the famous landmark in Montmartre looks even more breathtaking than in the photo, making me wish with every ounce of my being that Jules could be here with me to see this.

Squeezing the journal in my hands as we drive up through the hilly side streets, I remind myself that she *is* here, by my side. It was her voice, after all, that found me in the darkness last night, that led me back to the journal, and here to this magical city we dreamt of visiting long ago.

After we wind around the base of the basilica and down a few more side streets, the cab drops me off in a charming cobblestone square facing Le Consulat Restaurant.

"*C'est bon?*" the young French cabdriver asks with a smile.

"*Parfait,*" I say before handing him a stack of euros. "*Merci, monsieur!*"

And with that, I whip open the cab door and take my very first steps onto the quaint cobblestone streets of Paris' eighteenth arrondissement. To my right, two old men sit outside at the Café Montmartre, sipping their morning *tasses de café*, the rich scent of French coffee making my mouth water. Beautiful artwork speckles the sidewalk to my left underneath the green awning of the Galerie Butte Montmartre. A quick glance down the charming little *rues* which span in all directions around me reveals red flowers spilling over black balconies, tourists and French people alike combing the streets, marveling at the charm, the old beauty of this enchanting pocket of Paris.

And as for me, I am overwhelmed with emotion.

Already, *I love it here.*

Glancing upward, I catch a swirl of puffy white clouds floating calmly overhead while the morning sun beats down on my cheeks.

Confessions of a City Girl

How have I waited so long to make our dream come true, Jules?

And how on earth will I return to the concrete jungle of Manhattan after only one day in Paris—a city which so clearly deserves days, weeks, months of exploration?

"Vous cherchez quelque chose, mademoiselle?" Are you looking for something, Miss?

Blinking from the glare of the sun, I swivel around to find a man with a mess of light brown hair sweeping across his deep blue eyes. He has a smudge of flour on his scruffy cheeks, a white apron thrown over his shoulder, and a curious smile on his face.

"Yes, in fact, I'm looking for a crêperie where I can make a Nutella crêpe," I say in French.

"Ahh, you want to make a crêpe?" he responds in English, his accent thick and undeniably sexy.

"Yes, and then I'd like to devour it." I smile back at him, trying not to stare too long at the cut of his arms in the snug gray T-shirt he is wearing.

He certainly doesn't hesitate to give me the once over, though, as he lets out a charming laugh, his smile lighting up his eyes even more.

"Well, of course you will devour the crêpe…what else would you do with it?"

A nervous giggle escapes my lips when I realize that I, Olivia Banks, the woman who hasn't had time to flirt with anyone but the crew on the talk show where I live and breathe from dawn till dusk every day, am actually standing on a beautiful street in Paris flirting with an even more beautiful Frenchman.

"Not sure," I respond finally. "Can you point me in the right direction?"

"But of course, mademoiselle. I know just the place." He nods down the street, then takes off over the cobblestones, whistling a happy little tune as we walk.

"So, let me guess," he says. "You are American, and this is your first time in Paris." He sizes me up once more, this time brushing the hair out of his eyes to get a better look.

"That obvious, huh?"

He chuckles. "I watched you step out of the cab—your eyes, they lit up like you'd never seen anything so magnificent."

The depth of his observation catches me off guard. "I haven't," I admit. "I mean of course I've seen pictures of Paris—I've dreamt of coming here since I was young. But to be here, on these streets...I'm already in love."

"You American women, hopeless romantics," he says with a grin.

"I've met a few Frenchmen in my time...you're not so different, I'd say."

He shrugs. "Maybe not."

"You live here in Montmartre, I assume?"

We round a corner, squeezing past a few Italian-speaking tourists, then pick up our pace as we stroll down a winding little hill.

"Yes, live and work here. I've traveled the world, but I wouldn't want to call anywhere else home."

"Smart man," I say. "Where do you work?"

Just as I ask the question, he stops in front of a boulangerie, gesturing inside. The scents of buttery bread, sugary patisseries, and melted chocolate waft out its front doors, making me realize how hungry I am after my overnight flight.

"*Voilà,*" he says.

Suddenly the flour on his cheeks and the apron over his broad shoulders are making sense. "You work *here*?"

He plants his fists on his hips, puffing out his chest, proud...and adorable. "Yes, this is the boulangerie of my father. After he passed last year, he left it to me."

"So you're telling me you get to smell freshly baked baguettes all day long? And eat them?"

"Yes, that is right."

"Do you just walk out your door every morning and think you're the luckiest man alive?"

"With where I live, and the work that I do, yes, I am lucky. Other areas of my life..." he trails off, his big blue eyes suddenly pensive, "...not so lucky. But such is life, no?"

"*Oui, c'est la vie*," I say, thinking of the loss of my childhood home, my mom, my dad, and my sweet sister Jules. Not wanting to get into our sad stories on such a happy morning, I change the subject.

"So this must mean you're an expert on the *pain au chocolat?*" I ask.

"I thought you wanted a Nutella crêpe, but now you want a chocolate croissant?"

"Well, I need to make and eat a Nutella crêpe here in Montmartre, then I need to eat the best chocolate croissant in all of Paris, and there are a few other things I need to accomplish before my flight leaves tonight."

He nods down at the Paris journal in my hands. "A list of things you must do in the magical City of Lights? In only one day?"

"Exactly."

"Can I see the rest of the list?" he says, making a bold reach for the journal. "Maybe I can help."

I think of number five, immediately picturing a kiss with this sexy *boulanger* on top of the Eiffel Tower. Oh, Jules would definitely approve.

Just as his fingers brush the spine, though, I hug the journal tightly to my chest. "No you may not see the list—it's private."

"Oh, *excuse-moi*," he says, chuckling. "Well, if you only have one day, we better get started with the crêpe, no?"

"Can we make it here, at your boulangerie?"

"I want to take you next door to Jacques' crêperie—he is the expert. But first, you haven't told me your name."

"And you haven't told me yours," I say, so enjoying this early morning Paris flirtation.

"I'm Alex, short for Alexandre. And you? Wait, let me guess."

I place a hand on my hip, laughing. "Okay, shoot."

"*Belle?*" Beautiful?

I shake my head.

"*Jolie?*" Pretty?

"Well, that's nice, but try again."

"*Charmante, éblouissante, ravissante, magnifique, adorable?*" Charming, stunning, ravishing, magnificent, adorable?

Now a flush is creeping over my cheeks, but this smooth French guy just stands there, totally in his element, brushing his thumb over his chin, searching for another word that will flatter this boyfriend-less *américaine*.

"Am I getting close?" he asks.

"Nice try," I say, unable to hide my smile. "My name is Olivia."

He leans in and kisses me on each cheek, his dark stubble brushing against my skin, sending butterflies on a mad twirl through my already growling stomach.

"*Enchanté,*" he says.

"*Enchantée,*" I respond. *Enchanted, indeed.*

Damn, these Frenchmen certainly know how to seduce the foreign girls.

"Are you always this charming so early in the morning?" I joke, glancing at my watch. "It's only ten o'clock."

This time, he blushes a little. "Well, it is not every day that a stunning American woman steps out of a taxi in my neighborhood, and stops to look up at the sky like a lost angel."

"Well, can you take this lost angel to the crêperie? I'm starving, and I'm on a schedule here."

"*Mais bien sûr, mademoiselle.*" *But of course, Miss,* he says, not fighting the grin spreading widely across his scruffy cheeks.

Alex leads me inside the tiny crêperie where a short, plump man is flipping crêpes and joking with one of the servers. Patches of gray hair inch around the sides of his shiny, bald head, and the lines around his eyes are kind and welcoming as he smiles at us.

"Jacques, this is my new American friend, Olivia," Alex says in French. "She would like you to teach her how to make a Nutella crêpe, and then she would like to eat it."

Jacques places a hand on his pot belly and laughs heartily. "*Une belle américaine? Quelle chance!*" *A beautiful American girl? What luck!* "*Avec plaisir, mademoiselle.*" *With pleasure, Miss.*

Jacques shuffles toward us, greets both me and Alex with kisses, then ushers me back behind the counter to get started. "*Allez, viens.*" *Come on,* he says, stealing the journal from my hands and the purse off my shoulder before placing them on a nearby table.

Alex eyes the journal as Jacques ties an oversized apron around my neck.

"Are you sure I can't help with the list?" Alex prods. "I have to get to the boulangerie in a few minutes, but I can at least point you in the right direction since you are so new to Paris."

I couldn't imagine a more dashing Frenchman to share that kiss with atop the Eiffel Tower or to dance with tonight in the Tuileries, but just as I am considering asking what time he gets off work, a petite French woman swoops into the crêperie, swings her arms around Alex's neck and plants a big kiss on his cheek.

"*Bonjour, mon cher.*" *Hello, my dear,* she says, her eyes twinkling up at him.

He hugs her back and kisses her on both cheeks. "*Bonjour, ma petite Joséphine. Ça va?*"

The two of them chatter away in French, and as I am trying to concentrate on what they are saying, Jacques hands me a bowl of batter and begins instructing me on how to make my first crêpe. A few seconds later, Joséphine flies out of the crêperie as quickly as she appeared, and Alex lifts a brow in my direction. "So, can I help with the list?"

I shake my head, wondering why all the good ones have to be taken. "No, thank you, though. It was lovely meeting you, Alex."

He places a hand on the doorframe and shoots me a killer grin. "Well, if you change your mind, you know where I work. And I may be a little biased, but I do make a pretty good *pain au chocolat*..."

I am so entranced by Alex's sweet smile, by his ruffled hair and sexy jeans that I am now spilling batter all over the floor.

"*Oh mon Dieu! Ces Américaines!*" *Oh my Lord, these American women!* Jacques cries as he snatches the bowl and spatula from my hands and shows me how it's done.

"Enjoy your Nutella crêpe, *ma belle Olivia,*" Alex says before disappearing inside his boulangerie next door.

After Jacques helps me slather an unhealthy, but oh-so-enticing, amount of Nutella onto the crêpe, he makes me a plate, pulls out my chair and gestures for me to dig in.

"Bon appétit!"

"Merci," I say, before taking my first delectable bite of my warm, gooey, chocolaty crêpe. The taste of Nutella immediately carries me back to Sunday mornings in our tiny Ohio kitchen—my mother flipping crêpes, while me, Jules, and Dad devoured them as fast as she could make them.

I savor this one, though, as I listen to the elegant sound of the French language floating past my ears, and think of how much Jules would have loved this place.

Three

It is noon on my one and only day in Paris, and I am standing in the middle of the Champs-Élysées, watching the endless string of cars buzz and honk their way down to the grand Arc de Triomphe. The most famous avenue in the City of Lights is bustling with more vitality and verve than I ever could've imagined from simply looking at the postcards my mother gave to us as little girls.

I set off across the street and down the tree-lined sidewalk, noticing at least five different languages twirling around me as hordes of tourists comb the chic designer shops, lugging their heavy bags and snapping photographs in every direction. This is an entirely different scene from the quaint, village-like feel of Montmartre, but as I stroll down this iconic Parisian avenue, I find that I am smitten all the same with the bustling, lively beauty all around me.

Next on the Jules and Olivia agenda is #2 on the list:

Buy a pretty French bra on the Champs Élysées (ooh la la!).

This one was Jules' idea, as she was always the bustier—and more promiscuous—one of the two of us, but I can't say I'm not excited to buy a piece of beautiful French lingerie. Now, if only I had a man to wear it for…

Alex's sweet smile pops into my head, but I dismiss any thoughts of him quickly, reminding myself that he has that adorable little French woman—*Joséphine* he called her—and I was nothing more than his daily tourist flirtation.

Luckily, I don't have time to think about Alex or my lack of a love life for another second because I spot my first lingerie store on the Champs-Élysées—Darjeeling.

Inside, racks of delicate undergarments line the walls, and I am immediately drawn to a gorgeous, coral-colored bra and panty set.

Just as I am running my fingers over the lacy material, my phone buzzes inside my purse, setting my nerves on edge. Before I even look at the screen, I know it is, of course, Miranda.

She knows I have traveled to Paris for only one day to accomplish some "unfinished family business," but that would never stop her from calling me first thing in the morning when she wakes up.

Hoping it will simply be a quick check-in, I answer my phone.

"Olivia!" Miranda screeches into my ear. It is only six a.m. on the east coast, but her scary panic voice is already rearing in full force.

"What is it, Miranda?" I am an expert at staying steady amid the daily hurricanes of Miranda…but today as I stand in the middle of a Parisian lingerie store with four more items to check off my list and less than one day to accomplish all of them, I wish that just for today, Miranda would let me live my own life.

"First of all, I cannot *believe* you jetted off to Paris without me, but while you're there, I thought of a few things you could get for me…."

As Miranda rattles off more than "a few" designer items she would like me to bring home for her in my non-existent suitcase, then launches in on the latest talk show crisis—namely that she slept with today's guest, a hot young actor fifteen years her junior, and how will she ever be able to face him on set?—I pace in circles around the store, willing her to take just one breath so I can get a word in edgewise.

But she doesn't—breathe that is—and I don't get a word in…not until the end, anyway.

By the time I have finally managed to talk her down from the ledge and end the call, I have exited the store and made three laps around the Champs-

Élysées, wasting close to two hours of my Paris day. Exasperated, I find myself back in front of Darjeeling, staring at my own reflection in the window.

How have I let this go on for so long? Running someone else's life, and not living my own?

A firm hand on my shoulder startles me from my thoughts, and I turn to find a stylish older woman smiling warmly at me. With an elegant violet scarf wrapped loosely around her neck, a pair of dangling earrings which reach almost to her shoulders, and her tousled-but-pretty auburn hair swept back half-way, I am at once struck with her resemblance to Jules...if Jules had been given the chance to grow up, that is.

"Let's try this again, shall we?" she says in a strong British accent.

"I'm sorry, have we met?" I ask.

"No, dear, but I saw you in here earlier eyeing that beautiful coral bra, and I happened to overhear a bit of your conversation. I think a touch of French lingerie is just what you need right now. *Allons-y.*" Let's go.

I don't argue as she leads me back into the store and fills an entire dressing room with the most gorgeous bras, underwear, and nighties I've ever allowed myself to try on.

Before she closes me in the chic dressing room, she extends a hand. "I'm Mary."

"Olivia," I say, wondering where this wonderful woman came from.

"Lovely to meet you, Olivia. For the next hour, you must forget all about that horrid job of yours, and simply pamper yourself. I'll be in the dressing room next door if you need anything."

With that, my lingerie angel closes the door and leaves me alone with stacks of lace and and bows and bodices to try on. I pick up the elegant coral set I was eyeing earlier, hesitant, realizing that the notion of pampering myself is so utterly foreign to me...and yet it seemed to roll off this woman's tongue as if there were nothing more natural in the world than treating yourself to something beautiful and luxurious.

Of course I pamper Miranda *all the time*, I think.

Screw Miranda, I hear Jules' voice echo in my head.

That's right. Screw her. I deserve to have a little fun, too.

An hour later, Mary and I emerge from Darjeeling each holding our own bag of absolutely stunning French lingerie.

Turns out pampering myself wasn't so difficult, after all.

"You're glowing," she says with a grin.

"Am I?" I ask, laughing. "Amazing what a little lace can do for a girl." I turn to Mary. "Thank you so much. I needed that."

"I could tell. Where to next?" She gestures down the Champs, as if the entire city of Paris is our oyster.

She doesn't know about my list, or my twenty-four-hour time constraint, so I keep it simple. "I'd like to eat the best pain au chocolat in the city. Any suggestions?"

Mary stops walking, places her pointer finger on her chin and ponders as if she is trying to come up with a solution to world peace. "The *best* pain au chocolat, let me think…In a city that has a boulangerie on every corner, that's really quite a tough question, you know."

"Well, how about *your* favorite pain au chocolat."

Her eyes light up. "I've got it! Come with me." She takes off down the busy avenue, weaving around gabby tourists and handsome businessmen until we reach the artsy Parisian metro sign.

We jog down the stairs together, lingerie bags flapping while a gust of wind follows us down into the station. As we board the train, I am hoping that in a crazy twist of fate, she is going lead me back up to Montmartre to Alex's quaint little boulangerie. But not long after we've squeezed onto the crowded train, we emerge at rue de Passy only a few stops later. So, I remind myself *again* that Alex is taken, and I force that utterly adorable smile out of my mind.

"Welcome to my *quartier*," Mary says as we walk up a small hill onto a lively street filled with posh shops, sidewalk cafés, and chicly dressed women strutting down the narrow sidewalks. From the brief time I've known Mary, I can see that this trendy little *rue* fits her personality to a T.

"It's so charming," I tell her. "Like everything I've seen today." A pang of sadness hits me as I realize that I only have one evening left in this magical city before I have to head back to the rat race.

"She's already got you, hasn't she?" Mary lifts a curious brow in my direction.

"I'm sorry?"

"Paris—she's got ahold of your heart."

"Oh...yes, I suppose she has. The minute I stepped out of the cab in Montmartre this morning, I was finished."

She chuckles to herself, her eyes gleaming in the late afternoon sunlight. "Once that happens, my dear, there's no turning back. I remember when it first happened to me, when I knew my heart would always belong to this city. I wasn't much younger than you, if I recall." She pauses for a moment, a wistfulness passing through her gaze. "I'd managed to escape my hectic life in London for a weekend all to myself...Well, it wasn't *all* to myself of course—there *was* a Frenchman." A mischievous giggle bubbles from her red-lined lips. "The first of many...but that's another story."

Taking a quick peek at her left ring finger, I notice she isn't wearing a ring. She doesn't seem like the marrying type—too independent, too witty, too fabulous to be tied down.

"It was my first trip to Paris and, my God, I'd never fallen so hard before, not even for a man," Mary continues. "This city simply swept me away. I returned to London, went back to work, and tried to enjoy my life, but within a week—well, quite honestly within a day—I knew we had to break up...Me and London, that is. I gave my notice, packed my bags, and headed for the City of Lights. Haven't looked back since."

"Wow. You make it sound so simple."

She stopped walking for a moment, placing her hand on my arm. "My dear Olivia, it *is* that simple. One of the greatest lessons I've learned is that *we* are the only ones standing in our way. If you want to come to Paris, come to Paris! You certainly didn't sound as if you're in love with that crazy boss of yours on the phone earlier. The one who kept you from shopping, the cow. By the way, another important life lesson I've picked up is *never* to trust anyone who doesn't encourage you to do a little shopping."

At this, she gets a laugh out of me. "God, no, I'm definitely not in love with my boss," I say, not wanting to think about the barrage of calls that will surely pour in from Miranda after she has to face her most recent sexual conquest on live television. "But if you want the truth, my career runs my life."

Mary gives a disapproving nod. "Never a good way to live, darling. But often times we bury ourselves in work to avoid making the decisions that will make us truly happy, for *those* are usually the hardest decisions to make. Though I can tell you from personal experience that once they're made, the rest falls into place quite naturally."

A chilly draft sweeps down rue de Passy, carrying with it the delectable scents of butter, cake, and pastries.

Mary takes my hand. "Come along now, you'll forget all about that stressful world of yours as soon as you take a bite into this pain au chocolat."

A few moments later, Mary stops in front of a red awning that reads *Aux Délices de Passy*. The windows of the boulangerie are lined with rows of colorful macaroons and beautiful chocolate tarts, and inside, the chocolaty aroma takes me right back to mouth-watering heaven.

Mary orders us two pains au chocolat, and just as I am about to open my purse, she stops me.

"Don't even think about it," she says. "My treat."

"Thank you," I say, hoping she knows that I am thankful for more than the pastries. I am thankful that she has spent her afternoon with me, a perfect stranger, and has made me feel like I am not all alone in this world.

Outside, the warm spring air has dissipated, leaving a cool wind and an ominous sky in its wake. A few drops of rain fall as Mary eyes the dark gray clouds rolling in.

"I'm going to have to run off in a few," she says. "But let's take a bite together before we get drenched. I want you to see how all of your troubles can melt away with one taste of this most magnificent pastry."

This time, I don't hesitate to take her instructions. My first bite is an explosion of melted dark chocolate, butter—*so* much butter—and the softest, flakiest croissant I've ever tasted. Before I realize it, I've closed my eyes and a low moan is escaping from my lips.

"Orgasmic, isn't it?" Mary says.

"Totally." I open my eyes to find her smiling radiantly at me.

"You're going to be just fine, Miss Olivia. I can already tell." She reaches into her purse and pulls out a business card. "My contact info. Please get in touch as soon as you're back in Paris. I would love to see you again, darling."

"Thank you....Thank you for everything, Mary. I'm not sure when I'll be back in Paris, but I'll definitely be in touch."

She gives me a kiss on each cheek, and before she vanishes, she looks me firmly in the eye. "Oh, you'll be back soon, I can feel it. Or *perhaps*...you may never even leave."

With a wink, Mary takes off down the sidewalk, her auburn hair blowing wildly in the wind as she disappears from my view.

If only it were an option not to leave, I think as I set off in the opposite direction, my trip to the Eiffel Tower next on my list.

Four

The dramatic, stormy view of *la Tour Eiffel* from Trocadéro takes my breath away. Heavy gray clouds swirl around the tower, threatening to release their downpour any second. I take off down a long staircase, passing by a twirling carousel and reaching the Seine just as the cold drops begin to fall. My walk turns into a brisk jog, but just as I am half-way there, I notice that a few rays of sunlight have broken through the clouds and are shining down on the choppy River Seine.

I stop running and let the rain soak my hair, my clothes, even the half of pain au chocolat which I have yet to finish...because I know that in a few moments, there will be a rainbow.

And my sister Jules *loved* rainbows.

A few seconds later, the arch of colors appears, stretching over the Seine and ending right at the bottom of the tower. Before I realize it, tears are pouring down my face, mirroring the rain which is falling in sheets around me.

I am engulfed in beauty and loss, awe and sadness, all at the same time.

A rainbow leading to the Eiffel Tower—*Jules must be here*, I think. She must be watching this gorgeous scene unfold.

God, I miss her. And my parents. I miss them all so much.

A few minutes later, the rainbow vanishes into the sky, and the rain lets up, now only a light drizzle.

I reach into my purse for the journal; I want to hold it close to my heart as I make my way to the most iconic Parisian monument, which Jules never had the chance to see.

But when my search for the journal comes up empty, panic takes over.

In my romp around Paris, I have lost the last physical link I have to my sister.

I think back through my day, realizing it could've fallen out anywhere: in the crêperie in Montmartre, in the dressing room at Darjeeling, in the metro or even on the street. I am tempted to turn around and retrace my steps, but time is not on my side. I have to fly back to New York late tonight, and I still have two more things to accomplish: French kissing a Frenchman atop *la Tour Eiffel* and dancing with him underneath the full moon in *le Jardin des Tuileries*.

As I haven't garnered a single Frenchman prospect since Alex this morning, it's realistic that the kiss and the dance may not happen, but I power ahead all the same.

For Jules, for the dreams we had as young girls, I have to at least try.

I try to ignore the familiar feeling of loneliness that eats away at my insides as I take the elevator up to the top of the tower, but by the time I reach my destination, I feel about as lost and forlorn as a girl could ever feel in the most romantic city in the world.

Making my way over to the window, I squeeze in between groups of Japanese and Australian tourists—just little old me, a mere dot on the top of a tower, peeking down at the world, wondering what my place in it all is supposed to be.

It is this feeling—this hellish, desperate feeling of being so totally alone—that I have worked so hard to avoid feeling all these years. *This* is why I have chosen to devote my life to Miranda, a slave-driver in stilettos, rather than focusing on my own life—to *never* feel this way.

I think back to what Mary said earlier—that the decisions which will make us the happiest are often the hardest ones to make.

I want to quit my job.
I want to leave New York.
I want to live my own life, a life that resembles me.

As I lean my forehead against the cool glass and gaze down at the twinkling lights of Paris, I'm not yet sure what it will mean to live my own life, but I figure that having the intention must at least count for something.

"Olivia."

Before I can register the fact that a man has just called out my name on the top of the Eiffel Tower, his hand is on my shoulder, his whisper in my ear.

"You forgot something."

I swivel around to find Alexandre—his light brown hair soaked from the rain, a smoldering grin on his sweet face—holding my journal.

I reach for it, but he stops me. "Wait, there is something I must do first."

And then, this unbelievably sexy boulanger from Montmartre leans down and brushes his lips over mine. I am momentarily stunned, wondering if I'm imagining the whole thing. But when he uses his free hand to pull me tighter into his chest, then kisses me even deeper, sending a wave of passion down to my core, I know that I am definitely *not* dreaming.

Alex runs his hand up my arm, my neck, and finally finds a resting place on my cheek before our lips part.

"You read my list," I say with a grin.

He kisses my forehead and runs his hand through my damp hair. "Are you angry?"

"Do I look angry?" I tease.

"No, you look like you want me to kiss you again."

Before he goes in for a second round, I place a hand on his chest. "But what about Joséphine?"

"Oh, *that* is why you didn't want my help this morning. *Ma belle Olivia*, Joséphine is my sister."

I feel my cheeks blushing in embarrassment, but it's dark enough up here in the clouds that I'm sure Alex doesn't notice. And when he grabs me and kisses me again, I can tell he doesn't care, not one bit.

An hour later, the storm clouds have moved on to their next destination, and Alex and I are standing side by side beneath a glowing full moon in the middle of the Tuileries Gardens.

"So, only one more thing on the list..." He extends a hand. "Will you dance with me, Olivia?"

"I would love to." I take Alex's outstretched hand without hesitation and let him wrap me up in his arms.

As our dance begins, a soft hum escapes his lips. After a few notes, I recognize the tune as "I Love Paris in the Springtime."

I have only spent one spring day in this lovely city, but already I know that this is the perfect song. Being in Paris has given me hope—hope that I can move forward with life, with *my own life*, despite my past choices, despite the immense loss I have experienced.

Of course the charming Frenchman twirling me around the Tuileries doesn't hurt either...

Alex finishes his tune and rests his forehead against mine as we sway underneath the moonlight. "Your sister, Jules...she's not with us anymore, is she?"

I shake my head, swallowing the knot in my throat. "No, we lost her when she was only sixteen. Coming to Paris together was our dream."

"So you came for her, to make your dream come true."

"Yes...it took me long enough."

Alex pulls his face away just far enough so I can see the sincere look in his deep blue eyes. "I think you came to Paris at the perfect moment."

This makes me smile. "I suppose you're right..."

"If you didn't step out of that taxi right when you did, I may have never crossed paths with this beautiful American angel. And if you didn't leave your journal in Jacques' crêperie, I wouldn't have had the chance to kiss you atop the *Tour Eiffel* tonight." Alex leans down, laying one more passionate kiss on my eager lips.

"You see, *perfect*," he says, after he has sufficiently taken my breath away. "Now, about that pain au chocolat...I still think you have not tasted the *best* pain au chocolat in the city."

I raise a brow at him, knowing exactly where he is going with this. "Oh, is that right?"

"Yes...if you'll come with me, back to my boulangerie, I would like to make you one. A warm, buttery chocolate croissant fresh out of the oven—you couldn't possibly say no."

"But, Alex, my flight leaves in a couple of hours..."

Alex ignores my protest, dipping me back and running a string of kisses up my neck. He stops when he reaches my ear. "A midnight pain au chocolat sounds *so* much better than a long flight back to New York, does it not?"

"Oh, it really, really does...but—" Just as I am about to make an excuse for why I cannot stay in Paris with Alex, my phone rings.

As Miranda's name flashes across the screen, I think of Jules, of the list we made all those years ago, of the dreams we shared, and of all of the opportunities that were taken from her at such a young age.

Tonight, I know that I owe it to her, but even more so, to *myself*, to choose *life*.

So, I let go of Alex's hand, jog over to the pond, and toss my ringing phone and all of the responsibilities that come with it right into the water.

Alex is beaming when I turn to face him. "I take that as a yes?"

Laughing, I find myself in his arms once more, dreaming of the possibilities.

"*Yes.*"

Dear Reader

Thank you so much for reading my Confessions series. I hope you enjoyed the girls' spicy trips around the world as much as I've enjoyed writing them. All four of these stories were inspired by events in my own life*, and after writing the fictional versions, I knew it was time to tell my story. You'll find all the juicy details of my own true tale of love and heartbreak in the City of Light in my memoir, *Meet Me in Paris*. Read on for an excerpt of my memoir, and you can find the book on Amazon, Barnes & Noble, or iTunes.

If you are inclined to leave an honest review on the site where you purchased this book, I would appreciate it so much. Reviews are so incredibly helpful for authors, and I have been touched by the lovely reviews many of you have left for my books over the years. And if you're interested in receiving FREE books and release news, simply stop by my website at www.juliettesobanet.com and click on "Newsletter" to sign up. You can also check out all of my Paris romances and time travel mysteries on my website.

As always, I love hearing from you, so feel free to get in touch with a bonjour anytime! I also love doing book club visits, whether over Skype or in person if we happen to be in the same city. Feel free to e-mail me at *juliette@juliettesobanet.com*.

Thank you for all of your love and support! Read on for an excerpt my memoir…

xoxo
Juliette

*While these stories were inspired by events in my own life, I do feel it is important to note that I am not an undercover CIA operative, in case you were wondering. Of course, if I were, I couldn't tell you…

READ ON FOR AN EXCERPT
FROM JULIETTE'S BESTSELLING MEMOIR:

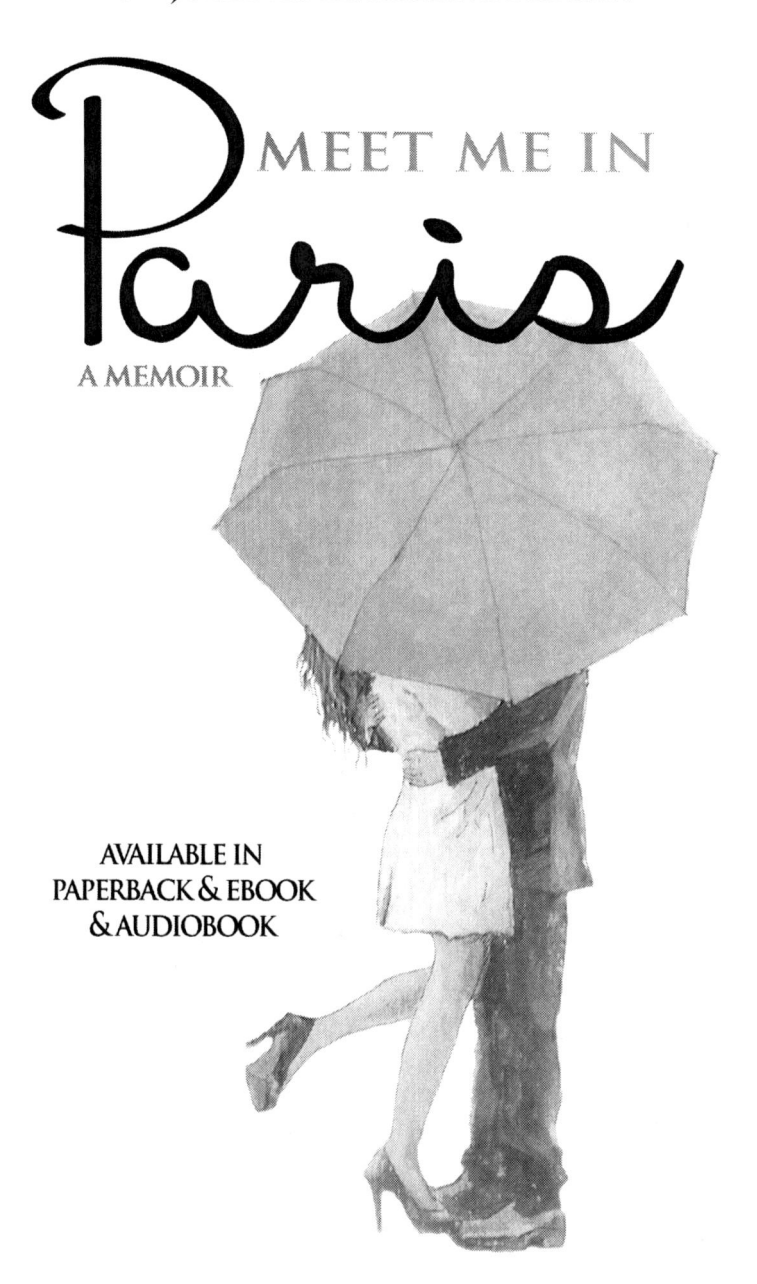

Meet Me In Paris

A MEMOIR

AVAILABLE IN
PAPERBACK & EBOOK
& AUDIOBOOK

Le Prologue

No matter the season, no matter the weather, love is *always* in the air in Paris.

And tonight is no different.

The autumn sun has been swept away by a splattering of gray clouds, blanketing the city's cobblestone streets in one of those inky, mysterious Parisian nights where lovers' secrets will be swept away by the choppy waters of the Seine, or captured whole by the Gothic towers of Notre Dame, or better yet, swallowed up by the bottle of red wine my own lover and I are sharing in a charming little bar near Châtelet.

Yes, I've taken a lover.

In Paris.

A Paris lover.

Oh, how I adore the taste of those delicious words.

The Merlot slips past my lips, smooth and rich, as I smile at this most disarming man I have by my side. I give him a look that is both coy and inviting, in lust and falling—well, more like plummeting—headfirst and harder than ever before.

It is only the third time we've been together, and already, this lover of mine has hopped on a plane from Chicago to spend a few days with me in Paris.

I'm not sure if he understands how much his presence by my side, in my beloved city, means to me. Or how each touch of his strong hands, each adoring smile, each endearing tilt of his head is healing this broken heart of mine.

Divorce has a way of shattering hearts like nothing else. And mine is no exception. It has only been a few months since I left my husband—the man I have loved for twelve years, the man I still love, despite my choice to leave our dying marriage—and I know these days in Paris with my lover will be my only happy ones for some time.

We've spent this crisp fall day strolling hand in hand along the hilly streets of Montmartre, devouring *croissants aux amandes* and *pains au chocolat*, stealing kisses in abandoned courtyards, sipping espresso at hilltop cafés, flirting with every word, every breath, and falling ever so hopelessly in love.

Although neither of us wants to admit it yet.

As my lover drinks his wine, he gives me a sly look that says, *Get up, go to the bathroom, let me slip off your jeans, and I'll take you right here, right now.*

I haven't known him that long, but I know what his looks mean.

"We're only a few blocks from our flat in the Marais," I say to this insatiable man. "And besides, French bathrooms are *so* tiny."

"That's a few blocks too far," he replies, sliding his hand up my thigh. "And *you're* so tiny. I think we'll be just fine."

"*Lover.* You'll just have to wait." I smack his hand, loving the way he wants me so.

The truth is, in the days since I left my marriage, I've been ravenous for affection, for sex, for love. A lioness let out of her cage. Raw, powerful, and in need.

I would let my lover take me anytime, anywhere. And he knows it.

But I *so* enjoy teasing him.

Suddenly my older, playful lover becomes all serious, taking my hand.

A long silence stretches between us as he holds my gaze. I have a feeling that whatever is coming will probably make me cry.

Finally, he speaks.

"No matter what happens with us in the future, whether you're finished with me after Paris or we can't stay away from each other for the rest of our lives, promise me…*promise me*…that at some point in the next five years, we'll meet again in Paris."

I glance down at my lover's silver wedding band, not meaning to, not wanting to, but my eyes go there, if only to remind myself of the reality of our situation. That I am falling in love with a man who is mine and who isn't mine. A man who is healing my heart and ripping it apart, all at the same time.

I can't stop the tears from rimming my eyes as I look up into his intense green gaze, the gaze that unhinges me completely, unravels my heart, makes me do all sorts of things I never would have dreamt of doing before he stormed into my life.

Or before *I* stormed into *his*.

It is here, lost in his eyes, where I forget all about my wounded heart.

"Hmm. Me, you, Paris, in the next five years…" I hesitate, pretending to consider my options.

"Promise me," he demands as he squeezes my waist and pulls me close so he can run those deadly lips of his along my neck.

He can't get enough of me; since the day I met him, he never could.

"Yes. I promise," I whisper, once I've caught my breath.

And then his lips find mine in this bar in Paris, where no one knows us, where no one recognizes the romance writer and her lover, holding on to each other, making promises we aren't sure we can keep, but making them all the same.

When we dash out of the bar moments later, I wonder how many secrets the wind is carrying as it whips past, waltzing over cobblestones, rustling through trees.

Quite a lot, I imagine, in a city this grand, a city this thrilling, a city so gloriously full of love.

Acknowledgments

I would like to thank my wonderfully talented design team, Blue Harvest Creative, for your incredible work. To all of my lovely family and friends, thank you for your continued love and support. And finally, to my loyal readers—my career wouldn't be possible without you. Thank you from the bottom of my heart.